A MOST TE

Lady Diana was in
—a period that ev
testing. Her husba
was trying to discover how much of her he
could totally control. And for her part, she
was trying to find out how much of her
freedom remained.

But now in the company of her husband's
handsome brother—on a journey into
France in search of a fiercely guarded hoard
of jewels—Diana faced a different kind of
test.

A test whether she was strong enough to
resist the most alluring of temptations—
and to survive the most brutal of dangers.

A test in which there would be no excuses
for failure—and no forgiveness. . . .

LADY ESCAPADE

LADY ESCAPADE

AMANDA SCOTT

A SIGNET BOOK

SIGNET
Published by the Penguin Group
Penguin Books USA Inc., 375 Hudson Street,
New York, New York 10014, U.S.A.
Penguin Books Ltd, 27 Wrights Lane,
London W8 5TZ, England
Penguin Books Australia Ltd, Ringwood,
Victoria, Australia
Penguin Books Canada Ltd, 10 Alcorn Avenue,
Toronto, Ontario, Canada M4V 3B2
Penguin Books (N.Z.) Ltd, 182–190 Wairau Road,
Auckland 10, New Zealand

Penguin Books Ltd, Registered Offices:
Harmondsworth, Middlesex, England

Published by Signet, an imprint of New American Library,
a division of Penguin Books USA Inc.

First Printing, January, 1986
12 11 10 9 8 7 6 5 4

REGISTERED TRADEMARK—MARCA REGISTRADA

Printed in the United States of America

For Terry, Ginger, John, and Lana
the spice of Scott life

1

The damp Wiltshire fog turned at last—as, indeed, it had been threatening for some hours to turn—into a steady drizzle, and the dismal gray light of the late December afternoon all but faded into darkness, causing the two lone riders on the Marlborough Road to urge their weary mounts to a quicker pace. The larger of the two, a man of middle years and medium bulk, his square face framed by salt-and-pepper sidewhiskers, was clad in gray-and-green livery beneath a thick drab frieze coat. As the raindrops began to fall, he reached to turn up the coat's broad collar to meet the drooping brim of his felt slouch hat in a futile effort to protect himself against the elements, but as he did so, he kept his dark eyes on the rapidly forming puddles in the roadway ahead. Though his expression was grim, he would not so far forget himself as to express his displeasure aloud.

His companion, stealing a glance at him from beneath long, thick black lashes, was conscious of a twinge of remorse when she noted the raindrops streaking his weathered face, despite the hat, and realized that even the heavy frieze coat would not long protect him from a thorough wetting. Though her own hat provided little protection and her elegant new blue riding habit would scarcely be the better for a soaking, Diana Warrington, Countess of Andover, didn't mind the dreary weather in the slightest. On the contrary, she found the experience of riding through the light rain an exhilarating one. To be sure, once the initial novelty faded, there would no doubt be discomfort, even irritation, but for the moment she reveled in the taste of raindrops upon her rosy lips and the smell of the soft, rainwashed air. So far, the English winter had been unseasonably warm, so although the slight chill in the air might well be the precursor of snow, at the moment it was merely a crispness, stimulating to the blood and to the high spirits of stolen freedom.

On the other hand, the black velvet lapels of her dashing habit would no doubt be ruined, and Ned Tredegar—who had been her groom since the day long ago when her father, the Earl of Trent, had carefully lifted her onto the back of her first pony—was not one with whom she wished to be at outs. Still, the rain was scarcely her fault.

"The turning is just ahead, Ned, I'm sure of it."

"Aye, m'lady," he returned curtly, his eyes still not leaving the road.

Diana sighed. But just then the black feather nestled between the crown and the jauntily upturned brim of her hat wilted and drooped, tickling her straight, broad-tipped little nose, and a sound perilously near a giggle escaped her lips. Even in the dim twilight, the twinkle in her wide-set blue eyes could easily be discerned, as could the roses in her cheeks and the flash of white, straight, well-formed teeth as she pushed the feather away from her face and grinned widely, saucily, at her companion.

"I daresay neither Lydia nor Ethelmoor will recognize such a bedraggled honey as I shall be by the time we reach the hall," she said lightly. Her words were clipped, well-enunciated, and her voice was lower-pitched than one might expect in a person of her small size. She was slim and straight-shouldered but, to her chagrin, of less than average height. It had often been said of her that the Countess of Andover had the best seat on a horse and the best hands, for a woman, in the country, that she rode with the lightness of thistledown but with the firm, seemingly effortless control of a Nonesuch. The same persons who said such things of her when seeing her on a horse, however, often expressed astonishment to discover, when she dismounted, that she was not taller. And when they heard her speak for the first time, those same persons were likely to suggest that such a voice would better befit a lady of greater stature. Such comments rarely disturbed Diana, but she was accustomed, generally, to receive a polite response when she spoke, particularly when she addressed one of her servants. When Ned Tredegar's only response to her conversational gambit was little more than a grunt, she straightened in her saddle, her eyes sparkling indignantly. "Give over, Ned, do. I'm prodigiously sorry you're getting wet, but how was I to know it would come on to mizzle like this?"

"Because I told you it would, Miss Diana," he retorted uncompromisingly.

She wrinkled her nose at him and wiped raindrops from her lashes with the back of one dainty York tan glove. "Well, of course you said it would. You always seek to put a rub in my way when you think I'm heading into the briars again. But the sun was shining when we left Wilton House. You know it was."

"Aye, but there was black clouds in the west, 'n' now they be upon us. And ye'd no business, any road, leavin' Wilton House like a willful gypsy, Miss Diana. Not when it was yer own birthday they was celebratin', 'n' not without the master had so much as a whiff o' yer intent," he added with the frankness of long and privileged acquaintance. "Like as not, I'll be losin' m' place over this latest bit o' tomfoolery."

"Pooh," Diana retorted. "Simon would never be so gothic. He'll know perfectly well that you have no power to stop me from doing as I please. If Papa never blamed you for my antics, you may rest assured that Simon will not."

Tredegar said nothing, but there was little in his expression to lead Diana to think he had much faith in her opinion of the matter. She knew he had no reason to fear the Earl of Andover, however, despite that gentleman's nearly legendary temper. The only person who had cause to fear him at the moment was Diana herself. A shiver raced up her spine at the thought, and she wondered if Simon had already set out in search of her. The likelihood was that he had not yet discovered her absence, for she had excused herself from the day's hunting on the pretext of a migraine headache, and even if it had come on to rain at Wilton House, a drizzle would scarcely have daunted the hunters. They would be coming in by now, of course, but as angry as Simon had been with her, it was unlikely that he would seek her out until she failed to appear at dinner. Even then, he might merely assume she was sulking. With such thoughts as these passing through her head, she made no further attempt to pursue her conversation with Tredegar, and silence prevailed until they reached the turning they sought. Fifteen minutes thereafter, the iron gates of her brother's house took shape in the gloom ahead.

The gates were open and they passed between the tall stone pillars supporting them and on down the gravel drive without bothering to announce themselves at the lodge. Less than a mile beyond, the shapely bulk of Ethelmoor Hall loomed ahead with warm, welcoming lights glowing through a number of large gothic-arched windows. Diana and Tredegar followed the drive as it circled around to the porte cochere protecting the main entrance.

Out of the rain at last, Tredegar dismounted, dragged his wet hat from his head, smacked it down upon his saddle, and moved quickly to assist Diana. Before her neatly booted feet had touched the ground, however, the front doors were pulled open, and the warm glow of a vast number of candles spilled across the low stoop to bathe the visitors in its light. A liveried porter peered out at them, then motioned to someone behind him. Seconds later, a footman stepped across the threshold, followed by the stately figure of my lord's butler.

"Lady Andover?" that worthy inquired doubtfully as he peered nearsightedly into the gloom from the stoop.

"Yes, Patcham," Diana replied cheerfully, " 'tis I, indeed, though a trifle damp about the edges. Is my brother at home?"

"No, my lady, but her ladyship is in the drawing room. I shall send at once to inform her of your arrival."

"No need to do that, Patcham," said a laughing voice from behind the butler. "The commotion stirred a most unladylike curiosity, I fear, so here I am." A slim, dark-haired young woman in a neat twilled evening dress appeared in the doorway as the butler stepped aside to make way for her. She shook her head in fond exasperation at the sight of her visitor. "Did Ethelmoor neglect to inform me that we were expecting you, Diana, or is this merely one of your starts? Where is Andover?"

"At Wilton House, no doubt amusing Pembroke and his bevy of fashionable guests with tales of my latest escapade," Diana replied easily. "It was my birthday party, but it grew to be rather tiresome, so I decided to visit you and Bruce instead. I'm sorry he is from home, but I hope I am welcome."

"Don't be foolish," Lydia, Viscountess Ethelmoor, told her. "He has merely gone into Marlborough for the night. You must be soaked to the skin, you unnatural girl," she added in brisker, scolding tones when Diana moved further into the light. "I shan't give you a proper, welcoming hug until you are dry, so do you come upstairs with me at once. Patcham will see to Tredegar whilst our people attend to your horses." Another thought occurred to her. "I say, have you brought anything else to wear, or do we take you as you are?"

Diana grinned, following her hostess into the elegantly-appointed, well-lit hall. "Does nothing faze you, Lyddy? I arrive on horseback, dripping water all over your lovely, polished floors, with no more than my groom for escort, and you wish merely to know if I have brought a change of clothes?" The speaking glance that Lydia threw over her shoulder told Diana clearly that there was a great deal more that lady wished to know, and she chuckled mischievously before adding in more virtuous tones, "As a matter of fact, Ned has just relinquished two entire bandboxes stuffed full of clothes to your footman, but as the contents are more than likely to be damp by now, I hope you can find me something warm to stave off the ague until they can be dried. An old robe of Bruce's will do," she suggested provocatively, "if you have nothing better to offer."

Lydia laughed, shaking her head. Refusing to be

diverted, however, she led the way into the stair hall and up the polished steps to the first floor and then to her own spacious bedchamber.

"Since we are nearly of a size," she said as they entered the cheerful primrose-and-gray room, "you may have whatever you like of mine until your own things are dry." Shutting the door, she stepped to the French wardrobe between the two tall, yellow-velvet-draped windows and began to sort through the gowns hanging within. A moment later she pulled out a medium blue, soft woolen gown with long sleeves and held it up for Diana's approval. "This will do for now," she said, "to warm you."

Diana wrinkled her nose. "Dowdy," she said flatly.

"Never mind, it's the warmth that matters now. Ethelmoor would throttle me if I allowed his precious little sister to expire for lack of a warm gown. Surely, you do not insist upon carrying London fashions into the country in wintertime, Diana."

"One must dress well all the time," Diana replied with a shrug, "but everyone suffers equally, so it scarcely signifies."

"Well, it signifies to me," retorted the ever-practical Lydia. "I cannot think of anything sillier than traipsing about a drafty country mansion in nothing more than a thin muslin gown with tiny sleeves and a less than adequate bodice, unless it's the damping of one's skirts under like circumstances. Pure foolishness. Not," she added with a complacent glance around the cozy, well-appointed room with its crackling fire and heavy curtains, "that Ethelmoor Hall is at all drafty. But here, you get out of that wet habit at once. I intend to maid you myself, for I mean to know without roundaboutation, if you please, what has brought you to us like this. Have you and Andover quarreled again?"

"Quarreled?" Diana's blue eyes glinted with sudden, bitter anger, and her voice when she spoke was brittle and higher pitched than usual. "Heavens, Lydia, we do not quarrel. Simon issues orders, and I obey them. Simon scolds, and I am contrite. We are the model modern married couple, the very talk of the *beau monde*.

Surely, you have heard the tales of the Earl and Countess of Andover and their merry match. Why, Lady Jersey informed me only yesterday that we provide all the best tit-bits for the gossip-mongers."

"Well, you need not heed such stuff from her ladyship, of course," Lydia said quietly, "and if she was able to say all that with a straight face after cuckolding poor Jersey all these years with the prince, I can say only that I have a smaller opinion of her than ever. She is a grandmother, after all, several times over. Such behavior is too absurd."

Diana shrugged, pulling off her bedraggled hat and flinging it onto a nearby chair. "Her ladyship's morals make little difference to the matter at hand. What she said was true enough."

"Well, I have heard things, naturally," Lydia admitted, "but I learned long ago to discount three-quarters of what I hear and to take the rest with salt."

"Oh, you may believe everything you hear about me," Diana said grimly. She reached to unfasten her spencer, muttering, "Surely, you of all people must know how spoilt I have been by my doting parents and what a hey-go-mad hoyden I was when Andover chose to cast the handkerchief to me. And now I am held to be a loose screw with no principles, besides."

"Merciful heavens," Lydia said in damping tones, "whatever can you be talking about? Open the budget, my dear, and quickly, for Patcham will have told them to begin laying the covers for our supper, and I mean to get to the bottom of this tangle before we leave this room. As I recall the matter, you chose Andover quite as quickly as ever he tossed any handkerchief. Why, everyone knew yours was the love match of the Season. And I have never heard anyone but Ethelmoor complain of your having been spoilt. As for your principles, well, that's naught but a bag of moonshine, as our John would say."

"How is John?" Diana asked absently, slipping from her damp habit and handing it to Lydia, who hung it on a wall-hook where her maid would be certain to spy it at once. "Does he like Eton, or do they beat him?"

Diana stood now in her thin chemise and York tan halfboots, a slim, athletic young woman, her sun-streaked blond hair darkened now by the dampness, her nearly turquoise eyes lightless under the long, thick lashes.

Lydia regarded her with concern. "Never mind John. He is well enough. What happened, Diana?"

Silently, Diana picked up the blue woolen gown from the high primrose-draped bed where Lydia had put it, and slipped it over her head, wriggling her hips to make the soft skirt fall properly into place. But when she would have turned her back to let Lydia do up the numerous tiny pearl buttons, the dark-haired woman stopped her with a gentle touch and a direct look.

"Tell me, dear."

"Simon thinks I have been engaging in an illicit affair with Rory," Diana said listlessly. Her gaze met Lydia's, and she was grateful for the disbelief she saw in the other woman's soft brown eyes.

"With his own brother? His *twin* brother? How could Simon be such a knock-in-the-cradle?" Lydia demanded. "How could he possibly believe such a thing of you, Diana? Or of Lord Roderick, for all that. Even that rascally scalawag would never do anything so reprehensible. Why . . . why, that would be incest! Simon deserves to be thoroughly shaken if he truly believes such stuff."

Involuntarily, Diana chuckled as the vision danced through her mind of Lydia, no bigger than herself, after all, attempting to shake sense into the tall, broad-shouldered Earl of Andover, a gentleman as well-noted for his abilities in the amateur ring as for his diplomatic prowess in political circles. A distinct twinkle lingered in her eyes as Diana shook her head fondly at her sister-in-law.

"He found us together, you see, and jumped—as, indeed, he always jumps—to all the wrong conclusions. But I'm fed to the back teeth with his temper and with his scolds," she added, turning now so that Lydia could attend to the pearl buttons, "so I simply ordered up my horse and Ned Tredegar and rode here to you, Lyddy dear."

Lydia had accepted Diana's rapid change of mood with a placidity born of long experience and had actually buttoned the bottom two buttons of the wool dress, but at these last, casual words, her hands went still, and a discerning eye would certainly have noted a paling of her cheeks. Her voice was carefully expressionless, however.

"Andover doesn't know where you are?"

Diana shrugged, saying in an airy tone, "I daresay he will find me if it suits him to do so."

"Merciful heavens," Lydia breathed, "he'll murder the lot of us."

Just then there was a scratching at the door, and a maidservant entered, bobbing a curtsy and saying politely, "M'lady, Mr. Patcham be wishful to know if y' want he should 'ave supper put back. It be ready t' serve, 'e says."

When Lydia hesitated, Diana smiled at her. "Do up my dress, Lyddy, and we shall repair to the dining room. Simon can't eat either of us, after all, and he may not even bother to come after me."

"Very well," Lydia said, her tone long-suffering. "Dory, tell Patcham we shall be down directly. But you, my girl," she added fiercely the moment the door had shut behind the maidservant, "are going to tell me the whole immediately after supper. How I wish Ethelmoor were here!"

"Why, Lyddy? So he might read me a scold? He scarcely ever does, you know."

"Well, he will if you've brought Andover's wrath down upon us all," Lydia pointed out. "Your brother is the kindest, most gentle man alive, Diana, but he does have a temper, and I for one would as lief you didn't stir it. Still, I cannot help but think he would have had the whole tale from you by now," she added wistfully.

Diana laughed. "Never mind, Lyddy. I'll tell you everything right after supper. But hurry now. I've scarcely eaten a thing all day, and I'm famished."

Obligingly, Lydia dealt with the rest of the pearl buttons, then waited patiently while Diana smoothed her damp hair into a neat coil at the nape of her neck.

These details taking a mere moment or two, the two ladies were soon seated in the large ground-floor dining room, attending to the first course of a tasty supper. With the servants in constant attendance, there was no opportunity for private conversation, but Diana had no qualms about entertaining her sister-in-law with some of the juicier bits of gossip she had collected during her recent round of house parties.

"For you must know, dearest, that although we have managed to visit Simon's father and Lady Ophelia at Alderwood Abbey several times since our wedding, Simon and I have scarcely set foot in Andover Court since the prince left Brighton at the end of September. First there was the hunting in Leicestershire, followed by a myriad of country house parties as we made our way south again, and then of course, I went into Hampshire to visit with Mama and Papa whilst Simon went to France with Mr. Fox and Lord Holland and the others last month."

"Do they truly expect this peace to last?" Lydia asked curiously. "Ethelmoor says that some of the news has been disquieting of late."

Diana shrugged. "The Peace of Amiens was meant to be the beginning of great things, but by all I've heard these past months, there has been a good deal of trouble over the bits and pieces of the treaty itself. Mr. Fox and the others are prodigiously disappointed by Mr. Bonaparte's continued aggressions, and I believe one purpose of their visit to France was to attempt to persuade him to behave himself, but all Simon would say was that they went there to pay their respects to the First Consul, as Mr. Bonaparte likes to call himself— seeing himself a prime minister, I daresay—and that they went there on behalf of Mr. Pitt. A state visit, in fact. But of course, Mr. Pitt is no longer the Prime Minister, and Mr. Addington is a loose fish, Simon says. So what Simon told me didn't make a great deal of sense, but then he rarely does when he talks to me of politics. And it isn't that I cannot understand, for of course I can, but he believes such things are not suitable for women's ears, or some such thing. In any case, that's all he told me of the matter. Of course, Lady Ophelia is furious with him—Simon, that is—for having any part of such a nasty piece of goods as that upstart Bonaparte fellow."

"I can hear her telling him so," Lydia responded with a gurgle and a wary glance at the hovering servants.

Diana's eyes twinkled, but she waved away the plate of creamed tripe being proferred by a footman and waited until the room was nearly clear again before continuing the conversation. "Her ladyship is *not* the diplomat in the family, to be sure," she said then, still twinkling. "She simply cannot conceive of any good reason why her nephew, who ought to be quite puffed up with his own vast consequence, after all, should have anything to do with an upstart commoner. And a French one, at that."

"He is Corsican, I believe."

Diana dismissed Corsica with a slight gesture. "He is a foreigner, which is quite enough for Lady Ophelia. She has no patience with foreigners. They are so very un-English, you know." Diana grinned. "The old marquess isn't nearly so outspoken, of course. I daresay he's waiting to see which way the wind will blow before plumping for one course or another."

"Well, at least he doesn't disapprove of Simon's activities," Lydia said comfortably.

"No, Simon can do no wrong in his eyes," Diana said, her thoughts turning inward again as she added musingly, "and poor Rory can do nothing right."

Lydia quickly cleared her throat and suggested that Diana might like to try some of the goose liver sauce. Diana refused with a little smile, but she accepted the hint willingly enough and began to relate a harmless anecdote from one of the house parties she had attended. Lydia encouraged this line of conversation, and by the time they had finished their repast, she had caught up on most of the pertinent *on dits* of the glittering *beau monde,* including the fact that the notorious Lady Jersey, who had been the Prince of Wales's *inammorata* for something more than seven years, since shortly before his unfortunate marriage to the Princess

Caroline of Brunswick, seemed to be on the lookout for an heiress for her eldest son.

"Not that Lord Villiers needs to marry money," Diana said, "but he's easily the handsomest bachelor on the Marriage Mart these days, so it doesn't hurt him to look about for the brightest star, and that certainly seems to be Lady Sarah Fane. She is, after all, the greatest heiress the *beau monde* has seen for many a day."

"They say her income will be forty thousand pounds per year when she comes of age," Lydia said in tones approaching awe. "I have never met her. Have you?"

"Briefly, the first day we were at Wilton House. She is pretty enough, and certainly her family is as well-connected as the Villiers, but I thought her rather wearisome. She is just seventeen, you know, and her manners are brash rather than pleasing—a schoolgirl drawing attention to herself, I think. You may judge for yourself if she and her stepmama condescend to visit Alderwood Abbey for Christmas. Lady Ophelia invited them, I believe. She likes Lady Westmorland but has no good to say of the earl, and I doubt she's even met young Sally. The Earl and Countess of Westmorland got married only two years ago, after all, and Lady Sarah's mama has been dead these nine years and more, so I cannot think how Lady Ophelia might have met her before." She paused, the infectious grin lighting her face again. "Her Christmas party is going to be something like, I can tell you. Besides Mr. Brummell, Lord Alvanley, Sir Richard Colt Hoare, and a good many others, including the prince and maybe the Duke of York, Lord and Lady Jersey are coming, and Viscount Villiers, as well. And I can tell you, you might have knocked me over with a feather when I heard that, for I would never have expected Lady Ophelia to allow Lady Jersey within shouting distance. They are of an age, of course, and have known each other for many years, but they are *not* bosom bows. However, Marimorse insisted because Jersey is an old friend of his. I believe they pranced about Almack's together in their macaroni days. And of course, Lady Ophelia can never stand out against her brother when he makes up his mind to something."

"Didn't they call Lord Jersey the Prince of Macaronis?" Lydia asked, smiling.

"Indeed, and the signs are all still there, I promise you. He lisps, and when he walks you'd swear he had high heels to his shoes. And I know for a fact that he still carries a lace handkerchief, though he makes do with a quizzing glass in place of a clouded cane these days to punctuate his conversation."

Lydia laughingly pointed out that his lordship, having served until recently as the Prince of Wales's master of horse, was still very influential in royal circles, then asked if Diana required anything more by way of sustenance. When that young lady insisted that she had eaten all she could reasonably hold, Lydia signaled to the footman behind her chair, and he immediately moved to assist Diana. Once she had risen, he stepped back to perform the same office for his mistress. Within minutes the servants had moved in to clear the table, and Lydia was inexorably leading Diana into the drawing room.

This room, quite the largest one in the house, was decorated in green and gold with modern, Egyptian-style furniture. The outer wall was glazed and in the light of day would present a picturesque view of rolling Wiltshire hills, the nearby woods, and a small lake. At present, the heavy green velvet curtains were drawn, a cheerful fire blazed in the marble fireplace, and Lydia led the way to two deep armchairs placed strategically near enough to the blaze to benefit from its warmth, yet not so near that the chairs' occupants might become overly warm. Firmly, Lydia pushed her guest into the nearer of the two chairs, taking the other for herself.

"Now, my dear, I wish you to begin at the beginning. We have seen too little of you since the wedding, since neither Ethelmoor nor I enjoy jauntering about the countryside as you and Andover do, but I had thought matters between the two of you to be marching along nicely. He loves you, Diana, and you love him, so the tales we hear from the rumormongers, despite what I said earlier, have distressed us. And now you say that

Andover has actually accused you of being involved with Lord Roderick, a thing I cannot and will not believe of you, and for that matter, a thing I would not have imagined Andover, in his worst temper, believing of you. So, clearly, things have come to a worse pass between you than I had thought." Lydia rested her elbows on the arm of her chair and propped her chin in her hands, gazing directly at Diana. After a brief silence, she said gently, "Please, dearest, won't you tell me what on earth can have happened these past months to set the two of you at odds with one another?"

2

Lydia's question was not the one Diana had expected to hear. Her thoughts were full of the events of the past few days, but the question forced her to take stock of herself and of her entire relationship with her husband.

For a moment, just trying to think back so far was disorienting, all the way back to March and the glitter and excitement of a London Season amidst the ecstacy of peace—the Peace of Amiens, secured at last, after years of war. The very notion had seemed magical. And as a young girl who had enjoyed several successful London Seasons without showing the least interest in settling down to marriage with any of the eligible or not-so-eligible gentlemen who had presented themselves to the Earl of Trent as desirable prospects, the Lady Diana Sterling had merely looked forward to another such spring full of laughter and good times. Then she had met Simon, Earl of Andover and eldest son of the wealthy, influential Marquess of Marimorse.

"I fell tail over top in love with him," she said now, speaking more to the cheerfully crackling fire than to

Lydia, "and I thought it was the same with him. It was the most incredible feeling, being in love. Simon was so magnificent. I remember thinking, the night I first saw him—at Bedford House, it was—that he was exactly what the knight in shining armor in all one's favorite fairy tales ought to have looked like. He's so big, you know, so handsome, and he looks so powerful, like he could slay dragons and rescue damsels from all manner of villains. And all the time his eyes look right through one like golden arrows piercing right to one's heart. There's such power, such authority, in those looks. When I first met him, everything in me would go weak whenever Simon looked into my eyes. Sometimes, it's still like that. There will be a stirring—no, more like a tingling. *You* know, Lyddy. Everything just catches fire. And then he'll smile, Lyddy, and he can look so gentle—"

"Diana, you're besotted with the man," Lydia cut in with a shake of her dark curls. "What on earth possessed you to run away from him?"

"I *was* besotted with him." Diana sighed, leaning back into the chair and regarding her fingertips as they laced together in her lap. "I felt that way right up until we got married, Lyddy, like Simon was a god or something, who loved me more than life itself and who would always take care of me. The love I felt for him filled me and was so strong it's a miracle it didn't consume me, but the feelings only lasted a few weeks after the wedding. I don't think his feelings lasted even that long. Little did I know what marriage to him would really be like."

"What happened?" Lydia asked quietly, serious now.

"He changed, slowly at first, so I didn't really notice. He would suggest I wear one dress rather than another or wear my hair confined in a snood rather than piled atop my head. That sort of thing."

"And then?"

Diana's jaw tightened. "Then he became unbearable, Lydia. It was absurd. He used to say—when we first met, you know—that he was charmed by my opinions and delighted by my independent spirit, but then he changed to the worst sort of jealous tyrant, constantly scolding and lecturing, giving orders instead of suggestions. He doesn't even permit me to have opinions anymore. Indeed, he expects me to devote myself to him without a thought for anyone or anything else. He even expects me to wait upon him, like some sort of scullery maid."

"Surely you exaggerate," Lydia said calmly, "and even if you do not, Diana, the blame cannot rest entirely with Simon. A good many of the tales that have reached our ears have little to do with him at all, you know, except insofar as he seems to be the victim of a rather willful young wife. That is plain speaking, indeed, my dearest," she added when Diana shot her a reproachful look, "but Simon is scarcely noted for his patience, except perhaps in diplomatic circles, and if any one of the tales I've heard is true, your behavior would have tried the patience of a saint. For that matter, you have had, for a number of years, the reputation for being a most accomplished flirt, so although I do not for one minute believe you have been engaged in criminal conversation with anyone at all, let alone Simon's own brother, perhaps you ought to tell me just what came to pass between yourself and Lord Roderick that caused Simon to jump, as you say, to all the wrong conclusions."

Diana bit her lip, avoiding Lydia's keen gaze, but when she spoke at last, she made an attempt to recover her dignity. "I don't know precisely what you may have heard, of course, but I make no doubt the tales were prodigiously embellished, Lydia."

"Oh, I'm perfectly certain they were exaggerated," Lydia agreed cheerfully. "I know for a fact that though you may very well have played the part of Lady Godiva at the house party at Badminton in September, you did not do so in a state of nature, for example."

"Lydia! Surely, you never heard such a thing!"

Lydia nodded, her eyes beginning to twinkle.

Nom d'un nom d'un nom, breathed Diana, choosing a phrase used by her French governess during moments of stress. "No wonder Simon was so out of reason cross when he arrived at Badminton. He had made one of his flying trips to London, you know, to confer with Lord Holland, and arrived two days after the theatricals. He must have heard a similar tale. That would certainly explain why he flew into a temper and scolded me so severely over the dress I was wearing when he arrived. It was a red gown with black lace trim, I remember. The bodice was perhaps a trifle low, and the whole effect was slightly improper, I suppose," she added, wrinkling her brow and thinking back, "but not so improper as all that."

"Did you truly empty a bowl of arrack punch over his head in the middle of that quarrel?" Lydia asked curiously.

Diana chuckled reminiscently. "That much of the tale was true enough. Lord, but Simon was furious. Standing there sputtering like a fool with punch streaming down his face and under his neckcloth. As I recall, an orange peel came to rest on the very top of his head. He looked perfectly ridiculous, but I do not like public jobations, you know, and he was idiotish enough to treat me to a regular bear-garden jaw right in front of the Duke of Beaufort and all the others. I had to do something. I got punch all over myself, as well," she added, chuckling. "The dress was utterly ruined."

A gurgle of delicious laughter escaped her hostess's lips. "I wonder Andover did not *do* something himself, my dear, like beat you soundly for treating him with such insolence."

Diana grinned at her, but she was remembering at the same time that it had been a near thing on that particular occasion. In her mind's eye she could still see the furious look on Simon's face, the ominous beetling of his thick eyebrows when the room around them grew apprehensively silent, just before the unexpected twinkle leapt to his golden-hazel eyes and his booming laugh burst forth. He had snatched her up into his arms then and had swung her about, to the huge delight (and relief) of the Duke of Beaufort's guests, calling her his make-mischief lady and wondering aloud what devilry she would next concoct to plague him. But when he had set her once again upon her feet, he had guided her with seeming gentleness but willy-nilly all the same into the winding staircase hall outside the ballroom, where he had informed her in a few pithy statements that if she valued her skin, she would never again subject him to such a scene. A shiver of fear shot up and down her spine now at the untimely memory, and she glanced over at Lydia to find that lady's soft brown eyes curiously upon her. Diana shifted in her chair.

"He is a temperamental man, but he is not much given to violence, I think. Lord knows, I have provoked him often and often, and though he bellows a good deal, he has never raised a hand to me."

"Is that why you provoke him, Diana? To seek out the limits of his patience?" Lydia spoke gently.

"He provokes me, too, Lydia. I *told* you how it is."

"Yes, I know you did, but it sounds to me as if the two of you are merely testing one another. You seem to be trying to find the limits of his temper whilst he seeks to discover how thoroughly he can master you. Such a testing is not at all unusual during the first year of a marriage, I believe, particularly in a love match."

"Nonsense, it is nothing so childish. At least, on my part it is not. I do not doubt you may be right about Simon, but I am determined that he shall never see me under his boot. Perhaps my methods have not always been precisely ladylike—"

"They call you Lady Escapade," Lydia murmured.

"Oh, that." Diana hunched a shoulder. "That came from that odious Vidame de Lâche. He is such a muck-worm, Lyddy. It astonishes me that he can have such a sweetly lovely sister as Mademoiselle Sophie."

But Lydia had ceased to follow the rapid twist of subject. "De Lâche? Sophie? Do I know these people?"

"No, probably not, though I'm sure they are perfectly respectable. Or Sophie is, in any case. Sorry, I'm dithering. They are French émigrés. The family name is Beléchappé, but their father is the Comte De Vieillard, and their mother the comtesse, of course. The vidame is a flowery fop with an evil tongue. He seeks to make his way by following Mr. Brummell's lead, I think, but unfortunately the vidame lacks both Mr. Brummell's charm and his wit. De Lâche had the temerity to call me *la dame des frédaines*, or the escapade lady, once in Brighton, and the Prince of Wales chose to be amused. Simon did what he could, of course, but I cannot be surprised to hear that the nickname has managed to stick in some quarters, at least. I am persuaded that no one can wonder at Rory's having a *tendre* for Mademoiselle Sophie, for she is shyly sweet and very charming— just the sort of innocent child to stir his protective instincts—though how she came to have *such* a brother, I'm sure I cannot—"

"Rory? Lord Roderick?" Lydia leaned forward, her mouth agape. "Oh, Diana, is he truly throwing out lures to an émigré's daughter? Why, the marquess will have an apoplectic seizure an he hears of such a thing."

"Oh, pooh, it is nothing so serious as all that," Diana said quickly, conscious of having been indiscreet in her wish to escape further discussion of her odious nickname. "Besides," she added with a mischievous gleam in her eyes, "there is a fabulous treasure hidden somewhere in the grounds of Château Beléchappé, their family seat in Normandy, and the vidame is hopeful of recovering it now that peace has come."

"Really, Diana," Lydia said, laughing, "you know perfectly well that every émigré family washed ashore on the south coast these twenty years has boasted of massive treasure left behind. 'Tis too absurd. Those who truly had disposable assets brought them along, and anything they couldn't carry away then, they are hardly like to snatch from under Bonaparte's long nose now. But tell me more of Mademoiselle Sophie. Is she frightfully beautiful?"

"She is lovely," Diana said slowly. "Light brown hair so soft and wispy it looks like spun silk, and huge blue eyes, like a China doll, but Sophie's loveliness is more than mere beauty. She is possessed of an innocence, a fragility, that makes men yearn to protect her."

"Men, maybe, but Lord Roderick?" Lydia's tone indicated astonished doubt. "You mentioned his protective instincts a moment ago, and I thought you must be joking. That madcap never gave a thought to anyone but himself in all his life, Diana. Now I know you have been roasting me. Innocence would merely bore him, so all this has undoubtedly been a ruse to escape confessing your own sins. *Were* you flirting with him? Truth, now."

Diana sighed. "No, Lyddy, I wasn't. But Simon certainly thought I was. Rory and I were in the Double Cube room at Wilton—"

"The room that is said to be all white with real gold trim and magnificent painted ceilings?" Lydia demanded. "I've heard it said that Inigo Jones went completely wild in designing that room."

Diana nodded. "The Herberts are proud of it, and I suppose it's very nice. Rory and I were looking at the Van Dyck portraits and just sort of talking. I said something he didn't like—I fear that, like you, I dared to doubt that he was truly serious about his love for Sophie—and he grabbed my shoulders to make me look right at him, just to emphasize whatever it was he was about to say, of course, and not for any other reason. His temper can be as volatile as Simon's at times. But of course Simon must choose that exact moment to interrupt our conversation. He knocked Rory down," she added with another sigh and a small, ironic smile.

"Well, that at least is nothing new," Lydia pointed out matter-of-factly, "whatever you may choose to think of Andover's not having a violent streak. They say the Warrington twins have been at it hammer and tongs since the day Lord Roderick first discovered that by having had the misfortune to present himself to the world some twenty minutes after Andover's arrival, he had done himself out of the title and anything other than what little his father or brother might choose to grant him from the unentailed property."

"But it need never have been that way if the marquess had not lavished all his attention on Simon and if Lady Marimorse had not dubbed him the good twin and poor Rory the bad twin before ever they were out of short coats. My mama said the marchioness's attitude was the source of the whole unfortunate business, and I've no doubt Mama has the right of it. I think it a most fortunate thing indeed that the marchioness is no longer around to shove her oar between them."

"Diana!" Lydia exclaimed, scandalized.

"Well, I won't unsay the words," Diana returned stoutly. "I think she must have been a dreadful woman.

I can only be glad she did not live long enough to cast a blighting influence over dearest Susanna. Goodness knows she's had enough to contend with in Lady Ophelia, but at least her ladyship means well."

"She is a bit overbearing at times, I daresay," Lydia said, diverted again.

"Not overbearing, merely a trifle weighty. Papa says she creates boredom, then causes others to suffer mightily. Mama merely calls her the platitudinous Lady Ophelia. But her ladyship is kind to Susanna, and the twins both adore their little sister, so she will come out of it all right in the end."

"Is not Susanna to make her come-out this year?"

"Indeed she is, and her letters to us have been full of nothing else. She was invited to make one of the Wilton House party, but both Lady Ophelia and the marquess forbade it, saying it would not be the thing, since she is not yet out. Not that that stopped Lady Sarah Fane from taking part. She does not make her come-out until spring either. But that is beside the point. We have prevailed upon the marquess to allow Susanna to emerge from the schoolroom for the Christmas festivities, and they are to be very grand, as you well know. My mama took up Susanna's banner when the marquess was loth to allow her to take part. Mama wrote him a charming letter, assuring him that his lovely and very well-behaved daughter could only profit from being granted such a treat, that it would be far better for her to try her wings for the first time on her home ground and under benevolent eyes. Simon also wrote to him," she added.

"Ah," said Lydia with an air of vast wisdom.

Diana made a face at her. "Getting him to write was one of Mama's knacky notions, too, if you must know everything. My mama is a very knowing one when all is said and done."

"She is, indeed," agreed Lydia, who made no secret of the fact that she adored her mama-in-law. There was a moment's silence before she added softly, "Did you explain the matter to Simon, Diana?"

Diana had no difficulty following Lydia's train of thought and realized, not for the first time, that while it was easy enough to divert her sister-in-law's attention for moments at a time, it was rarely possible to put her off the scent entirely. She grimaced. "I couldn't explain other than to tell him it wasn't what he thought, that we were merely talking."

"It is well known that Lord Roderick has always wanted whatever Simon had," Lydia said slowly, musingly, "so perhaps—"

"No!" Diana interrupted explosively. "I won't listen to such stuff, Lyddy, even from you. If Rory is bitter, he has cause to be, but much as they have fought over the years, he loves Simon and Simon loves him. He covets nothing of Simon's—not anymore—only what should be his by right. Even Simon was beginning to see that, before he had to tow Rory out of River Tick again only a week before we reached Wilton—"

Lydia's laughter interrupted her. "Oh, forgive me, Diana," she said, attempting unsuccessfully to stifle her mirth, "but you jump about so. One moment I'm nearly persuaded to feel sorry for Lord Roderick, and the next you paint a perfectly clear portrait of poor Andover coming home from France to be met by the news that his scapegrace twin is under the hatches again and must be rescued from a sponging house. Then, as thanks for the rescue, Lord Roderick is caught making love to Andover's wife. Andover ought very likely to be ripe for Bedlam by now. One must hope that Lord Roderick did not choose to fly into the boughs after that little scene you described to me, and leave Wilton House on your heels, else Andover will think the two of you have run off together."

Diana tossed her head. She hadn't considered the possibility of Rory's taking flight, too, but if the thought disturbed her, she would never admit as much to Lydia. "So what if Simon does think I've made a conquest of Rory?" she demanded. "He's accused me of flirting often and often, just as though he himself had not left a string of feminine conquests from Calais to Paris on this latest trip of his."

"Goodness, did he, indeed? A whole string of them? How very tired he must have been," Lydia said sympathetically. "I daresay he quite collapsed at Mr. Bonaparte's feet, which perfectly accounts for their mission having gone so well. No doubt that odious man merely counted Andover's behavior as proper obeisance from a potential subject."

Diana choked. "Lydia, will you, for the love of Heaven, be serious?"

"But I am serious, my love, perfectly serious. If I mouth absurdities, 'tis only because the thought of Andover making love to countless Frenchwomen, one after the other, can be nothing *but* absurd. I've seen the way he looks at you, Diana."

"The way he *looked* at me, you mean. I tell you, Lyddy, the man stifles my very spirit. His jealousy is ridiculous. Even if I do flirt a little, we all do. Such behavior is expected. It is also perfectly harmless, as everyone but Simon seems to know. And he *does* flirt, too, whatever you may think, so he has no business to tell me to stop when he won't stop himself."

Lydia gave her a long look, and Diana felt sudden tears springing to her eyes. But the older woman made no attempt to press the issue, giving instead a quick look at the elegant, gilt Cafieri clock on the Nash mantelpiece. With a ladylike shriek of dismay she exclaimed, "Good gracious, Diana, only look at the time! I'd no notion the hour was so far advanced, and I must be up with the birds, for I promised to visit the dairy in time for the milking. We've a new dairymaid, you see, and I promised Ethelmoor I'd keep watch till she's found her way about. A nice child from one of the tenant families, and she'll do well enough, but it is always difficult being new at something. Never mind feeling you must get up any earlier than you would have done at Wilton House, however," she added, still speaking rapidly. "We shall feed you whenever you choose to show your face abroad."

Diana smiled, her equilibrium restored. "You are a love, Lyddy," she said impulsively. "I think the smartest thing my brother ever did was to entice you into our family."

"Pooh," said Lydia. "If you think your doltish brother did the asking, then you still do not know me very well. He had some of the oddest notions of proper courting—

all pomp and circumstance and stuffy proprieties. But I managed to turn all that to good account in the end, for very fortunately my grandpapa fell ill, so I was able to urge Ethelmoor to come up to scratch in case Grandpapa should cock up his toes and do us out of a timely wedding."

Diana shook her head. "And to think," she said in righteous tones, "that you were taking me to task less than twenty minutes ago for my irreverent words regarding the late Marchioness of Marimorse."

"Ah, but Grandpapa recovered," Lydia pointed out, "so it was not at all the same thing. And since I knew perfectly well that he was suffering from nothing more serious than a slight chill caught whilst wading up to his hips in an icy brook in order to catch the one that always gets away . . . well, there you are. Not the same thing at all."

"Sometimes," Diana said awfully, as Lydia got to her feet and shook out her skirts, "I think you are a more unprincipled madcap that I am, Lyddy."

"No, do you?" replied Lydia demurely. "But how could I be, dearest, with a sturdy ten-year-old at Eton and a scrambling three-year-old in the nursery? I've no time for mischief, nor would you have time for it, my girl, if you and Andover would but begin your nursery." Seeing the gathering frown on Diana's face, she added quickly, "Never mind, my dear. 'Tis none of my affair, and I'll indulge in no more lectures. I'll see you to your bedchamber and then, just to show what a love I am, I'll send Madi along to you the moment she's put my things away."

Diana declined at first, insisting she had no need of a lady's maid to see her to bed, but she gave in without much argument because she liked Madi and because it would give her a chance to practice her French. Madi was another of the numerous émigrés from war-torn France, but hers had not been the comfortable life of the Comte and Comtesse de Vieillard and their children. Her parents had fled the Terror when Madi, then Mademoiselle Madeleine de Flétan, had been but a child. Her father, a minor nobleman (but not minor enough to escape the attention of the Committee for

Public Safety), had died before ever reaching safe harbor in England, and Madi's mother had arrived with one small child and no money. Fortunately, however, she had managed to find a position as chambermaid in Lydia's parents' household, so Lydia had known Madi most of her life.

When the plump Frenchwoman arrived to help Diana, that young lady greeted her in fluent, idiomatic French, and Madi, knowing well that Diana enjoyed practicing the skills learned from a doting French governess, made no attempt to turn the conversation to English, although she now considered herself every inch an English citizen.

Once the maid had gone, Diana snuffed the remaining candle by the bed and snuggled down to sleep. But sleep eluded her. Whenever she closed her eyes, her mind filled with a vision of the Earl of Andover, large and furious, his eyes flashing, his voice aroar. She had half expected him to have arrived by now. Perhaps this time, however, he had chosen not to confront her. Perhaps this time she had outraged him beyond what he would tolerate.

She could still see the expression on his face when he had caught her—no, not that—when he had walked into the Double Cube room so unexpectedly. He had said nothing at all at first, merely striding across the room to grab Rory with one iron hand before knocking him to the floor with the other. Then, hauling him to his feet again, he had ordered his twin to make himself scarce while he could still move under his own power. And Rory had fled, leaving Diana to her husband's tender mercies.

She had made no particular attempt to justify her actions, because she had not felt she could do so without betraying the subject of their conversation, which Rory had particularly asked her not to do. She had not even (though she had told Lydia otherwise) tried to tell Simon he was in error in believing she held a tenderness for his twin. Instead, she had held her tongue while he read her a severe scold. Not until he had begun berating her for past misdeeds, not until he had accused her of flirting with a list of men long enough to count as a squadron, if not an entire army, had she lost her temper and lashed out at him, accusing him of worse things, taunting him until she had thought for a moment that he would lose all control over his temper, that he might even strike her. At that point she had fallen silent, and Simon, after one parting blast, had left the room.

The episode had taken place after supper the previous night, and Diana had not seen Simon afterward. She had slept alone in a very large bed, and the next morning her headache had been only half imagined. Sending a chambermaid to tender her excuses for not taking part in the day's hunting, Diana had packed her bandboxes, ordered Ned Tredegar to saddle her favorite mount, and ridden nearly forty miles through a drizzling rain to Ethelmoor Hall.

Now, as these images faded and she began to remember her talk with Lydia, she was besieged with visions of Simon as he had been when she had first become acquainted with him—at Bedford House, the night they first met, when Simon, a golden giant in a dark blue coat, golden waistcoat, and cream-colored knee breeches, had swept down upon her and informed her with his charming smile that he *needed* her company at supper.

"You need me?" She had laughed at him, feeling very sure of herself simply because his eyes told her that she was the most beautiful, the most fascinating creature he had ever seen.

"Indeed I do," he assured her, his low voice like music to her enchanted ears. "You are exactly the sort of young lady my aunt would approve of, so if you will go down to dinner on my arm, she will not attempt to foist the daughter of one of her bosom bows upon me. Boring, every one of them, I assure you. You will be doing me a signal service, thereby putting me forever in your debt."

How they had laughed, and how much they enjoyed themselves that night and a host of other nights afterward. For the young Earl of Andover suddenly seemed to appear everywhere she went, and Diana, who had never been tempted to marry any of the young men who had pursued her through several Seasons, suddenly found herself hoping and praying that Simon would approach her father to seek permission to court her. In those days Simon had only to suggest that he liked her best in pink for her to discard every gown in her wardrobe that was *not* pink. And if, on a whim, he decided the following week that pale yellow would become her, Diana had sent for her long-suffering dressmaker to effect the change. She grimaced now, thinking about how he had changed after the wedding.

The wedding itself had been the highlight of a sparkling Season. It was as though the marriage of Andover and the Earl of Trent's lovely, fickle daughter had presented the *beau monde* with the perfect way to celebrate the Peace of Amiens. After a succession of lesser celebrations, they had gone all out with a special fete at Ranelagh Gardens and even a grand display of fireworks in Hyde Park.

There had been fireworks afterward, too, Diana remembered, squirming a little in her bed. Not immediately afterward, though she had been annoyed when Simon had refused to take her into France on their bride trip, saying it was still much too dangerous, when everyone knew people were simply flocking to Paris again. He had taken her to Scotland instead, to Edinburgh, where they had visited the castle and where they had stayed with friends of his. But the change had been setting in even then.

She had no longer had quite the same urge to flatter his every whim by then, of course, but he had seemed to go right on expecting her to bow to his slightest suggestion, and, worse, he had begun to take umbrage when she did not. And he had objected, loudly, every time she had so much as smiled at another man. Diana's independent spirit had rallied quickly under such Turkish treatment, and a not so private war had raged between them ever since, much to the delight and consternation of friends in the *beau monde*. They were an *on dit*.

Her thoughts came back to the present, and she wondered if Simon would arrive during the night. The rain still drizzled steadily, so he had probably racked up for the night by now, but he would no doubt arrive in the morning. She would need a good night's sleep if she was to deal competently with him in an angry confrontation.

That was her last sensible thought before sleep finally claimed her, but her dreams were by no means peaceful, and the muted clatter and crunch of horses' hooves and carriage wheels on the gravel drive beneath her window the following morning snapped her to an upright, wide-awake position straight out of her troubled sleep.

"Simon," she whispered, snatching back the covers and springing lightly from the bed to hurry, barefoot, across the chilly floor to the window. Hastily, she pushed aside the heavy curtains and shoved open the casement to peer anxiously down at the sunlit scene below.

3

Bright sunlight from a cloudless blue sky sparkled on puddles and green grass, on glistening bare shrubbery, and on the irregular, picturesque landscape designed some years before by Humphrey Repton for the Viscount Ethelmoor. Ethelmoor Hall had been designed by the architect John Nash to settle comfortably into the broken landscape of the Wiltshire valley in which it was situated. The viscount had desired to build a modern house in a parklike setting for his bride, and that was exactly what Nash had built. Repton, his partner at the time, had designed the landscaping to suit the same modern taste, which demanded that one's house be incorporated into its natural setting. Consequently, the park at Ethelmoor came practically up to the house itself, separated from it only by the drive, a broad still-green lawn, and an informal garden, barren of flowers at this time of year, but still sporting neat hedge-rows and rich, well-cultivated earth. The view was the thing, and the view this morning was magnificent. Through the thicket of gnarled oak trees at the southern end of the garden, Diana might easily have seen sunlight dancing on the waters of a small lake, had she been at all interested in doing so.

But Diana had eyes for nothing other than the yellow chaise rolling to a stop near the conservatory entrance. A man leapt from the vehicle even before it came to a complete halt, and as he strode toward the house, he reached up and snatched the chapeau bras from his head, clapping it flat under his arm. Crisp yellow curls were thus thrust into view, and Diana let out a long breath of relief. Her brother had come home.

The tingling apprehension that had propelled her to the window subsided rapidly, and she was conscious of a sense of disappointment that deepened when, glancing at the little clock on the dressing table, illuminated by a shaft of light from the window, she noted that it was already half past ten o'clock. Perhaps Simon would not come after all.

Diana opened the pale green curtains properly, letting the morning light flood the cheerful room. A floral carpet of greens and golds covered a good portion of the polished oak floor between the high, sea-green-draped bed and the door into the hallway, but the boards between the bed and the window were bare and, now that she noticed, quite chilly beneath her feet. She shut the casement and skipped back to the bed to tuck her toes underneath the eiderdown. Hugging her knees, she considered what she would do if Simon failed to come for her. Recognizing her disappointment for what it was, she remembered certain things that Lydia had said to her the previous night. Was she merely playing bride games with her husband? Could their frequent quarrels be the result of such childishness as that? Diana grimaced, wriggling her toes in order to hasten the warming process, not liking the turn her thoughts were taking. Surely the fiery nature of their relationship was not entirely her fault.

Where was Simon, anyway? Why did he not come for

her? He would be furious, of course. At least, she
certainly hoped he was furious. Her thoughts seemed
suddenly to suspend themselves as she turned the last
one over in her mind to examine it more thoroughly.
Would she truly be disappointed if Simon were not
angry with her?

Stretching, she pushed the disturbing thoughts to the
back of her mind. It was no use to wonder what would
or would not happen or how she would or would not
feel. The sensible course was to await the future and to
deal now with the present. And that meant it was time
to cease her idleness and get dressed to greet her brother.

Ringing for a maid, Diana quickly accomplished her
ablutions and within half an hour, clad in one of her
own morning gowns, a turquoise-and-green sprigged
muslin with silk mistake ribbons banding the high waist
and a ruffled flounce decking the hem, she made her
way downstairs to the magnificent conservatory, which
was the family's customary daytime gathering place even
in the wintertime.

During the past ten years, as turnpike roads and fast
coaches had made country living more accessible and
subsequently more fashionable among the members of
the *beau monde,* their houses had begun to reflect their
changing tastes, and in the conservatory at Ethelmoor
Hall, both John Nash and Humphrey Repton had com-
bined their considerable talents to make the room at
one with the surrounding landscape. For some twenty
years the trend had been moving away from the notion
that the servants' day rooms in a noble house needed to
be beneath the main rooms. In newer homes, such as
Ethelmoor Hall, it was therefore now possible to put
the servants in a wing of their own so that the main
rooms of the house could be at ground level.

Symmetry was no longer fashionable either, so the
rooms on the ground floor of the Hall had been grouped
to enjoy the sun and the view. All of the main rooms
opened directly onto green turf or gardens, and each
of these rooms had windows down to the floor. The
furnishings, even in the Egyptian-style drawing room,
were simple, so as not to compete with the view, and
while the dining room, drawing room, and Ethelmoor's

study all had curtains framing their gothic-arched windows, the conservatory had none.

As Diana passed through the drawing room toward the door into the conservatory, she heard her brother's deep voice.

" 'I wish you will tell Mama,' " he said, amusement coloring his tone, " 'that when she directs my letters, she must remember to direct Mr. Sterling and not Master, for every boy's letter is now directed Mr. Thingabob. It is only a week to the holidays now, and that will soon be gone. I am to tell you—' Good morning, Diana, I trust you slept well."

Ethelmoor stood in the center of the spacious room, peering at her over a sheet of flimsy paper, crossed and recrossed in schoolboyish scrawl. He was a gentleman of slightly more than thirty years and was generally accounted to be a handsome man. Certainly his figure was well enough, though with his better than average height, long legs, and broad, rather bony shoulders, he had a tendency to look lanky rather than graceful when he moved. The expression on his face spoke of a sweet disposition, his eyes were wont to twinkle, and he possessed a smile of singular charm. The latter came into play now as he looked his sister over with his head cocked a little to one side.

Diana grinned at him. "I slept wonderfully well, thank you. Is that letter from the hope of the house?"

"From John, yes. His observations on life at Eton are always amusing. I picked up the morning's post at the lodge as I came in. But I can finish reading this later, of course," he added reluctantly.

"Not unless it contains messages unsuitable for auntish ears," Diana replied, taking a seat which provided her with a splendid view of the oak thicket and the grassy park. "I should adore to hear what he thinks of your old school."

"Yes, darling, do go on," Lydia put in encouragingly. "I am glad to know he has got over his cold," she said, adding for Diana's benefit, "The whole middle fourth seemed to be ill when last he wrote. What is it that he is to tell us, sir?"

"That he has been a good boy and has still not given

them cause to flog him," her husband replied, chuckling as he scanned to find his place again. "He is certainly well again. Listen to this bit. 'We are all playing at marbles now. The bigger boys play at hockey, fives, and single stick, which is beating one another about as hard as you can with sticks. I should not think it was a very agreeable game.' " Ethelmoor laughed heartily, but his wife frowned.

"That does not sound at all safe to me," she said. "What can the masters be thinking about, to let them do such things?"

"It sounds," said Diana, "like precisely the sort of thing John will adore to do when he is one of those bigger boys, himself. Is that the lot, Bruce?"

"One more bit. 'Cousin Dick'—that's Lydia's brother's eldest—'tells me to tell you that he has not had occasion yet to throw me downstairs, and that I do not make much noise.' "

"Good gracious!" Diana exclaimed, laughing. "Young Dick must be quite a ruffian."

"Not a bit of it," Ethelmoor retorted. "He's been at great pains to look after our John. 'Tis merely that I wrote some time ago to inquire as to whether the task had proved overly arduous. This is my reply. John signs off now, informing us graciously that we need not write him again as he will soon be at home." Ethelmoor folded the letter, moved to lay it upon a side table next to his chapeau bras, then bent a surprisingly piercing glance upon his sister. "What's this Lydia tells me about you running away from Simon, Diana? Tantrums again?"

"Oh, 'tis nothing at all of consequence," she assured him with an airy, dismissive wave of her hand. " 'Tis merely that I have tired prodigiously of his scolds and sought to enjoy a repairing lease with you and dearest Lyddy."

Despite the gesture and her casual tone, she was watching her brother warily. As Lydia had pointed out the previous night, he was not at all a temperamental man, but there had been one or two occasions in the past, which Diana remembered now with reluctance, when he had said some very uncomfortable things to her.

The twinkle in his eyes, which were much the same turquoise-blue as her own, reassured her. "You alarm me," he said easily, gathering up his things from the side table. "I trust we are in momentary expectation of Andover's arrival?"

She shrugged. "As to that, I'm sure I wouldn't presume to hazard a guess."

"Well, I would. Seems to me it's dashed well inevitable. But he won't trouble me, and I daresay that, given enough time, he's still the man to teach you to obey him, chit." He grinned at her, ignoring the stormy look she cast him as he turned to his wife. "I shall be in my study, sweetheart. Mind," he added with a mock-fierce frown, "that you don't send any more letters to Eton directed to Master Sterling."

"Yes, my lord," replied Lydia demurely.

"Baggage. Get up from that chair and give me a kiss. I know I've been away only the one night, but Lord, I missed you." He pulled her out of the chair and gathered her into his arms, kissing her heartily.

Diana watched them, thinking how easy it seemed for them to express their love for one another and feeling a little wistful.

Ethelmoor set his rosy-cheeked wife back on her heels, grinned again at his sister, and strode from the room. Lydia, still blushing, smiled. "You must be famished, Diana. Shall I ring for them to serve you right here on a tray? I rarely eat a nuncheon in the country, you know, so we do not dine again until four o'clock. Or I can accompany you upstairs to the morning room, if you prefer."

She spoke rapidly as though her speech could cover her blushes, and Diana laughed at her. "Pray do not be so conscious, Lyddy. I promise I was not dismayed by Bruce's unhusbandly display of affection. No one who knows him can fail to realize how very much he loves you."

"But 'tis prodigiously unfashionable," Lydia protested. "A man and wife are not supposed to live in one another's pockets, and I promise you, Diana, we shall do nothing to embarrass you or Lady Ophelia when we visit Alderwood Abbey after Christmas."

"Fustian. Lyddy, pray do not be such a goose, I implore you. You'll never stop Bruce from looking at you as he does, no matter how hard you try, and no one will mind a bit. The two of you make other people feel good. Why, if Simon—" But she broke off at once, realizing that such a change of subject might well carry her into waters she had no wish at the moment to explore. "Dear me," she said instead, laughing, "how I do carry on. I should adore to have something served to me here, Lyddy. This is quite the most charming room in your very charming house. With three sides all glass, clear from ceiling to floor, as they are, one quite has the feeling of being outdoors. And how *do* you contrive to keep the park and the hedgerows so green in winter. I am persuaded Alderwood and Andover Court must both be looking quite sickly by now."

Lydia answered glibly as she rose to ring for a servant. A few moments later, tea and a light repast having been ordered for Lady Andover, they were alone again, but Lydia made no attempt to turn their conversation back to Simon, and Diana was grateful. She was also grateful that her brother had taken her arrival in stride, but she had to admit that his amusement didn't sit too well with her. Nor did his casually-expressed assurance that the Earl of Andover would soon find a means by which to ensure her obedience to his will.

Her breakfast soon arrived and the conversation continued desultorily, covering a myriad of topics from Master John Sterling and his little sister, Amy, to the new dairy maid and the latest London fashions.

"Are you certain you are not cold in that thin dress?" Lydia asked anxiously.

"No, of course not," Diana replied smiling her thanks to the maid who had come to remove her tray. "How could anyone be chilly, sitting in this sunny room?" But just then, as if to belie her words, goose bumps rose on her arms and a tingling chill raced up and down her spine. She froze, her lips parted slightly as she stared at Lydia. Then the sound that she had heard almost subconsciously grew louder, the sound of carriage wheels on gravel, and Lydia returned the anxious look with one just as anxious when the sound reached her ears.

Diana had been sitting with her back to that portion of the carriage drive that swept past the east side of the house, but she turned now, nearly certain of what she would see.

Four horses hove into view, drawing a light tan chaise, its wheels and edgings picked out in yellow, a familiar crest emblazoned upon the door panel. A large trunk was strapped onto the front of the chaise, and a liveried footman stood up behind. The two postboys mounted on the lefthand horses wore the same blue and green livery with yellow jackets and beaver hats. As they brought their charges to a plunging halt just outside the conservatory, the nearside door of the chaise was flung open from within before the footman had time to jump down from his perch, and a pair of well-muscled, buckskin-clad masculine legs swung to the ground.

The footman leapt to hold the door, and the Earl of Andover, a large, bronze-haired man with broad shoulders and a heavy torso that gave him a somewhat bullish appearance, presently attired in a loose but well-tailored brown jacket over his close-fitting buckskins and shining topboots, emerged from the interior of the chaise. When he straightened, looking purposefully toward the French doors leading to the conservatory, Diana came involuntarily to her feet, barely conscious as she did so of her sister-in-law's stammered excuses.

"I-I think I'll just run upstairs to the n-nursery to see if Amy requires anything." Lydia was already moving toward the door into the drawing room as she spoke, and the sight of the Earl of Andover striding from the drive across the short stretch of turf to the French doors sped her on her way.

The footman swung up behind again, and the chaise moved away toward the stables, as Diana braced herself. Then Andover pushed open the doors and fairly erupted into the room.

"So here you are, indeed," he boomed, crossing the room in a few long strides. His large hands gripped her shoulders, and he gave her a hard shake. "I might have guessed you would come here. Are you all right?"

"Y-yes, of course I'm all right," Diana snapped, her fears dissipating as her temper rose to meet his. "Do stop shaking me, sir!" She tried to pull away from him, and the attempt merely earned her another shake.

"You deserve that I should do a great deal more than shake you, you idiotic wench. How dared you serve me such a trick! You frightened me nearly witless. Are you quite certain you have not come to grief? The roads are treacherous in the wet, and one never knows what sort of scoundrels might be encountered along the highroad."

"Simon, let me go," Diana commanded, trying once again and just as unsuccessfully to free herself. "I tell you I am quite safe. The road from Wilton is in excellent condition, and the distance is scarcely more than forty miles, after all. And as for scoundrels, there are few footpads on the Marlborough Highroad at the best of times and certainly none at all in a rainstorm."

"Much you would care if there were," he snarled, shaking her again. "And even if you met with no mischance on the road, you will still be well served if you have caught your death from the elements. You must have been nearly the entire afternoon in heavy fog and rain."

"Well, and what if I was? I am not made of anything that will dissolve from a wetting."

"By God," he said wrathfully, "I *shall* beat you this time. You haven't the sense God gave a goose, my girl. And what reason, may I ask, had you to hare off like that in the first place?"

"What reason?" she repeated, her voice going up dangerously on the last word in a squeak of near fury. "How can you even ask me such a question after accusing me—yes, and your brother, as well—of the most disgusting things?"

He held her away, silent for a moment as his gaze raked her from tip to toe. "Your cheeks are over-red," he said at last. "I am persuaded you have a fever."

"Simon, I am not feverish," she said firmly, measuring her words as though she spoke to a halfwit. "If my cheeks are red, 'tis because I am angry." She twisted again in his grasp, but still he would not let her go. She had been watching his eyes, knowing their golden-hazel depths to be the best gauge of his temper. They narrowed now, and a glint appeared that made her cease her struggles and draw breath rather quickly.

"*You* are angry?" he said, his voice steadier but with a note of implacability that had not been present before. "You?" he repeated. "Let me tell you that your anger is as nothing compared to mine. How do you think I felt, my girl, when I went to your room, expecting to find you indulging in a fit of the sulks, only to find you not at all?"

"I don't know how you felt," she told him. "I never know."

"Fustian. You know very well. Had you not intended to frighten me, you would at least have left me a message."

She was still watching his eyes, but his words gave her pause. She had not even thought about leaving him a note. She had known he would find her. A note would have seemed unnecessary, supposing it had ever occurred to her to write one.

"I was angry," she said. "I didn't think."

"Rubbish."

"What? I *was* angry."

"Perhaps. But you didn't leave Wilton House in a fit of anger, Diana mine. I know for a fact that you left yesterday morning, so you had had all the previous night to think about what you were doing. Yes, and that brings to mind another small detail. I shall have a thing or two to say to your precious Ned Tredegar that he won't wish to hear."

"You mustn't." Diana raised one hand to touch his jacket sleeve in a half-pleading gesture. She felt the muscular forearm beneath. "Please, Simon, you know Ned wanted nothing to do with my flight. He came with me only because he knew I'd come alone if he refused to accompany me."

"No doubt, but he could have stopped you," her husband said stubbornly.

"How? He never has been able to stop me from doing as I please." When the golden eyes narrowed again, Diana wished she could unsay the simple state-

ment. Simon now looked very much as she imagined a
bull might look if one were foolish enough to wave a
red flag under its very nose.

"No one can stop you, it seems," he said ominously.
"At least, you choose to think that is the case. And so
you attempt to make a fool of me whenever the fancy
strikes you, even to playing dangerous games with my
own brother—"

"Oh, Simon, no! You can't think—"

"What I think or don't think is small beer compared
to what the rest of the world thinks, my lady. The time
has come for you to cease your foolishness. We have
provided the *beau monde* with grist for its rumor mills
long enough. This last escapade of yours will see an
end to it."

He had her full attention now. She went perfectly
still, her face paling as she attempted to decipher the
purposeful expression in his eyes.

"What are you going to do?" she asked at last, speaking with forced calm.

"We are going home."

"To Andover Court? You are sending me home?"
She had not thought he would do anything so drastic.

"To Alderwood," he said quietly, "and I'm not sending you anywhere. I am going with you."

Diana gave a sigh of relief. "Well, of course we are
going to Alderwood, but not until next week. Surely,
you cannot have forgotten the hunt party at Stourhead
to celebrate the completion of the new wing?"

"Richard," he said, referring to Sir Richard Colt Hoare,
the dilettente and great collector, whose house was his
pride, "will do well enough without us. We are going
home." He released her at last, but she made no attempt to move away from him, and after a searching
look down into her face, he added almost coaxingly, "It
will not be so bad, Diana. You will enjoy seeing Father
and Aunt Ophelia and little Susanna, after all."

"She will not thank you for calling her 'little', sir,"
Diana muttered. "She is a young lady."

"So she is," he agreed, still watching her closely. "We
shall tell them that after all the festivities of the past

months, we both have need of a week to repair our constitutions before Christmas."

"You forget that I had quite a nice rest in Hampshire with Papa and Mama whilst you were enjoying yourself all over France," she said grimly.

"I was scarcely enjoying myself," he retorted, "and I was not 'all over France.' Merely in Paris, and it was a very wearing journey, as I have told you before. Moreover, you were not precisely idle in Hampshire. If Holly Manor was not teeming with guests during the entire course of your sojourn there, it must be for the very first time."

"But I do not—"

"We will not argue the point. I am too tired to bandy words with you, my lady. I have been to Holly Manor and back to Wilton House on horseback in heavy rains before ever packing up to make the journey here, and my temper is on a shorter rein than usual, so I'd advise you to tread warily."

Seeing clearly that he meant every word, she drew in her claws. "You went to Holly Manor? Were they dreadfully worried about me?"

"Not dreadfully. Your father wanted to know what I'd done to vex you, of course, but your mama, dear lady, wisely recommended that I ride to Ethelmoor and shake some sense into you. At the time, I can promise you, I meant to do a deal more than that."

She swallowed carefully. "Will not Lord Marimorse and the Lady Ophelia wonder why we are come before our appointed time? You will humiliate me, sir."

"If 'twere so, 'twould be no more than you deserve for your antics, but they will not indulge in idle curiosity. They will accept the fact that we are worn to the bone from a full and overfull schedule of house parties." When she opened her mouth to protest further, he stopped her with two fingers gently laid upon her lips. "Not another word, Diana. This time you will obey me as any good wife obeys her husband."

"That I should live to see the day." The chortling voice from the drawing room doorway caused them both to start, then to turn as one to face Viscount Ethelmoor. He grinned at Simon. "Welcome, Andover.

You must forgive my tardy appearance, but from one cause or another, my people neglected to inform me that you had arrived."

Simon accepted his hand ruefully. " 'Tis rather I who should beg forgiveness for trading on our kinship to enter your house so informally. My excuse, such as it is, is that I expected to find you all gathered here at this time of day."

"No matter," Ethelmoor told him, still grinning. "I daresay you found the only one you truly wanted to find. I trust you've given her a proper trimming."

"Why, as to that—" Simon began, only to be interrupted by his indignant wife.

"If the two of you wish to converse as though no one else were present," she said coldly, "I shall be only too happy to oblige you. I am persuaded that Lydia must be wondering why I have not come to her before now."

"Oh, no doubt she is in a dreadful pucker of worry," her brother agreed, his eyes atwinkle. "You certainly must find her at once. That is," he added more softly, "if Andover here has nothing further to say to you."

Involuntarily her gaze shifted to Simon, who met the wary look with an appreciative smile.

"You may go, Diana," he said kindly, "but you will oblige me by being prepared to set forth for the abbey by first light."

She grimaced, saying sarcastically, "It must ever be of importance to me to oblige you, my lord."

"Ah," said Simon, getting in the last word, "you begin to understand your duty to me, sweetheart."

Diana gritted her teeth but made no effort to reply, not being entirely certain that she could rely upon Simon to restrain his temper merely because her brother happened to be present. Going upstairs, she did not seek out Lydia but went instead to her own bedchamber to fetch a warm shawl. She then left the house and enjoyed a long, rambling walk through the park, telling only one young footman whither she was bound. She did not return until it was time to dress for dinner, but no one scolded her for her long absence, and she could not be certain anyone had even missed her.

At dinner the other three talked amicably, but Diana

was uncomfortable and spoke stiffly when she spoke at all. It didn't help matters when she informed the others that Simon had no doubt brought messages from Holly Manor. "For you must know," she added with a barbed glance at her husband, "that he most foolishly thought I must have flown home to Mama and Papa after the dreadful things he said to me."

"Only because Holly Manor lies nearer to Wilton House than this place does," Simon said grimly, his eyes warning her that to pursue the subject would be unwise.

Diana lapsed into silence again while Ethelmoor filled the breach by reminding Simon that he wanted to show him a promising young hunter he had recently acquired. They went out to the stables together directly after dinner while Diana joined Lydia in the drawing room, where young Amy had been brought by her nanny to spend some time before bedtime with her mama.

Miss Amy Sterling was a bouncing, curly-headed moppet whose coloring exactly matched her mother's but whose brown eyes danced with her father's mischievous twinkle. The three women—mother, nurse, and aunt—watched with doting expressions while the child scampered here and there, holding imaginary conversations with assorted pieces of Egyptian-style furniture and pulling a small wooden dog on wheels back and forth across the Aubusson carpet. When the men returned, young Amy let out a banshee shriek of delight and flung herself at her father's long legs.

Ethelmoor snatched her up and tossed her, squealing, into the air, catching her easily amidst a flurry of lace petticoats and cuddling her to his chest. Half an hour later Nanny took the child away again, and the men settled down with a bottle of port and a pack of cards to play picquet.

The tea tray was brought in to them at nine-thirty, and no sooner had it been cleared away again than Andover got to his feet and approached his wife, who was curled in a chair near the fire prepared to continue her earlier conversation with her sister-in-law. "We want an early start," he said quietly, "so I think Bruce and Lydia will excuse us now."

Diana looked up at him, prepared to protest, but the expression in his eyes stopped her. "As you wish, sir."

Allowing him to help her up, she gave her brother's appreciative chuckle no heed whatsoever, merely wishing him a cool good night and her sister-in-law a much warmer one before following Simon to the stair hall and up the winding stairs. At her door, she paused to bid him a good night, expecting that he had been allotted one of the other bedchambers on the same floor, but to her dismay, he merely reached past her to open the door and waited patiently for her to enter the room.

"I-I thought you—"

"I know what you thought," he said, "but I have had my things put in here, and here is where I mean to sleep, Diana, with my wife."

4

The bedchamber, with Simon in it, seemed much smaller than before. He filled it, not just by his size alone, Diana decided, glancing at him, but by the power of his presence. She remembered Lydia saying something about his being accustomed to commanding those around him, and the observation was an accurate one. As heir to the powerful Marquess of Marimorse, Simon had been raised to believe himself master of all he surveyed. Right now, she realized, he was surveying his wife.

"Simon," she said a little breathlessly, "whatever else you may believe of me, you cannot truly have believed I was trifling with Rory. What he had to say to me in the Double Cube room was of a private nature or I would explain the whole to you, but I assure—"

"I have no wish to discuss that incident further," he said, his voice low, a near growl. "What I said to you on that account that evening I have no wish or reason to retract. Your behavior—aye, and his—lent credence to the worst the busybody tabbies may wish to believe of you, and that is why I was angry. This passion you have for flirting—"

"Well, and what if I have? Lots of women flirt, and many of them carry matters a good deal further than that. If I have been accused of flirting, at least no one of sense has actually accused me of more. And why is flirting so dreadful? Men do more—certainly you have done more—and no one so much as lifts an eyebrow in disapprobation."

"*I've* done more?" They were glaring at each other now, standing on opposite sides of the floral carpet, Diana near the bed and Simon still near the door. He took a step toward her. "Just what the devil do you mean by that remark?" he demanded.

"You know perfectly well what I mean," she told him recklessly. "Why, if the streets of London are not littered with your cast-off women, then the road to Paris certainly is!"

He had taken another step even as she spoke, but he paused now, regarding her with astonishment. "Where on earth did you come by such a crazy notion? Diana, you cannot possibly believe that nonsense."

She didn't. Not really. But she wanted to hear him deny the accusation. "Why should I not believe such stuff, sir? You certainly had a reputation for charm before we were married, and I have seen the way too many women look at you even now, as though they know you intimately. And your behavior, let me tell you, does nothing to put them off."

"You're all about in your head. I haven't so much as looked at another woman since I met you. You're imagining things."

"Rubbish, sir. You flirt constantly, and you know it." But she was reassured, and a warm glow filled her. She knew he meant the words he spoke, that he honestly believed them. His flirtations were as natural to him as breathing. But if it annoyed him to watch her flirt, then he must learn to recognize the fault in himself. Still, she was sorry when he turned from her to light the ready-laid fire in the little fireplace. She had seen the glint of anger in his eyes and knew he had no liking at all for this particular argument.

Suddenly, watching him as he knelt down upon one knee setting a taper from the chimneypiece to the paper in the fireplace, she felt tired, lonely, and a little sad. Simon looked worn to the bone. His very posture spoke volumes. She moved to stand beside him, resting her hand first upon the soft bronze hair and then upon his shoulder.

"Simon," she said quietly, "I'm sorry, my lord."

"We could deal together better than this, sweetheart." Flames burst forth in the fireplace just then, consuming paper and small kindling, gaining energy to attack the logs above. Simon turned his head to look up at her. "What say we call a truce in this war of ours?"

She knelt beside him, her hand moving from his shoulder down the lapel of his jacket and then to the buttons of his waistcoat. Playing with the top button, she murmured, "It was just too much, you know, to think you would believe such a thing of me as that I would betray you with your own brother."

He caught her small hand in his and gave it a hard squeeze. "I may have exaggerated my beliefs, sweetheart, in the heat of the moment."

Though his words could scarcely be construed as an apology, she knew they would have to do. He was unlikely to say more. So when he pulled her to her feet and guided her toward the bed, she made no objection, merely giving her thoughts up to anticipation of what was to come. One aspect at least of their marriage brought her nothing but delight. When Simon held her in his arms, she could forget the other, more distressing aspects, and when he was not by to hold her, her bed seemed much too large for one small person.

Now, as he helped her to take off her dress, then moved to rid himself of his own clothing, she watched him in the light from the flickering fire and the glow of candles on the dressing table and chimneypiece. The muscles in his back rippled as he pulled off his shirt, tossing it onto a nearby chair. His boots presented a slight problem since he was not accustomed to removing them by himself, but she helped, and between them, they managed to pull them off without doing more than smudging their glossy surface.

Simon chuckled ruefully. "Pettyjohn will have a fit," he said, referring to his toplofty valet.

"Did you send him on to the abbey?"

"Aye, and young Marlie and that awesome Miss Floodlind of yours, along with Forsham, who will see to it that my phaeton and the hunters get there safely, as well. I brought only Fairburn to arrange accommodations on the road for us if we had need of them. I daresay we shan't. I had thought at first to go straight on today and rack up at Marlborough. But even if we travel slowly, we ought to make Bath easily enough by suppertime tomorrow and Alderwood soon after dark. Are you quite ready for bed, Diana mine?"

In answer she lifted her arms and slid them around his neck, breathing in the familiar scent of him, feeling a tingle when the tips of her breasts touched his bare skin. She leaned against him, savoring the moment, then let out a sigh of pleasure as his hands moved down her sides, tracing the curves of her body as though he would refresh his memory after two nights without her.

He bent his head to press his lips against her hair, murmuring, "I missed you these past nights, sweetheart."

"I never sent you away, sir," she whispered. "You just didn't come to me."

His hands tightened at her waist, and she feared for a moment that she had succeeded in arousing his anger again. But a moment later he lifted her into his arms and carried her to the bed.

Diana felt warm inside, and as he began to caress her, finding first one then another of the most sensitive parts of her body, the warmth grew until every fiber of her seemed to ache for him. She decided he was toying with her, even perhaps punishing her a little, but she had learned over the months just how to tantalize him in much the same way, and so now she exerted herself until he was groaning with the attempt to restrain the heat of his passion. Suddenly, he moved over her, taking her swiftly, but she was ready for him, and the culmination of their efforts came in long waves of pleasure.

"I thought you were suffering from exhaustion, sir," she said demurely a moment or two later as she lay within the shelter of his arm, her head resting in the curve of his shoulder.

"And so I am," he retorted, "and all these sirs of yours sit mighty unnaturally upon your lips, I'm thinking."

She chuckled. "At the moment I'm feeling submissive, my lord, but the attack will pass, I daresay."

He grunted, but the sound was a contented one. They lay quietly then, not speaking, until Diana knew by his even breathing that Simon had drifted into sleep. Lying there beside him, she was unaccountably reminded of their first night together.

After all the excitement and festivity of the wedding, held at Trent House in Grosvenor Square, it had come as a shock to find herself suddenly and completely alone with Simon in his own house in Duke Street. But Simon had been so loving, so gentle, so careful of her sensibilities— She nearly chuckled aloud at the last thought. She could scarcely have laid claim, even then, to many sensibilities, only to a vast curiosity. And Simon's first touch had sent veritable flames racing through her body.

Not that their first experience had been altogether successful, she remembered, smiling. One might even have described certain moments as awkward and others as definitely painful. But the pain had passed and the awkwardness had diminished in time until they had learned how best to please each other. And the fact that Simon had truly set himself to please her was one of the things she liked best about him. He still made the effort—in bed, at least. But in other ways, their relationship had deteriorated drastically.

Why, she wondered now, staring into the glowing coals of the dying fire, had they fallen out of love? For surely, despite anything Lydia might say or anything that might pass between them in bed, they no longer truly loved each other. The mighty flame of passion that had burned so brightly between them almost from the moment of first meeting had gone out. At best there was little more left than coals like those smoldering now in the little fireplace. Perhaps they had tumbled so quickly into love that it was merely a surface thing that had consumed itself.

If the love between them had not died, then how could Simon treat her as he did now? He had not been used to scold her for every little thing she did. And she! Diana squirmed, thinking of some of the things she had done in the past months, things she had said, belittling things, things meant to hurt and ridicule him, even before his friends. Once, after three glasses of champagne, she had even told the tale of Simon's first kiss, of how he had practically dragged a young cousin into the folly at Alderwood. She had made it sound as though he had attacked the poor girl, and she had quite neglected to mention that Simon had been ten and the cousin eight at the time.

She had not done anything quite so reprehensible since, but she could not honestly deny the fact that she had done things she ought not to have done. Nor could she deny flirting, even with Lord Roderick Warrington. Rory was quite as much fun to flirt with as any other man, and perfectly harmless, of course, though Simon could scarcely be blamed for thinking otherwise. He did not realize that his twin was tail over top in love with the beautiful Mademoiselle Sophie Beléchappé.

Just before Simon's untimely entrance into the Double Cube room at Wilton, Rory had been confiding his fears to Diana that the lovely Sophie's beauty was being exploited by her detestable brother, the Vidame de Lâche, in his peacetime efforts to regain possession of the family château. De Lâche had recently sent for both his mother and sister, Rory told her, to spend Christmas at Versailles, where he was pleading his case with the First Counsul. Why else, Rory had demanded to know, would de Lâche, a scoundrel if ever he'd known one, wish for his sister's presence, if not to use her beauty and innocence to achieve his own ends? Poor

Sophie was defenseless, he had added, because the comte, a victim of the gout, had been unable to accompany her, and madame la comtesse, though quite a grand lady, would be no match for her unscrupulous son.

Thinking the matter over as she lay now beside the gently snoring Simon, Diana was conscious of a wish that she could tell him the whole. He still believed his brother to be a competitor for her affections, and until his jealousies could be laid to rest, she was certain the road ahead of them would be a stormy one.

On the other hand, she told herself, her flirtations were perfectly harmless, as were her so-called escapades in general. Simon was merely attempting to force her into the sort of submission he believed proper for the future Marchioness of Marimorse to show her husband.

He must be taught that she was made of sterner stuff. After all, he had fallen in love with an independent Diana, one as unaccustomed as he was himself to having her will crossed. And she had fallen in love with a man who had seemed at the outset content to love her as she was. But then he had begun to try to change her to suit some patterncard he had designed for his wife.

If she were to allow him to effect all the changes he seemed to want, neither one of them would ever be happy. Better that she remain true to herself. He would not divorce her, after all. Such a course was scarcely heard of among their set. So they would be stuck with each other for many years to come. With this last thought lingering, she slipped out of the circle of his arm, pushed him hard enough to make him roll over, so as to stop his snoring, then curled up against the warmth of his back, where she quickly fell asleep.

Simon woke her early the next morning. "Bustle about, sweetheart. The chaise will be at the door in an hour and a half."

She stretched, regarding him sleepily. "What time is it?"

"Nearly half past seven."

Diana groaned. "I've rarely been up before midday in months, Simon. Surely we needn't leave before ten."

"You were asleep before midnight, my girl, and you have managed to be up before, early enough for the occasional hunt breakfast at half past nine."

"Oh, Simon, you know perfectly well that whenever breakfast is ordered for half past nine, the servants know better than to set anything out before ten or even eleven o'clock, and the hunt scarcely ever begins before noon even in the most well-appointed houses, no matter what good intentions everyone expresses the night before."

He chuckled, admitting the truth of her words. "But that doesn't matter today, Diana mine. I nearly wore that team out yesterday, and I've no wish to injure any of them, so today we travel by easy stages."

"You could hire a team in Marlborough and send someone back for yours later," she pointed out.

"I could, if I wished to do so. If this were spring or summer, I'd even have my own cattle stabled there with my own lads to look after them. But it is winter, and I've no great opinion of the stables, even at the Castle, and I've no one to leave with them. We've plenty of time to travel slowly if we get an early start. So, up you get. I've already rung for a maid."

Diana sighed. Behold the master, she thought. But now that she was wide awake, she had no real objection of getting up and getting dressed. She noticed that Simon was already fully clothed and decided he had been up for an hour or more. He wore his buckskins again and the dark brown jacket, but they had been brushed and pressed, and his topboots seemed none the worse for their smudging but were as glossy as ever. His shirt and neckcloth were fresh, both snowy white and the latter neatly tied, although Rory, who was more of a dandy than his twin, would no doubt have scorned its simple arrangement.

Simon wore no jewelry other than his carved gold signet ring, refusing to adopt the prevailing fashion for wearing a number of rings, fobs, and jeweled stickpins scattered about one's person. He even refused to carry a snuffbox, saying that he thought the habit a filthy one.

Once, when Diana had acquired a snuffbox of her own from Friberg and Tryer's and had cajoled Lord Petersham, the acknowledged snuff expert of the polite world, who was actually said to possess a different snuffbox for each day of the year, into mixing a recipe for her called Lady Andover's Sort, Simon had promptly pitched the lot of it onto the nearest fire.

Since she had privately practiced the delicate art of taking snuff for untold hours until she knew she could carry it off with flair no matter who was watching her, Diana had been properly incensed to have her first public attempt so ignominiously spoilt by her domineering husband. That the stench caused by Simon's precipitous action had called everyone's attention to them both had not helped the matter, and the row that erupted between them on that occasion still rated among their friends as one of their most fiery efforts.

With a reminder to make all speed, Simon left the room as soon as the maid arrived to help Diana dress. Since the girl had overheard his curt command, Diana was tempted to dawdle just to teach him that he should not issue his orders to her so peremptorily in front of mere servants, but she knew his temper to be uncertain, and she had no wish to initiate a further dispute beneath her brother's roof. Thus it was that she joined the others in the morning room some moments before her appointed time.

Breakfast was soon over and farewells said, and by ten o'clock the Warrington chaise, followed by Ned Tredegar in charge of Diana's horse, was bowling along through the streets of Devises. Two hours later, they were driven into the yard of the Castle and Ball, the lovely sixteenth-century inn in central Marlborough where the Marlborough Highroad intersected with the main London-Bath Road. A mere thirty miles lay before them now, twenty-six to Bath and then four more along the Bristol Road before they would reach the abbey.

Luckily the side-pocket of the chaise contained a traveling chess board, so after refreshing themselves and the horses at the Castle, they settled down to while away the slowly passing miles over several games of chess. As Simon had predicted, they reached Bath in time for supper at the York House, and less than an hour after they had finished their tasty repast, they arrived at the gates of Alderwood Abbey.

The sun was setting almost directly behind the great house as they approached it along the broad, tree-lined avenue, throwing the shape of the magnificent building into bold relief against the reddened western sky. There was nothing churchlike about the outline.

As Diana had learned during her first visit to the abbey many months before, Alderwood was indeed one of those remarkable country houses made out of the monastic buildings shut down by Henry the Eighth when he closed all the religious houses in England between 1536 and 1540; however, in the case of Alderwood, the actual church had been demolished. The present house had begun its life as a rather select and very influential convent, founded in 1232, which because of its influence was one of the last of the religious houses to be dissolved.

In 1539 the church, convent, and surrounding lands had been sold for seven hundred thirty-eight pounds to Sir William Warrington, who had excellent connections at court. Warrington had immediately pulled down the church for fear of committing sacrilege. In its place he had built a magnificent courtyard and an elaborate hedge garden with meandering pathways that eventually led to the stableyard.

Sir William had moved himself and his belongings into the upstairs rooms of the convent and had put the downstairs rooms, which had been the nuns' main quarters, to more menial use. The calefactory or warming-room, which had originally contained the only fireplace accessible to the nuns, had been converted to a kitchen, and the series of vaulted rooms off the cloister were used for storage, the laundry, and for servants' bed-chambers. Succeeding Warringtons had made various changes in the main house, and Sir William's hedges had grown tall and stately, but the cloister, roofed by an exquisitely graceful fan vault of the fifteenth-century, had remained untouched throughout the centuries of change. It was now considered to be one of the finest examples of its kind in England, and the Warrington family, as Diana knew well, were justifiably proud of it.

Their pride in the interesting Sir William was another matter and not, in Diana's opinion, quite so justifiable. Sir William, though he possessed exquisite taste, as could be seen in his many remaining contributions to the present-day abbey, had undeniably been a bit of a crook. As a result of his misdeeds, however, he seemed to be quite the Warrington's favorite ancestor. Since, as they cheerfully explained to anyone who had not yet heard the tale, Sir William had earned his fortune as vice-treasurer of the Bristol Mint by the simple expedient of clipping the coinage—that was to say that he actually clipped the edges off the coins and re-smelted the clippings while the remains of the original coins, which bore the mint's impression, were returned to circulation.

As if that were not enough, Sir William used the proceeds of these activities for various questionable enterprises, not the least of which seemed—from information still extant among the many documents in the abbey's vast muniments room—to have been a plot against the crown. Warrington had actually been arrested for this interesting crime in 1549, but he had wisely turned king's evidence, putting all the blame for their activities upon his cohorts, who were subsequently hanged. For such signal service to the crown in this matter, Warrington got off with his life, a fine, and the loss of his property. Undaunted by the setback to his fortune, he had recouped his losses, including the abbey, in what Diana, for one, thought to be a disgracefully short period of time. He then returned to his home, wealthier than ever, as the first Earl of Andover, and had lived to enjoy a ripe old age.

His grandson, another enterprising gentleman, whose portrait graced the library just off the great hall, was created first Marquess of Marimorse some forty-five years later by Henry's younger daughter, Elizabeth, for services which were not, so far as anyone had yet discovered, documented by anything in writing among

those endless records in the muniments room. Since
that time, the Warrington family had continued to pros-
per, each succeeding generation displaying, when necessary, that same gift as their ancestor had shown for
eluding disaster at royal whim.

Diana glanced at Simon as the chaise rolled to a halt
before the impressive east entrance to the abbey. He
was certainly involved in a good many political affairs,
not all of which met with royal or, for that matter,
family approval. But times were safer now. She had no
fear that he would be clapped up in the Tower for his
efforts, or that he would lose his head as a result of any
disagreement he might have with the King.

The footman, Fairburn, opened the chaise door just
then and let down the steps. Diana accepted his hand
and stepped gracefully to the ground. By the time
Simon had followed her, the front doors had been
opened and flunkies appeared to deal with the trunk
strapped onto the chaise. Mounting the lefthand side
of the broad, split stairway leading to the entrance,
Simon and Diana stepped into the great hall to be
greeted by Figmore, my lord's elderly butler.

The great hall, with its magnificent grand, winged
staircase, still bore such reminders of its ancient origins
as a stone floor and iron wall sconces that had once
held torches but which had been adapted to contain
branches of candles. To the left of the entrance was a
pair of double doors leading to the large book-lined
library. To the right was a matching pair of doors, and
it was to these that Simon and Diana were directed by
the butler. An obsequious footman leapt forward to
open the doors.

The gothic chamber thus revealed, having served a
number of Warringtons as a grand saloon, had been
redesigned some fifty years earlier for the eighth marquess by Sanderson Miller, the Warwickshire squire
who carried a taste for architecture so far as to become
an amateur architect, providing designs for friends and
friends' friends. The so-called "new hall" at Alderwood
was considered by many to have been his greatest con-
tribution to the Gothic movement, comparable to some

of the gaudier highlights of Horace Walpole's Strawberry Hill.

Miller had been greatly influenced by the Kent school, but the hall showed evidence of his own tremendous originality of thought, including such minor touches as the pierced parapet and the rose window at the southern end, and more noticeably, the walls plastered to imitate stone and provided with many ornate niches filled with amusing Rococo terra-cotta statues by an Austrian sculptor whose name Diana could never remember. The ceiling was painted with the coats of arms of many of the eighth marquess's friends (all of whom, according to his detailed diary, had been invited to a great dinner in the hall when it was completed). With a crackling fire in the huge marble fireplace, the cheerful furnishings, and the bright red Turkey carpets dotting the marble floor, the new hall provided a cozy place which had long been the family's favorite place to assemble.

The persons in the room when Diana and Simon were announced numbered three—a plump, gray-haired dame swathed in an awe-inspiring gown of purple satin, who sat comfortably ensconced in a wing chair near the fire with her feet propped up on a gros-point footstool; a thin, elderly gentleman in a white periwig, tied at the nape of his neck with a black ribbon, seated at a large Buhl desk near one deep, gothic-arched window; and a dark-haired young lady in a long-sleeved, cream-colored wool gown cut primly high to the throat and unfashionably tight at the waist. At their entrance, the latter leapt to her feet, casting her tambor frame and silks aside, and ran to meet them, chattering as she went.

"Simon! Diana! Oh, I told Papa I was sure it was you when we heard the carriage, but he would have it that you were in Wilton or some such place and would not so much as draw back the curtains to look out, though he might perfectly well have done so, sitting by the window as he is. Oh, how perfectly delightful to see you both!"

So saying, she flung herself into Simon's arms and he caught her, giving her a hearty hug. "So, you've missed us, Susanna, have you?"

"A proper lady," declared the stout dame near the fireplace, lifting her long-handled glasses to peer at them all and speaking in damping tones, "does not shriek, nor does she leap about like a gypsy, nor fling herself into a gentleman's arms. I cannot think how you come to do such things, Susanna."

"No, aunt, I beg your pardon," Lady Susanna Warrington said quickly, her cheeks reddening at the rebuke, as she freed herself from Simon's embrace.

"Hoydenish manners," said Lady Ophelia. "You put me to the blush. Whatever will people think of your upbringing an you behave so in company?"

"I shan't do it again, Aunt Ophelia," said Susanna in a small voice.

"How do you do, Simon?" inquired the elderly gentleman from his place at the desk.

"Well enough, thank you, sir," Simon replied, putting a protective arm around his sister's shoulders. "Come, come now, child, don't be downcast. There's naught amiss with a little enthusiasm. No one would think the worse of her for it, Aunt Ophelia, I assure you. You certainly look to be in fine fettle, I must say, ma'am," he went on hastily, thus forestalling any rejoinder her ladyship might have made. "That cap becomes you mighty well." He released Susanna then and moved to take his father's hand. "You're looking well, too, sir."

That was certainly true, Diana thought, as she stepped forward to take her part in the amenities. The Marquess of Marimorse was approaching his sixtieth year, but he was still a fine figure of a man. His dress was neat and precise, and if he wore a deal more jewelry than his son, he wore it with a dignified grace. Though he retained his wig, he had traded in the brocades and silks of his salad days for the more sober-hued attire now becoming fashionable among the masculine social set, but he still had something of the air of an exquisite, and his manners—when his temper was not aroused— were very refined. He did not rise, but he inclined his head, greeting both his son and Diana and begging her pardon for not getting to his feet to greet her properly.

"My rheumatism, you know," he told her. " 'Tis a sad

fact that the cooler months seem to make a martyr of me, my dear, and by the way my old bones have been complaining these past two days, I fear the mild weather is about to desert us to make way for a more wintery chill. Susanna, girl," he added more tartly, "either sit yourself down with your sewing or take yourself off to bed. You're fidgeting me."

"I beg pardon, Papa," that young lady said, quickly retiring to the chair she had so precipitately forsaken and gathering her silks and tambour frame into her lap.

Diana, feeling, as she often did, a sympathy for the young girl, left Simon to enjoy a chat with his father and settled herself into a chair near Lady Ophelia, intending to draw Susanna into their conversation but knowing that she would offend her ladyship if she did not make her overtures first to that punctilious dame. Obedient to Diana's signal, Susanna moved her chair closer to the other two, folded her hands primly in her lap, and held her tongue.

Diana smiled at her. Lady Susanna Warrington, just on the point of emerging from the schoolroom, showed all the nervousness of a young filly and none of the poise that Diana thought the daughter of an influential marquess ought to possess. Susanna's experience of the world was very small and came, for the most part, from the animadversions cast upon it by her aunt, who spent much of her time deploring modern times, and from the caustic remarks of her father, who criticized everything and everyone in the political world. Diana felt sorry for her.

"What have you done with you shawl, Diana?" Lady Ophelia demanded suddenly in the midst of one of her own sentences. "You young things, always showing yards of gooseflesh, then denying that you feel the least bit chilled."

"I'm perfectly comfortable, ma'am," Diana assured her, wondering how anyone seated so near to the roaring fire could possibly be cold.

"Nonsense. Susanna, do you go at once and ring for someone to bring your sister a shawl."

"There is no need, my lady, truly," Diana protested,

but she might as well have spared her breath, for Susanna had already moved to do her aunt's bidding. There was nothing to be done but to thank the footman who presently appeared carrying a heavy pink wool shawl. At least, Diana told herself, it was not a color that would clash horribly with her green and lilac gown.

"There now," said Lady Ophelia with satisfaction, "I am persuaded that that will be a deal more pleasant. There is always a draught in this room. Move the firescreen a trifle to the left, Susanna, if you please. We shall enjoy a comfortable coze."

5

Susanna obediently moved the firescreen to protect her aunt from the fierce heat of the blaze, then resumed her seat, smiling shyly at Diana, who asked as though she did not already know the answer, "Are you looking forward to your come-out?"

"Oh, yes," the young girl replied, her smile growing wider. "Aunt says I shall go to Almack's and to Ranelagh, and even perhaps by water to Vauxhall Gardens."

"The gardens," said Lady Ophelia, smoothing her purple satin skirts and adjusting her own peach-colored shawl more securely about her plump shoulders, "are become dreadfully public nowadays. I don't know what my sainted mama would say to some of the goings-on one hears about. They seem to let just anyone into those places, you know. Not Almack's, of course, but the public gardens."

"Oh, pray do not say I may not go after all, ma'am," Susanna protested, subsiding at once into confusion when her aunt disapprovingly lifted an eyebrow.

"I was speaking to Diana," her ladyship said in quelling tones.

"Yes, ma'am."

"The gardens are really very nice, ma'am," Diana said quickly before Susanna could beg pardon again. She wished that her ladyship would not so consistently stifle the girl's natural high spirits. Diana felt a kinship for Susanna, knowing perfectly well that Lady Ophelia did not approve of Diana's high spirits either.

"No doubt," her ladyship said now, turning a basilisk eye on Diana as if she suspected her of attempting to shield Susanna from deserved reprimand, "I expect you enjoy the sort of romps one hears about only too often."

"No ma'am, I don't," Diana replied calmly, having no doubt that her ladyship's "only too often" was meant to qualify her enjoyment and not the rumors flying to her ladyship's ears. "Not if you mean, as I think you must, the public masquerades and ridottos that are held both at Ranelagh and at Vauxhall during the Season. Such events often become rowdy and unpleasant, but there is nothing amiss in a private excursion with one's particular friends and relations to enjoy a concert or a display of fireworks. Such occasions are perfectly harmless, I assure you."

"I daresay," returned her ladyship in tones that bespoke doubt. But she would not lower herself to engage Diana in a debate on the subject. Instead, she shifted a little in her chair, bent a more benevolent eye upon her, and suggested that since Diana had been traveling about for the past three months she would no doubt like to entertain them until teatime with all the latest crim-con stories.

Although a little daunted by her ladyship's suggestion, Diana nevertheless made an effort to comply with the request by describing the places she had visited and the people she had met. Since most of these were well-known to her ladyship, she was ably assisted in her endeavors, and Lady Ophelia expressed particular gratification to learn that the Duke of Beaufort had rebuilt the ancient conduit houses at Badminton so that one was no longer prone to find bits of limestone in one's washwater, and to learn as well that the Wilton House remodeling was nearly completed. Diana managed to keep the conversation on an amiable key until she chanced to mention Lady Jersey's name along with those of the other guests at Badminton soon after telling Lady Ophelia that the Prince of Wales had numbered among the company.

"That *woman*," pronounced her ladyship in awful tones. "Do not speak of that dreadful woman to me. I do not know how I shall support my spirits whilst she is present in this house." She glanced rather quickly just then at her brother, but Diana, her own gaze following Lady Ophelia's automatically, noted that the marquess and Simon were still involved in their own conversation. As she returned her gaze to Lady Ophelia, she chanced to notice that Susanna was attempting to hide a smile. No doubt the child realized as well as she did herself that the marquess would not approve of his sister's comments.

"Will it truly be so dreadful, ma'am?" her evil genius prompted her to ask. Even if it brought the marquess's wrath down upon them all, the subject would serve to keep Lady Ophelia from criticizing Susanna or herself, and it was always more gratifying to hear criticism of others. Moreover, if she were not successfully diverted, Lady Ophelia was bound before much more time had passed to demand a more narrow account of Diana's own activities during the past months.

"Having that woman here will be intolerable," her ladyship said. "I do not know how you can ask such a question when you know perfectly well that his highness means to honor us by celebrating the New Year at Alderwood. He will think I am hand in glove with that woman."

"No, no, ma'am, how could he when he knows that Lord Jersey is a friend of my Lord Marimorse?"

"Well, that is as may be, but I will not tolerate *goings-on* in this house," pronounced her ladyship with a grimace of distaste.

"Nor will you be asked to do so, ma'am. Although Lady Jersey does indeed persist in throwing herself at the prince's head, her star is definitely believed to be on the wane, you know, for the prince makes no secret of the fact that his affections are once more engaged by Mrs. Fitzherbert, a fact which cannot but gladden the hearts of those who know them. He scarcely pays any heed now to Lady Jersey."

"As if that should please me. Knowing Frances as I do, I can tell you that being ignored must merely stimulate her to more outrageous behavior than ever. And he, a married man. He should be ashamed of himself, whomever he chases. And you needn't tell me he is married to the Fitzherbert woman, for that cannot signify in the slightest if the match was never approved by his father. His proper wife is the Princess of Wales. In my day, such doings were not tolerated, I assure you."

Diana repressed a chuckle, wondering how in the world Lady Ophelia at the tender age of fifty had managed to suppress all memory of the excesses of her younger days. Considering that the prince had turned forty only last summer and had been engaged in scandalous activities for more than half his life, surely her ladyship was well aware that such goings-on were not isolated to the present new century. According to Diana's parents, the last twenty years of the old century—and indeed, the twenty years before them—had been wilder by far than those of the present. But she murmured commonplace reassurances, knowing it would be unwise to remind Lady Ophelia of the facts.

"Moreover," Diana added with a smile, "I believe Lady Jersey will be on her best behavior when she comes to Alderwood, particularly if the Earl and Countess of Westmorland have also accepted your invitation."

"Lady Westmorland is coming," said Lady Ophelia. "Had a message from Brymton d'Evercy only this morning. Bringing that eldest chit of his along as well, and since the girl will make her come-out in the spring and has already been included (most improperly, if you ask me) in a number of parties, I could scarcely tell Jane to leave her at home. But as to whether Westmorland will come, I'm sure I have no way of knowing. Although Lord Alvanley very properly sent his regrets—some matter of business, he said—Westmorland's manners are not so nice. He has not honored us with any response, and Jane did not mention him."

"Why do you dislike him so, ma'am? By all I've heard, he's perfectly respectable. He is the King's Lord Privy Seal, after all."

"That's as may be, but there's bad blood in the Fanes, and the chit's inherited it. Not much good to be said about her mother's family either, for that matter. Can't imagine what Frances Villiers, so high in the instep as she pretends to be, sees in Sarah Fane. Oh, I know what Frances is about, same as everyone else, of course. Thinks to add the girl's fortune to the Jersey estates by making a match for the young viscount. I've heard about her schemes. I daresay she thinks the girl's money will make up for all the rest. It won't. The old tales will be bruited about as quick as the cat can lick her ear, if they haven't begun already. Then she'll be smiling out of the other side of her face. See if she don't. I cannot imagine how she thinks to escape the unpleasantness."

"What old tales, ma'am? I confess, I've seen some sly looks and noted a bit of whispering, but my own friends seem to know nothing."

Lady Ophelia glanced at Susanna. "No need for you to await the tea tray, my dear," she said kindly. "You bid your papa and Andover good night and run along upstairs."

Disappointed but obedient, Susanna made her curtsies and left the room. When the door had closed behind her, Lady Ophelia nodded placidly. "No need for her to hear such stuff. Unsuitable. Moreover, she's a bagpipe, and I confess I'd just as lief she not blurt something when the house is full to the rafters. I know you will not say anything."

"No, indeed, ma'am, but do go on."

"John Fane carried young Sarah's mama off to Gretna Green and married her in the teeth of her father's opposition, that's what," said Lady Ophelia with an air of divulging the worst. "Her father was a mere banker at that. No family to speak of, though I believe his brother was a baronet. Died in mysterious circumstances, however, so he don't count for much. Not one of our kind."

"But Robert Child was scarcely a *mere* banker, ma'am," Diana said, stifling laughter. "There's hardly a penny to choose between Child's Bank and Hoare's, after all, and Sir Richard Colt Hoare is accepted everywhere."

"Indeed, I am very fond of Sir Richard. Now I come to think of it, wasn't you meaning to go to Stourhead from Wilton House?" her ladyship demanded disconcertingly.

"Yes, indeed, but we decided, as Simon said, that we had had enough racketing about for the moment, and we knew you would welcome our assistance here, what with all the upheaval for so many guests."

"That I shall. Not that there's much to do, of course," Lady Ophelia added complacently. "The servants see to everything."

"Under your very able guidance, ma'am. I know. But do, please, tell me about Lady Sarah Fane's parents."

"Well," said Lady Ophelia obligingly, "Miss Child— she was Sarah, too, as I recall—was no better than she should be, I daresay, but John Fane wanted her, and her papa's fortune, of course, despite the fact that Child wanted a man with a head for business and not a flighty earl for a son-in-law. So what does Westmorland do but ask Mr. Child what he'd recommend to a young man who couldn't gain parental permission to wed the girl of his heart. And Child—more fool, he—up and tells him he'd elope with her. So that's what Westmorland did. Even shot a horse from under one of the Child grooms who pursued them, they say. And the two of them was married over the anvil after no less than three nights on the road together. Needless to say, despite the fact that they tried to put a good face on it by having a proper ceremony later, *she* was never received. Westmorland carried her off to Ireland as soon as ever he could manage it, and she died there at Phoenix Park when young Sarah must have been about eight or ten. He married Jane Saunders two years ago, as you know. She can't be much older than her stepdaughter, I'm thinking, but she's a proper lady."

"They say Lady Sarah Fane is a great heiress," Diana prompted, having no wish to discuss the current Lady Westmorland.

"Ought to be, seeing as how Robert Child left her his

entire fortune, including his houses at Swanscombe and Osterley Park."

"But surely he died before she was born, ma'am. How is it that the Fane family did not acquire everything? Was not that her papa's purpose in marrying Child's daughter?"

Lady Ophelia chuckled, causing her plump bosom to ripple beneath her low-cut bodice. "That may have been his purpose, but Child made sure that no Earl of Westmorland would ever see a penny of his money."

"You mean Mr. Child entailed everything in the female line?"

"So some said at the time, but that was not the case. He merely left it all to his eldest granddaughter. And that's why Frances Villiers hopes to see Lady Sarah as the next Viscountess Villiers. She would add Osterley Park to the Jersey estates."

"We are invited to Osterley the end of next month," Diana confided. "I've never been there before, but Lady Westmorland has invited everyone, saying it will be more convenient to entertain at Osterley than at Brymton d'Evercy."

"Well, you will no doubt enjoy yourselves, and Frances will be surveying the whole park with a proprietary air, or I miss my guess."

"Perhaps when she learns the truth about how Lady Sarah's parents were married, she will change her mind about the suitability of a match with her handsome son," Diana suggested, eyes twinkling.

"Not she. She knows the tales as well as I do," said Lady Ophelia sardonically. "She just won't like hearing them retold. But when all's said and done, she's no more than a reverend's daughter herself—a bishop, her father was, but only an Irish one, and dead two months before she was born. It was her stepfather, General Johnstone, who provided her entry to the polite world, him plus a generous bit of money left her by her reverend papa. But for all my Lady Jersey holds herself so proud, the lack of proper breeding shows in the way she—a grandmother, for pity's sake—flings herself after the prince. Not that she didn't have a precedent or two for such behavior. The Villiers women have cuckolded their lords with royalty since the days of Charles the Second, after all. Very wicked of them, I'm sure."

Knowing her ladyship was perfectly capable of re-hashing the entire conversation, Diana made haste at this point to change the subject by reminding her that they had come to Alderwood from Ethelmoor Hall and by extending greetings from her brother and sister-in-law. From there it was but a natural step to lead the conversation into family matters, where it rambled ami-ably until the gentlemen chose to join them when the tea tray was brought in.

"Been enjoyin' a gossip, I daresay," said the mar-quess in his cultivated tones as he settled himself cau-tiously into a chair near Diana's. He used a cane when he walked and propped it now against a low parquetry table near his chair. When the cane began to slide, Diana caught it and replaced it more securely. The marquess thanked her. "You're looking well," he said, "not a bit as if you've suffered from all this racketing Simon tells me you've been doing."

"Oh, I'm perfectly stout, sir," Diana told him, grin-ning saucily. " 'Tis only Simon playing at master that brings us here. He would have it that a repairing lease was in order."

"Not increasing, are you?" demanded the old man.

"No, sir." But, caught off her guard, Diana blushed, avoiding her husband's eye.

"Will you take tea, Marimorse?" asked Lady Ophelia haughtily.

"Well, of course I shall," said the old man tartly. "Always do, don't I? What a thing to ask. What was I saying before?"

"You were telling me, sir," Simon put in quickly, "just before we joined the ladies, that Parliament is once again considering the income tax issue. I know that Diana, at least, would be most interested to hear your views on that matter."

Diana knew perfectly well that Simon meant to divert the marquess before that gentleman remembered what he had asked her and further offended Lady Ophelia, and she was grateful to him, particularly since she knew he was annoyed with her for her earlier words and had enjoyed her discomfiture when the marquess demanded to know if she was with child. Consequently, she responded instantly to her cue, expressing great interest in what was now to be done about the dreadful income tax.

"Aye, dreadful it is, and so you may believe, my dear," said the marquess, accepting his cup of tea and glaring at them all. "Imagine taxing one's income. A vile, Jacobin, jumped-up, jack-in-office piece of impertinence is what I have always said. That's what it was when they inflicted it upon us three years ago, and that's what it is now that they *say* they mean to do away with it."

"I daresay more money was needed to support the war effort," said Lady Ophelia placidly, helping herself to a cake from the silver tray at her side.

"Fustian," retorted the marquess. "A good number of wars have been fought without recourse to such a thing in our history. I ask you, is a true Briton to have no privacy? Are the fruits of honest labor and toil to be picked over farthing by farthing by the pimply minions of bureaucracy?"

"For all the world," Diana told Simon when they were able at last to retire for the night, "as though your papa has been making and scraping and hoeing the weeds in his own fields."

"Shame, shame, Diana mine," Simon said softly against her curls. "Papa feels strongly about many things, though he has long since left the responsibilities of the estate to me. He washed his hands of Pitt, of course, after the Catholic issue, and he despises Addington for being poor-spirited. Still, he wields a deal of influence in some quarters and keeps his fingers in a number of pies just by virtue of his overwhelming correspondence."

As the days passed swiftly by, Diana saw the truth of Simon's words. The marquess paid scarcely any heed whatever to the upheaval all around him as the servants prepared for the Christmas festivities. Instead, he spent his days contentedly at the large desk amidst the gothic splendors of the new hall, writing letter upon letter.

Diana spent her own days helping Lady Susanna to decide which of her new gowns would be most suitable to be worn once their guests began arriving, and assisting Lady Ophelia in directing the servants' activities. She saw little of Simon during the day, for he spent his time with the bailiff, going over accounts and hearing complaints and recommendations for improvements to be made on his father's vast estates. The fourth day after their arrival, the marquess's prediction with regard to the weather was fulfilled. Rain began to fall steadily soon after breakfast, and by late afternoon the temperature had dropped noticeably. Simon, returning from a tour of the succession houses, informed them that the ground outside was turning icy and that they would likely have snow before morning. Only Lady Susanna was gratified by the information.

"We shall have a white Christmas," she said happily.

"One must hope," said her aunt dampingly, "that the roads continue to be passable for another week at least, and that we do not find ourselves either bereft of company or enduring rather too much of it. I cannot think our guests will like to travel in bad weather."

Despite the fact that snow fell during the night, the inhabitants of the abbey were brought to realize that the roads had at least remained passable enough for the mail coach from London when Lord Roderick Warrington arrived shortly before supper, announcing that he had taken passage on this conveyance as far as Bath, where he had prevailed upon a farmer to carry him to Alderwood in an ancient gig.

"Good Lord, Rory, whatever possessed you to have recourse to such a mode of travel?" demanded his sister when she learned of his experience. "You and Simon never travel any way but by post chaise!"

"Pockets to let," explained her scapegrace brother, grinning at Diana, who entered the hall in time to hear the exchange. "Hoped to impress the almighty Andover and the even almightier Marimorse with my wonderful sense of economy, don't you know?"

"They are both more like to scold you for making a cake of yourself, as I've no doubt you did," Diana said, teasing him as she allowed him to give her a brotherly hug and helped him to divest himself of his heavy but stylish traveling cloak.

Lord Roderick Warrington was nearly as tall as his twin, but there the resemblance between them ended. Rory's hair was lighter and his eyes more green than golden. His figure, too, was more graceful than Simon's, and his attire more modish. He had little liking for the sports that Simon loved, though Diana knew that he was nearly as much of an expert as his brother with the small sword and foil. But Rory's talents were more appreciated in the ballrooms and salons of the *beau monde*. He was a favorite dancing partner with all the ladies, and he played a good hand at whist. That he preferred to play for larger stakes than were allowed at mixed card parties was unfortunately the case, and the fact that he had an even greater liking for the wheels and bones of the more rakish gaming halls was also unfortunate. These favored pastimes had brought him more than once within ames ace of finding the bailiffs at his door and had earned him the rough side of his brother's tongue and more than a few uncomfortable letters from and private audiences with his parent. The marquess considered his younger son to be a scapegrace ne'er do well, and consistently refused to increase his allowance beyond the pittance—as Lord Roderick assured everyone it was—that was granted to him.

"Simon ought to appreciate my efforts," Rory assured the two young women now as he rubbed his chilled hands before the hall fire. He looked down at his trouser leg, frowning. "Damn, I've a crease in these breeches." He rubbed at it ineffectively, then looked up at them with a grimace. "Travel by mail is an abominable experience. Innkeepers are insolent, hostlers are sulky, the maids are pert, and the waiters impertinent. I dined last night at the Angel in Reading, and the meat was tough, the wine foul, the beer hard, the sheets wet, the linen dirty, and the knives seem never to have been cleaned. Assure you, any home would be better. Hello, aunt," he added as Lady Ophelia entered the room, "I've just been telling them I came to Bath on the mail coach."

Lady Ophelia lifted an eyebrow. "Indeed, I trust you

had good reason for such a thing. I cannot believe it can have been an edifying experience."

"Oh, but it was," Rory assured her. "The first stage was enlivened by the quarreling among the roof passengers over who would get to tool the coach. All very frolicsome, but one fellow was knocked off, and we had to stop for him, which did not please the coachman, I can tell you."

Rightly guessing that Lord Roderick had numbered among the quarrelsome roof passengers himself, Diana could only be grateful to learn that driving rain had forced him to seek shelter inside on the next stage of the journey. By the time he had reached that point in his description they had been joined by the marquess and Simon, who had learned of his arrival. Diana did not think Simon or his father looked to be much impressed by Rory's choice of vehicle, but both laughed when he told them that traveling with two women had proved harmless enough, though one of them had threatened eternally to be sick.

"All went well enough, however," he said cheerfully, "until the off leader shied at a fox dashing across the road. The coach lurched, then tumbled into a ditch, the road being soft with mud and slick with ice."

"Good gracious me," said his aunt, settling into her favorite chair to hear the rest of his tale. "I trust you were not injured. That sounds very dangerous to me. I cannot think what the coachman was about to let it happen."

"Not a bit of it, ma'am. The ditch wasn't deep, you know, but the two women, curse them, started shrieking fit to wake the devil, and one gentleman was thrown clean off the roof into the hedge. He was pulled out later by your obedient servant and the guard, but the horses were in a tangle, backing and struggling, so it was as much as the coachman could do to calm them. The guard and a gent in a bottle-green coat went to aid him and after twenty minutes and much hard swearing of oaths, the horses were got free of their harness and taken up on to the road where it was discovered that the leader was lame in the near fore. I did what I could to bathe the swelling with water from the ditch but it wasn't much use, since I don't chance to carry spermacetti lotion on my person when I travel."

"Indeed," Simon said wryly. "What then? Did you rescue the ladies?"

"Oh, someone pulled them out, though with all the shrieking and complaining I'd as lief have left them where they were," Rory replied, twinkling. "The coach was firmly wedged in the ditch, you know, and no amount of effort would move it. The females remained hysterical, and the man from the coachtop—the one in the hedge, you know—seemed to be suffering from concussion. But no one paid him much heed, for an argument blew up between the coachman, who insisted upon staying with his horses, and the guard, who insisted upon staying with his mails, as to who should go for aid. Neither would give way, so finally the gent in the bottle-green coat took one of the horses and went into Newbury. It was drizzling by then, so we were all pretty miserable, I can tell you. It was a full hour before he returned with fresh horses and we were able to pull the coach out. Then, since one wheel was found to be insecure, only the ladies rode. The men walked. It took us another hour to reach the inn, and our reception was scarcely of a nature to encourage me to favor that hostelry again."

"What an adventure," said Lady Susanna appreciatively, when he paused for breath.

"Easy for you to say, miss," retorted her brother. "You'd have been riding in the coach. I ruined a perfectly good pair of boots walking through all that mud, wasted half a morning in Newbury waiting for the coach to be repaired, and I have reached the melancholy conclusion that my second best breeches will never be the same again."

"What have you done with your valet?" Diana inquired.

"Gave him and my tiger two days' leave in Reading," replied Rory carelessly. "They will arrive with my curricle tomorrow."

"So much for your economy," Simon told him amid laughter from the others. "By the time you pay their expenses and repair your precious wardrobe, you might just as well have hired a post chaise and four."

Rory grinned at him, unabashed. "Well, you might at least appreciate the gesture after all you said to me less than a week since."

To Diana's relief, although the marquess demanded an explanation of these words, Simon diverted him with an offhand remark and the incident passed off harmlessly. But when she commented later to her husband that his twin seemed at least to be making an effort to mend his ways, Simon refused to discuss the matter, his expression indicating that his jealousy lay very near the surface.

Not wishing to upset their present amicable relationship, Diana dropped the subject, but she had no intention of letting Simon's foolish jealousies keep her from enjoying a comfortable chat with her brother-in-law. Thus it was that when she found Rory alone the next day in the blue parlor, a charming room lined with early eighteenth-century paneling and numerous family portraits (including one of the irrepressible Sir William Warrington), she made no effort to elude him but demanded instead to know if he had heard anything further about Mademoiselle Sophie.

"As a matter of fact," he confided, "I broke my journey in Reading purposely in order to visit with the comte. He has a house near there at Langley Marsh, you know—at least, I daresay you didn't know, but he has. In any case, I spent a good part of yesterday there, and as I'd no wish to set their tongues wagging, I thought giving my men leave and taking the coach the rest of the way was a rather knacky notion. But, Diana," he added with a frown, "you may imagine my consternation when the comte informed me that he hasn't heard a word from his family since madame wrote to inform him they had arrived safely at Calais."

"Well," Diana said practically, "that cannot have been more than a week or so ago, after all. No doubt they are having bad weather in France, too, and the mails have been delayed accordingly."

"'Tis possible, I suppose," he admitted, "but I took the liberty of inviting de Vieillard to join us over the New Year all the same. I cannot rest easily, Diana, until I know that Sophie is safe."

She realized that he was seriously worried and forebore to tease him, even going so far as to submit to hearing a catalog of his Sophie's numerous virtues, although she had heard them all before. It was at such times as these, whether he waxed enthusiastic over a horse or a woman or merely a new suit of clothes, that she found herself hard-pressed to recognize that Rory was Simon's twin and not a much younger brother. And it was not only his enthusiasms but his complaints as well. He railed over the fact that both his father and brother refused to recognize that he was a gentleman grown and no longer a child, but even as he was complaining he managed to infuriate one or the other of them by indulging in childish excesses. Diana had wished more than once that she could help him, for in some ways she understood Lord Roderick better than she understood her husband. Simon could be positively stuffy about some things, while Rory never was. And Rory never scolded.

Under his enthusiastic influence the atmosphere at the abbey grew more festive, and he and the Lady Susanna set the servants to decorating the house with a vengeance. Evergreens were brought in, holly, ivy, laurel and bay, as well as sweet rosemary, and cypress. Mistletoe was strung above every doorway, and holly berries were strung together and wound through the evergreen branches decking all the main-room chimney-pieces as well as the grand staircase in the great hall. A huge kissing bough in the form of a crown of greenery adorned with lighted candles, red apples, rosettes and ribbons, with mistletoe hanging below, was suspended from the ceiling of the gothic new hall and Lord Roderick, Lady Susanna, Simon, and Diana busied themselves with tying small, gaily wrapped parcels at the ends of the long ribbon streamers.

On Christmas Eve the Ashen Faggot, that enormous bundle of green ash sticks, very thick in the middle and tightly bound with bands of ash and hazel, that was Somerset's traditional substitute for the Yule Log, was carried in and placed in the huge new-hall fireplace with great ceremony and as much excitement as was possible with Lady Ophelia making part of the company.

Simon supervised the lighting of the fire with a fragment from the previous year's bundle. "Be certain you have sufficient tinder and kindling," he told the young footman who knelt to help guide the heavy bundle into place, "and do not let them set it in such a way as to smother the fire before it can take hold. A fire needs air to burn as well as fuel, you know."

"As if the poor lad has never built a fire before," Diana said, shaking her head at her husband.

He grinned back at her, but Susanna spoke up at once. " 'Tis prodigiously important that the thing be done correctly, Diana, for the fire must burn the whole twelve days of Christmas if the Warringtons are not to suffer ill luck the rest of the year through. And there must be a bit left of the ash bundle, too, to light next year's fire, you know."

Diana did know, although the custom was slightly different in Hampshire. But here in Somerset, during the feast of Twelfth Night, the fire would be quenched, and of the bits of ash that were left, one or two would be carefully put by to use in kindling next year's fire to ensure a continuity of blessing in the house. Such had been the tradition at Alderwood Abbey since Sir William Warrington's first Christmas in the house, and she had a warm feeling that she would watch her grandchildren continue the tradition.

Christmas Day passed peacefully, with prayers led by Lady Ophelia's chaplain in the chapel, followed at midday by a magnificent meal that was set before the family in the large first-floor dining room. The final course, as always, was a huge, flaming Christmas pudding, and even Lady Ophelia joined in the merriment when she discovered the wedding ring in her portion. Lord Roderick, biting down upon a silver coin, jubilantly waved it about and informed the others that now his fortune was sure to be made.

After the meal they retired to the new hall, where they were soon joined by all the servants, who had come to drink a toast to their master and to receive their gifts. The gaily wrapped parcels were removed from the kissing bough and distributed, after which there was much merrymaking and singing of carols, followed by evening prayers, before the household retired at an early hour to replenish their energies for the morrow.

6

Boxing Day dawned in a blaze of sunlight upon a light crusting of snow. Looking from her window soon after rising from the warmth of her bed in the cheerful blue and silver bedchamber, Diana gave a small sigh. The world outside looked crisp and clean, stimulating, invigorating, inviting. Suddenly she felt as though she had been confined indoors, hemmed about by family, forever, and she longed for a taste of solitary freedom. The thought lingered, was savored, and a glint of mischief leapt to my lady's eye.

No doubt Lady Ophelia would have a list of chores for her to see to before the first of their guests began to arrive soon after midday, but her ladyship could scarcely set her a task without first laying eyes upon her. Accordingly, Diana rang for her maid, moving at once to pull a nut-brown velvet riding habit from her wardrobe, then scrabbling through the oddments on the floor for her riding boots.

"Whatever are you about, m'lady?" demanded a soft voice from the doorway.

Diana, on her knees before the wardrobe, glanced ruefully over her shoulder. "Looking for my boots, Marlie. I've a mind to ride before breakfast, and I'm in a bit of a hurry."

"Well, all the same, Miss Diana, you'll not find them boots down there," said her handmaiden, shutting the door behind her and stepping swiftly toward her mistress. "As if I'd put your boots down amongst them hatboxes and such. No, nor Miss Floodlind wouldn't neither, being so niffy-naffy in her ways as she be." Marlie reached up to the top shelf and pulled down a bundle carefully wrapped in white paper. "Here they be, where they belong to be, safe and sound, where naught can put scratch or smudge upon 'em. Now, do you get up from that cold floor, m'lady, before you catch an ague. 'Tis mighty cold outside fer riding, I'm thinkin'."

Marlie stood over her mistress, her lips folded primly in disapproval. Her feelings were likewise evident in the way she held her sturdy body, for Marlie had been with her mistress nearly as long as Ned Tredegar had, and she was not one to mince her words. Diana also employed a very expensive dresser, Miss Floodlind, but that haughty dame, a good deal higher in the instep than her mistress, rarely showed her face abovestairs before midday unless the occasion particularly warranted her skill. So, unless Diana wished to cut a dash, she infinitely preferred Marlie's services.

"Quickly," Diana said now, ignoring the maid's disapproval. "If anyone comes in search of me, I'm sped. It is not too cold for riding, either, Marlie. Doubtless the Duke of Beaufort will have his pack out by eleven. And unless I miss my guess the ground will be perfect, neither frozen nor slushy, but just right for a good ride. So do hurry." As she spoke, Diana stepped quickly into a short, thin chemise, then pushed her arms through the sleeves of the soft lawn shirt Marlie held for her. The shirt was made doubly thick for warmth, but because of the thinness of the material, it was still a good deal softer next to her skin than linen would be and more practical than silk for riding.

Next came her stockings and garters, then the heavy velvet skirt, and lastly the riding coat, designed à l'Écuyère with small lapels faced like the collar in deeper brown velvet. Seated upon her dressing chair, Diana allowed Marlie to pull on her boots, then spoke quickly when the maid picked up the silver-backed hairbrush from the dressing table.

"Just brush it out and stuff it into a gold net, Marlie. I've no wish to sit still for more."

Marlie obeyed, expressing her opinion of such laxity with a small sniff. But moments later Diana was ready, her golden curls confined in a net and tied at the nape of her slender neck with a brown grosgrain ribbon. She tilted her plumed, velvet hat rakishly over her right eye, gathered up her whip and gloves, and slipped from her bedchamber after Marlie looked outside the door to be sure the gallery was clear. Once she had made her way safely from the second floor, it was an easy matter in that large house to evade other family members who might be up and about at that early hour and to make her way through the tall, mazelike hedge garden to the stables without encountering the slightest check.

She found Ned Tredegar brushing one of her favorite mounts, a dappled gelding some fifteen hands in height. The groom looked up from his task. His eyes twinkled.

"Escapin' again, Miss Diana?"

She chuckled. "You may well say so, Ned. Is Crispin fit for a gallop?"

He rubbed the gray's cheek. "Aye, mistress, 'n me bay as well."

"Well, I don't want you," she said bluntly but with a smile. "I want to gallop the fidgets out of myself so I can be a lady again when our guests begin to arrive. I am quite as full as I can hold of family togetherness, and I've a good many days more of it before I shall manage another opportunity such as this one, I daresay. So bustle about and fling a saddle on that gentleman. He looks as if he feels the same way I do."

Crispin tossed his beautiful gray head just then and pawed the ground with one dainty hoof as though to second her words, and Ned Tredegar smacked him fondly on the rump.

"Aye, he's fit t' go, 'n no mistake, but I'm thinkin' the master won't like it much an ye go alone, Miss Diana."

"Pooh, I'm only going through the home wood and about the park a little. No one will molest me, and I promise not to be out above an hour. I just want to be alone, Ned. I've had little privacy these past months."

Tredegar argued no more but saddled the dapple gray and tossed her up. Only as she was leaving the stable did he warn her to keep a tight rein and to mind her wits didn't wander. "There be a good crust, but ye'r like t' find a patch 'r two of ice as well, mistress."

"I'll take care," she promised. Looking back over her shoulder a moment later, she was not surprised to find him standing in the stable entrance watching her. It gave her a good feeling to know that Ned cared about her safety, but a moment later she put all thought of him out of her mind as Crispin, practically champing at his bit, made it clear to her that he had no wish to dawdle along like a carthorse. Accordingly, having seen by now that the snow was little more than a thin white crust and that Crispin would have no difficulties with ice, she dropped her hands and leaned forward slightly over his arching neck.

"Let's go, then, boy," she murmured. He understood even without the light touch of her heel against his flank, and she could feel his muscles gathering beneath her like coiling springs. His stride lengthened quickly until the chill air was like a wind against her cheeks, and she could feel her blood stirring with the familiar sense of excitement as the horse moved into a distance-eating gallop that quickly took them across the open, snow-covered field and into the home wood. The trail was wide and hard-packed, and the snow no deeper than it had been in the open field, so she scarcely checked Crispin's pace, all but letting him have his head, letting him run until he began to slow of his own accord. When she turned him at last, her cheeks were flushed and her eyes were glowing from the exhilaration of the ride. She tossed her head, raising her face to the sun and drawing in long breaths of the cool fresh air. Thus it was that she did not immediately perceive the rider approaching her along the path.

When she did see him, some of her joy faded, and she nibbled unhappily at her lower lip, for she had no difficulty recognizing her husband in the large, broad-shouldered horseman so rapidly nearing. She remembered Tredegar's warning. No doubt Simon would scold her, either for riding alone or for not taking proper care with regard to the snow on the ground. But even as these unpleasant thoughts crossed her mind, she thought how well he rode and how much to advantage he appeared upon a horse. Squaring her shoulders, she urged Crispin to a quicker pace. Let Simon scold if he wished, she told herself. He had been too busy to do so for days, so perhaps it would be better to let him vent a little temper before their guests arrived. She had had her ride, and he would be less likely, perhaps, to stir up a scene later. To her astonishment, however, she realized as they drew nearer to each other that her husband was grinning broadly.

"Good morning, sweetheart," he called. "Tredegar said I would find you along this ride."

"And so you have," she replied, watching the golden eyes carefully. "Did you wish to see me particularly, Simon?"

He chuckled, drawing in and turning the huge bay he rode to fall in beside her. "Aunt Ophelia wished to consult with you on some matter of grave importance. You see in me her courier. I was dispatched to rouse you from your slumber. Only you were not there, so I tracked down Marlie, who told me you had gone riding, whereupon I promptly discovered an overwhelming urge within myself to do likewise. Hence, my discussion with Tredegar."

"What did Lady Ophelia want precisely?"

"How the devil should I know?" he retorted with another laugh. "That woman insists she leaves everything to the servants, but to my notion she's set them all at sixes and sevens when by rights she ought not even to have left her bedchamber yet. It is scarcely nine o'clock."

"I know." Diana sighed. "She truly is a very good woman, Simon. It is a rare pity she never married. Instead, she has done her duty, first by raising you and Rory after your mama died and secondly by taking charge of dearest Susanna from the cradle."

"Fudge," said the undutiful Simon. "That is what she gives the world to believe, right enough, but Rory and I were already at Eton when my mother died shortly after giving birth to Susanna, and Aunt saw us only during holidays from school. She did her duty then by bringing every one of our youthful peccadilloes to my father's notice. Poor Rory certainly suffered from that sense of duty of hers more than I did, but I, too, had my moments. As for her oft-touted devotion to Susanna, I wish I may see it. What there is of it is certainly of a recent nature. For the most part the child was raised by her nurse and her governess. I think Aunt pretty well terrifies her, for she was used to be a sprightly child, not nearly so shy and unsure of herself as she is now."

"Well, I've seen her only in company for the most part, of course," Diana said, "but I have seen indications of spirit from time to time when her ladyship is not close at hand. Must we go back at once?" she asked reluctantly.

"We most assuredly must not," he replied, twinkling. "I've a wish to ride round the entire park, and I command you to attend me as a good wife should."

She grinned saucily. "Sometimes your commands are very gratifying, my lord."

"So I should think," he returned with a leer that was only half mocking.

Diana blushed, shaking her head at him. They rode together in perfect harmony for some time, breaking off their conversation occasionally in order to enjoy a brisk gallop, then slowing again to talk. Diana tried to think of the last time they had ridden together like this, and failed to remember a single occasion after the first few weeks of their marriage. More often than not they were surrounded by others, and their time together seemed to have been filled with arguments and stiff, unpleasant scenes. But now Simon was laughing, relating a tale from his youth, the memory stirred by a gurgling, brook-fed pond they had just passed.

"And when I told them back at the house," he said,

"that the fool fish had jumped right onto the shore in his enthusiasm to snatch a mosquito out of the air, and that *that* was how my uncle chanced to catch it, Uncle Tom picked me up, threw me over his shoulder, and carried me straight back here, where he pitched me, fully clothed and screeching, into that icy pond."

Diana joined in his laughter, then made a saucy face at him when he warned her sternly but with his eyes still reflecting his laughter that he didn't wish to hear that tale repeated to a ballroom full of interested listeners.

He chuckled again, then eyed her more narrowly. "Are you warm enough with just that light jacket?" he demanded.

"Yes, Simon."

He regarded her doubtfully, and she waited for him to say more, but beyond muttering that he hoped she didn't make herself ill all for the sake of following a stupid fashion or two, he didn't.

"Afraid I shall leave you in the lurch to support Lady Ophelia and the marquess through the coming festivities, sir?" Diana asked, teasing him.

"You'd best do no such thing, Diana mine, unless you want to see your wretched husband clapped up in Bedlam."

"Rory and Susanna would help you," she told him.

"Help me to Bedlam, more like," he retorted. "No, thank you, I prefer your assistance."

Having thus successfully introduced his brother's name to the conversation, Diana decided Simon's mood was receptive enough for her to attempt to follow through on a half-promise she had made her brother-in-law. Lord Roderick had no independent income of his own but was wholly dependent upon his father and his brother for his finances, a fact that, he assured Diana repeatedly, did not sit well with him. Though he admitted when pressed that the marquess made him an adequate if not generous allowance and that Simon was usually willing enough to "tip over the ready," as Rory put it, whenever he outran the constable, he also pointed out that Simon more often than not offered an unwelcome sermon with the money, and insisted that the entire situation had become loathesome. Moreover—and here, Diana realized, was the crux of the matter—the Comte de Vieillard had demanded, not unnaturally, to be reassured of Lord Roderick's capability to support Mademoiselle Sophie before he would permit an alliance to be made between them.

"And how can I possibly give the old man such an assurance when Papa could as easily cut me off on some whim or other as not?" he had demanded. When Diana had assured him that she could not imagine the marquess doing such a thing, Rory had said, "Perhaps not, but the possibility does exist, and you know it, so long as I have no proper income of my own. If only Papa would give me the opportunity to prove myself!" He had gone on then to assure her that if such an opportunity came into his hand, he would promptly cease his irresponsible ways and become a paragon of every virtue. Though Diana was not by any means certain that he would succeed in that final endeavor, she knew he meant well, and she was determined to help him.

She eyed Simon carefully, and since he showed no sign of bristling at the mention of his twin's name, she dared to introduce the subject of that gentleman's precarious future. However, she decided an oblique approach might answer better than an outright demand for his assistance.

"Does Susanna have money of her own, Simon," she asked curiously, "or will the marquess provide her dowry when she marries?"

"She will have an independence," he responded readily enough, though he glanced at her searchingly. She did not generally display such curiosity in matters that did not concern her. "My mother left her fortune to any daughters she might have had."

"And Rory?" she asked, emboldened by the fact that he had not reproved her for her curiosity. "Will he always have to depend upon the marquess?"

"He will be left several of the unentailed properties when Father dies," Simon said more curtly than before.

"Not until then? Your father has a little rheumatism, Simon, but it is scarcely like to kill him. He may well live another twenty or thirty years."

"Indeed, I hope he may do so," Simon replied coolly.

"Well, you know I wish him no harm," she said, her indignation rising at his tone, "but surely you cannot expect Rory to hang on his sleeve—or upon yours, either—for so long as that. Why was he never pressed into some sort of occupation, for heaven's sake, the church or the military?"

With an involuntary crack of laughter, Simon demanded to know if she could actually envision his dandified brother in a country parson's black coat reading the Bible each Sunday to a flock of pious parishioners.

"Well, perhaps not," she conceded, a smile hovering upon her lips at the thought.

"I should think not! Why, 'tis all Aunt can do to get him to family prayers three or four nights out of a week when he's at Alderwood."

"But I *can* picture him in a red coat, Simon, or better yet, a blue one," Diana said quietly. "I think Rory might enjoy a cavalry regiment."

"He might well enjoy the way he'd look in full dress, mounted on a handsome charger," Simon agreed, "but if he's ever evinced the slightest inclination for a military career, I, for one, haven't noticed it."

"He's no coward," she retorted stiffly.

"Of course not." His expression was grim now. "I never said he was. I merely said he'd never expressed an interest in following the drum."

"Then why cannot you convince the marquess to deed over one or two of those properties to him now?" Diana demanded, her temper astir. "It would give him something to do. He wants occupation, Simon, and some control over his own income, for that matter, and it is not right that a grown man—he's nearly thirty after all—should be treated like a schoolboy."

"I am well enough aware of his age," Simon said coldly, "but since you have assured me that you have no interest in him, I should like to know how it is that you've become so thick with him as to presume to know his wants and needs." His eyes had narrowed, and when he looked at her, Diana had the feeling that his gaze was piercing through her, as though he would see into her very thoughts.

"It is not what you're thinking, Simon," she said wearily. "I never said I had *no* interest in him, only that my interest was not of a sort that ought to rouse your jealousy. I care for your brother because he *is* your brother, but you must see that it isn't fair for him always to stand in your shadow. A mere twenty minutes the other way and you would be where he is. Would you be any more resigned to the position than he is, sir?"

"He shows no sense of responsibility," Simon said. "Had I been in his place, I'd have made a push to prove myself before now."

"Would you, sir? Would you, indeed?" Her tone was sarcastic, her glance withering. "If you had never been given the slightest responsibility, if indeed you had always been held to be inferior because of a simple accident of birth—for that's all it was, my lord, he might as easily have been the one born first—would you really have been the man you are today? I think not. Had you been taught to be dependent instead of taught to think yourself a crown prince of some sort, you'd have been as Lord Roderick is. Take care, sir, that between you, you and your father do not push him into doing something utterly outrageous."

"Enough, Diana!" It was an order, snapped angrily as he reached out to catch Crispin's bridle and bring both horses to a standstill. "You've no business to be putting your oar into what is for the most part my father's business and to some extent my business."

"It is mostly Rory's business," she said, contradicting him without thought for possible consequences. "You do not listen, Simon, not to him and not to me—"

"I will not listen to more of this prattle, that's certain enough. You would do better, Diana mine, to remember your place."

"A mere female, you mean, with no business to discuss men's affairs? Is that indeed your meaning, my lord?"

"No, it is not. But I am your lord, madam, and it

would be as well for you to remember that before you concern yourself with my brother's so-called needs."

The anger had reached his eyes, and his voice was ominously calm now, so she knew she had pushed matters as far as she dared. With a little grimace, she reached out a hand to touch his arm.

"I am sorry to have annoyed you. That was not my intention. Nor is it my intention to run away, sir. You need not hold Crispin's bridle."

The muscles in his jaw relaxed slightly, and he did release the bridle. "You do know how to stir the coals, sweetheart," he said ruefully. "To think that I promised myself that I would not quarrel with you this morning."

A smile trembled upon her lips. "A foolish promise, Simon."

He agreed, then suggested that they ought not to keep the horses standing in the chill, and the moment was past. Diana made no attempt during the rest of their ride to return to the subject of Lord Roderick's difficulties. She knew that to do so would be most unwise, particularly since she had promised Rory that she would say nothing to Simon or to anyone else about his wish to marry Mademoiselle Sophie.

No doubt both Simon and the marquess would disapprove of the match, since Rory had assured her that the marquess, at least, wished for him to marry well. Unless there was some truth to the tale of the Beléchappé treasure, Mademoiselle Sophie would have scarcely a penny to bless herself with, let alone a proper dowry, and the marquess didn't hold with foreigners any more than Lady Ophelia did. Rory had confided to Diana that he hoped further acquaintance with the comte would convince his parent, at least, that the family was a respectable one. Diana, not knowing the marquess well enough to form an opinion on that head, and unable to discuss the matter with Simon, could only hope that Lord Roderick knew what he was about.

By the time they returned to the stables, Simon and Diana were in charity with one another again, and Diana quite happily took his arm when he offered it to her on the way back to the house. Both had forgotten by that time that the Lady Ophelia had expressed a wish for Diana's company, and so it was that when they entered by way of the courtyard hall, they met that formidable dame emerging from the blue parlor.

"Well, so you have found her at last, Simon," said Lady Ophelia, lifting her long-handled glasses to peer at Diana as if to be certain of her identity. "No doubt it has escaped your memory, my dear child, but we are in hourly expectation of receiving a number of visitors. I should have thought you would realize I might have need of your support at such a time, but I know how it is with you young people. Susanna is just such another. Laid down upon her bed since ten o'clock with a headache. Or so she says. I was just this moment going up to her to tell her that now is not the time for such foolishness. The child is merely shy, and so I told Marimorse when he first suggested she take part in these festivities. She is too young, I told him, and not yet out. She should not show her face. But he would have it that it was better for her to make her first appearance amongst her family, and I do not set my will against his, for to do so would be most unbecoming in me, and I trust I know my way better than that. But it is as I said, and she will disgrace the family if care is not taken."

Her ladyship finally pausing to take an indignant breath, Diana leapt into the breach, saying quickly, "I'll go up to her at once, ma'am, shall I? You will not wish to trouble yourself, not with your guests no doubt arriving at any moment. I'm so dreadfully sorry that I didn't realize you wanted me. I was certain you would take advantage of the lull this morning in order to recruit your energies by indulging in a lie-in. But I should have known that you would not do so. Do, pray, but tell me what you wish me to do first."

"First," put in Simon with a grin, "you are going to change your dress, Diana mine. It would not suit my consequence to have my beautiful wife greeting our guests in her riding dress. Aunt must agree with me." He turned the grin upon her ladyship. "Do you not, ma'am?"

"Indeed, it would not be suitable for you to be seen

in all your dirt, and you must change your clothes, too, Andover, for your papa wishes you to attend him in the hall, you know. At least, I make sure he will wish it, for he will bury himself in his letters and forget to greet our guests unless he is nudged on to do so by you," she added a little more tartly.

"Then, since I will be in my own rooms, and since they are quite near dear Susanna's," Diana said firmly, "I shall attend to that little matter, Lady Ophelia. You need not trouble your head further. I'll see to it that she is ready to greet the very first arrivals."

"Well, as to that," her ladyship said doubtfully, "there is no real reason for her to show herself before dinner if she wishes not to do so."

"Nonsense," said Diana briskly, "she may as well begin as she means to go on. And if that," she added to Simon as they climbed the stairs together a moment or two later, "doesn't spike her ladyship's guns, I don't know what will. I wonder what she did to frighten poor Susanna into a headache."

"Heaven knows," he replied. "Are you sure my little sister is ready for all this, sweetheart?"

"Of course she is. It is only a family party, after all."

Simon laughed. "A family party, Diana? With Lord and Lady Jersey, the Countess if not the Earl of Westmorland, their interesting offspring, Mr. Brummell, Lord Alvanley, at least a day's worth of the Duke of Beaufort, ditto the Earl of Pembroke, Sir Richard Colt Hoare, and the Prince of Wales, possibly a look-in by York, your family, and God knows who else, I would scarcely call this get-together a family affair."

"Lord Alvanley sent his regrets," she reminded him, "and you know perfectly well what I mean. Susanna will do very well if she is allowed to be herself, and I depend upon you to second my efforts to protect her from Lady Ophelia."

He chuckled. "First you prove to me that you can produce Susanna," he said.

Tossing her head, she assured him that there would be no difficulty about that. He only laughed again, and she watched him disappear into his dressing room, thinking that she liked his laughter very well, even when—as now—it was little more than the sound of a challenge being issued. Well, she would show him. Susanna would be as wax in her hands. But first, since she had no idea how long it would take her to deal with the young girl, she decided to prepare herself for the afternoon ahead. Lady Ophelia and Simon were both right about one thing—it would never do for her to receive guests in her riding dress.

Finding both Marlie and Miss Floodlind awaiting her convenience, she soon rid herself of the riding habit, had a quick bath, glad that she had managed to wash her hair only two days previously, and dressed as quickly as possible in a becoming round gown of pale orange Indian muslin trimmed round the bottom with a wide, colorfully embroidered border. The dress was made with full sleeves to the elbow, tied with coquelicot ribbons. A matching ribbon banded the high waist, and both the front and back of the bodice plunged low. Even in the bedchamber with its cheerful fire and the windows curtained to block the draft, Diana was chilly, so when Miss Floodlind suggested a shawl, she agreed, deciding to wear one that Simon had brought her from Paris the previous month. It was made of the softest white wool, embroidered all over with gold thread, and Simon had assured her that the fashion of sporting such shawls was all the crack in Paris. She could not deny the wearing of it would keep her a deal warmer.

Since the dinner hour would be put back to at least eight o'clock, she would have time to change again later; therefore, she wore her hair simply, à l'Anglaise, and in less than an hour from the time she had entered her dressing room, she was ready to leave it, looking the fashionable young lady.

Trusting that Simon would not come in search of her but would go instead to lend his support to Lady Ophelia and the marquess, and that he would furthermore somehow contrive to prevent his aunt from sending someone to fetch her if guests began to arrive, Diana gathered her pretty shawl about her shoulders and went forth to attend to the small matter of the Lady Susanna.

7

Lady Susanna's bedchamber was three doors along the second-floor gallery from Diana's dressing room, and Diana pushed open the door quietly without knocking, thinking the younger girl would very likely be laid down upon her bed in a darkened room recovering from her headache, and not wishing to disturb her overmuch. Instead, however, she discovered Susanna, curled up on a French seat in the deep window alcove, a book upon her lap, her curly dark head bent as she read. She looked up sharply when Diana chuckled.

"Good gracious, Diana, you frightened the liver and lights out of me!"

"My, what elegant phrases your governess has taught you," Diana said teasingly.

Susanna blushed. "I had that one from the boots, actually," she said. "He's the most engaging creature. You must make his acquaintance."

"Do you actually converse with the boots?" Diana inquired, her eyes dancing. "Even my mama would never have countenanced such familiarity with the servants as that."

"Well, he's the son of one of Papa's tenants, so I knew him even before he began working here at the abbey," Susanna told her. "He was such a funny, laughing little boy that I recognized him at once the first time I saw him on the gallery, returning some guest's boots to his valet."

"Not a particularly finicking guest, if he entrusted his boots to anyone but his valet," Diana replied.

"No, indeed. Papa certainly would never do such a thing."

"Nor Simon, generally, though I do think someone else must have polished them at Ethelmoor, since Pettyjohn was not with him."

"Oh, well, Simon scarcely cares what he looks like, you know, but fancy Rory arriving here without his valet!"

They chuckled together over the vagaries of the opposite sex, and then Diana regarded her young sister-in-law rather sternly. "Why are you not dressed, my dear? Her ladyship said something about a headache, but that cannot be the case. You look to be in prime twig."

Susanna blushed again. "I-I merely wished to keep out of her way, you know. Diana, I cannot feel that I am quite ready to appear in public yet. Not yet."

"Pish tush, my dear, you are as ready as you will ever be, and you are merely suffering from a case of nerves. Trust me. My own mama practically had to drag me to my first affair, and I was in alt for weeks before with the excitement of anticipation. But when push came to shove, she had to shove. I was very glad of it afterward, I can tell you, and so will you be. You will not wish to miss the fun. This is no formal presentation as mine was, you know. You will merely conduct yourself as befits the daughter of the house, not putting yourself forward, you know, but merely observing and being polite when you are noticed at all. It will not be so difficult."

Susanna regarded her doubtfully. "You must have forgotten that the Prince of Wales means to honor us," she said. "Surely, I will be presented to him. Aunt said—"

"Never mind what Lady Ophelia said," Diana put in quickly. "If his highness requests an introduction, you may be certain that her ladyship will present you, but he is not at all likely to do so, you know. If he stays above a day or two, he will be more interested in speaking with his particular friends than with a young girl recently come from the schoolroom. More than likely he will take no notice of you. If he were to be accompanied by the Princess of Wales, that would be altogether different, of course."

Susanna giggled. "It certainly would!"

"Yes, well, never mind about that. You have no royalty to worry about today, for the prince will not arrive before Thursday at the earliest. Since many people choose not to travel on a Sunday, you know, we may expect only those persons today who do not entertain such scruples—my brother, Ethelmoor, and his family and possibly one or two others. The rest will begin arriving in force tomorrow. So you see, my dear, today will be little more than a family gathering. You will not wish to miss seeing little John or Amy, you know. Though I suppose," she added with a smile, "that I had best stop calling him 'little.' He will not appreciate such words now that he is getting so advanced in years."

Susanna laughed again. "Indeed, I should not like to miss seeing them. Is Amy talking yet?"

"Yes, and such a prattler. Only wait till you see her."

After that it was a simple matter to persuade Susanna to ring for her maid, and Diana stayed to see her rigged out in the white muslin round gown that Lady Ophelia had decided would be proper for her to wear the first afternoon. She, too, had a shawl from Paris, a gift from her brother. Susanna's was of palest pink with silver embroidery, and since she chose to wear pink ribbons threaded through her hair and pink satin slippers upon her feet, Diana decided the total effect was bound to impress any young man she might chance to meet. Lady Susanna was going to take London by storm if only she might learn to deal more competently with the well-meaning Lady Ophelia.

They went downstairs together and joined Simon and the marquess in the new hall, where they learned that no guests had yet arrived. Rory entered some moments later, dressed nattily in the French style in tan breeches, a well-cut coat of dark blue with highly polished steel buttons, a gaily embroidered scarlet brocade waistcoat, and lace frills at his collar and cuffs.

Simon shook his head. "Very pretty, twin. A new rig?"

"Not so new as all that, but 'tis all the crack. What do you think?"

"Fluffy."

Rory laughed. "I should know better than to ask you,

Simon. You've no more notion what a gentleman ought to wear than . . . well, than Diana's Tredegar does. Just look at you. That coat of yours is too loose, your neck-cloth is tied all by guess, and your waistcoat is mighty dull and drab. Don't you agree, Papa?"

The marquess gave the question some thought, then pronounced that both his sons looked well enough. "Can't understand the modern fashions at all, myself," he said. "So little color, even in yours, Roderick. Why, in my day, a gentleman spent the larger part of his day perfecting his appearance. No detail was too small to go unnoticed."

His sister, entering the room in time to hear his words, agreed with him heartily. "Indeed, Marimorse, one cannot tell what the modern world is coming to when a man appears before a woman not only with his head bare of powder but bare of hair as well. All this cropping. Even the ladies, though I am glad to see that Diana has not been so foolish as to chop her lovely curls off."

"I told her I would beat her an she dared such a thing," Simon murmured provocatively. But when Diana turned to glare at him, she found him regarding her with twinkling eyes. He made her a little bow, gesturing subtly toward Lady Susanna. "I make you my compliments, my dear," he said. "Very nice, very nice, indeed."

The gesture caused a small flip-flopping sensation in her breast, and Diana felt warmth rushing to her cheeks. She knew perfectly well that he referred to her victory in producing the Lady Susanna, but his tone and the twinkle seemed to be doing odd things to her insides, nonetheless.

"Yes, she does look charmingly," agreed Lady Ophelia, misunderstanding Simon entirely, "and I'm sure Susanna looks well, too, but as for allowing her to cut her hair, I can tell you that I should never agree to such a thing. Nor would Marimorse be so lacking in his sense of duty to his daughter as to permit it. We do not feel it necessary to follow every foolish fashion here, I can tell you," she added unnecessarily, as she smoothed her full, purple satin skirts and adjusted the net veil that covered her gray, rigorously ordered curls. "I like that rig of yours, Roderick," she said then, raising her long-handled glasses to peer at him. "Shows a bit of imagination, and I like a touch of lace. So sad to see lace going out."

"Not in France, it ain't," Lord Roderick assured her. "Wouldn't wear ruffles for morning dress, of course, but you wait till you see the shirt I wear with my evening rig. Rows of ruffles. Assure you."

"Oh, Rory, no," Susanna said with one of her giggles. "Why, I was reading in the *Lady's Monthly Museum* only last week that ruffles for men are quite out. Simon is dressed much more the way they said a gentleman should be dressed."

"Poppycock," said Lord Roderick. "Simon don't know the first thing about it. Not that the idea ain't right if he means to follow the English way of things, but no one would ever mistake him for a member of the well-dressed set. You only wait till Brummell gets a look at him. Now, there's a fella knows how to dress."

"But not in lace, twin, never in lace."

"Well, no, but I daresay he couldn't carry it off, anyway. Just look at him. Fella looks best as he is, and he's got the body to carry off that stark, simple look. Wants to set a fashion, so he does it in a way that others can't follow without a lot of padding and nipping-in. Look at poor Prinny, for example. With all his bulk, he'd much rather dress with a few ruffles—aye, even with long, full skirts to his coats—but will Brummell let him? Not a bit of it. 'You call that thing a coat?' he says, and poor Prinny well nigh weeps."

"I cannot approve of such flippant talk about a member of the Royal Family," said Lady Ophelia in measured tones. "It is not becoming, particularly with Susanna present."

"True," Rory agreed, twinkling at his sister. "Can't be saying things about Prinny's girth, not when he means to honor our humble house with his august presence."

"Well, as to that, I cannot agree," said his austere aunt. "It is his highness who should feel honored, for although the prince and his brothers had the good fortune to be born on English soil, I'm sure they are quite the first members of the Hanover family to have done so."

"Aunt, you know perfectly well the family dates back to the Conqueror."

"Only by way of a female and very obscurely, I'm sure," said his aunt, unimpressed. "I shall always hold by the true line."

"As if she knew the Pretender personally," Simon murmured in his wife's ear.

Diana choked back a laugh. "Pray, do not suggest such a thing, sir."

"What's that you say?" demanded Lady Ophelia.

"Only that the Hanoverian line seems fairly well entrenched now, ma'am," said Simon without missing a beat. "Won't you take a chair? You have been in such a bustle all day that I'm persuaded you ought to put your feet up."

She agreed to his suggestion and allowed him to pull up the gros-point footstool for her comfort after she had seated herself in the deep wing chair near the fire. Rory took the opportunity to shoot a questioning look at Diana, and she was sorry to have to shake her head, grimacing slightly at the same time in order to let him know that although she had indeed tried to speak to Simon on his behalf her efforts had gone unrewarded. His cheerfulness faded somewhat, but the expression was brief, and a moment later he was happily engaged in relating a humorous anecdote to his sister.

Diana was pleased to see that Susanna looked relaxed. Even her aunt's stern pronouncements seemed to have little effect on the girl and Diana hoped that so long as she was not left alone for any length of time with Lady Ophelia, Susanna might do very well. Diana's stomach chose that moment to remind her that she had not eaten all day, and she glanced quickly about to see if anyone else had heard the embarrassing noise. No one was paying her any particular heed, however. She wondered idly if Simon had eaten breakfast before going in search of her.

Lady Ophelia being settled at last, he glanced up just then, catching Diana's eye. She smiled at him and felt a glow of delight when he grinned back at her.

Having nearly decided to risk incurring Lady Ophelia's displeasure by going in search of sustenance, Diana heard the approaching carriage wheels outside with mixed feelings. If guests were indeed arriving, some refreshment would soon be served. On the other hand, it would most likely be of the cakes and tea variety; whereas, if she had had the opportunity to slip away to the kitchen, she might well have talked the cook out of something more sustaining. A moment later, however, her hunger was forgotten when her brother, his wife, and their two children were announced.

Ethelmoor and Lydia came in with their usual calm dignity, and young John Sterling, entering behind his parents, carried himself with much the same dignified air. But Amy, seeing her favorite aunt from her perch in her nanny's arms, gave a shriek of delight and made it clear that she wished to be put down immediately.

Noting Lady Ophelia's outraged expression even as that lady began to rise from her chair to greet the arrivals, Diana hastened forward to take the young offender from her nurse.

"There, there, Amy, quietly, if you please. Ladies do not shriek in drawing rooms," she said, allowing herself to be well nigh strangled by her niece's fierce hug.

"I'm so sorry, Lady Ophelia," Lydia said, moving to make her curtsy to that lady. "She has no manners to speak of as yet, and Diana is quite her favorite relative, you know."

"Indeed, my dear, I shan't refine too much upon it," said her ladyship, looking down her nose. "Ah, here is Figmore now. Figmore, do see that Lady Ethelmoor's nurse is shown immediately to the nursery wing with the children."

John's expression threatened to become mutinous, but Diana saw Lord Roderick bend to speak into his ear, whereupon the boy immediately became more cheerful and was able to shake hands with his host and make his bow to Lady Ophelia with his dignity unimpaired.

"What on earth did you say to him?" Diana demanded in an undertone a moment later as the children made their exit and Lady Ophelia ordered the long-awaited refreshments.

"Merely that I'd see he didn't suffer untold boredom this week. Promised to take him shooting if nothing else appears on the horizon to interest him. Daresay Uncle Tom will bring his offspring, but they're mostly female, as I recall. Won't be much good to young John."

"Well, it was kind of you to offer to take him out," Diana said. "I did talk to Simon. It's no use, Rory."

"Figured as much. I'll come about, though. See if I don't."

His attitude worried her, for she could think of no way by which he might win his point with either his twin or the marquess. There were other arrivals during the afternoon, including Lord Thomas Warrington and his lady, some twenty years younger than Lord Thomas, and their three daughters, all of whom were still relegated to the nursery or the schoolroom. Diana had little time for quiet reflection after that before it was time to change for dinner, but she managed to change quickly, checked to see that Susanna was still in good spirits, and then went downstairs in case any of the guests might be wandering about unattended. No one was in the great hall when she came down the stairs, but she discovered the marquess at his desk, making an entry in his journal.

"Oh, I beg your pardon, sir. I am intruding."

"Not at all, Diana. Come in, child." He was dressed in evening attire, satin knee breeches, a frilled shirt, an intricate neckcloth, and a dark coat. He wore his wig tied in a little silk bag at the nape of his neck with a black ribbon, and he removed his spectacles as she approached, laying them upon the desk. "Very tiring, all this entertaining, don't you think?" he asked, smiling.

"Oh, no, sir, I've become accustomed to it, you know," she told him, taking a seat in the Kent chair across the desk from him. "Despite anything Andover may have told you, I really do enjoy all the festivities. I scarcely know what to do with myself when there is no company about. Nor does Andover, for that matter."

"You two should take a month or two to get to know each other," recommended the marquess with a slight smile. "I daresay with all the gallivantin' you do, you've scarcely become acquainted. People don't these days. Noticed it often."

Diana regarded the old man a little wistfully, wishing suddenly that she could open her heart to him, that she could tell him exactly what had been happening between his son and herself, but the moment passed as quickly as it appeared, and she found herself telling him a rather naughty piece of gossip instead. The marquess quite enjoyed the tale, and the two of them talked amiably for some fifteen minutes before it occurred to Diana that the opportunity was a perfect one for pleading Lord Roderick's case.

"Sir, may I confide in you?" she asked, eyes innocently wide.

"To be sure, child, I should be honored."

"Well, it is nothing at all to do with me personally, but I think Lord Roderick is a little afraid to mention the matter to you himself, you see, so I thought perhaps . . . well . . ." It was not so easy as she had thought it would be, Diana realized when the marquess's eyes began to narrow much as Simon's did when he was annoyed. Odd that she hadn't noticed before how alike their eyes were.

"You were saying . . ." the marquess prompted, his tone not nearly so inviting of confidence as it had been only moments before.

"Only that Lord Roderick wishes you would place more reliance upon his capabilities, my lord," she said quickly. "I know it is none of my affair, indeed, I do, but I thought that perhaps, since you are so near to him, you know, you might not see things as clearly as someone else might, so if I could just explain the matter to you, perhaps you might see your way clear to helping him prove himself."

"Indeed."

Neither word nor tone was at all encouraging, but Diana, now that she had taken the plunge, was determined not to be daunted. Leaning a little forward in her chair, she said, "Yes, sir. Lord Roderick truly wishes to mend his ways, you know, and I think if he but had some responsibility of his own—a bit of property to look after or the like—he would soon prove to be as capable a man as Simon is."

The marquess had been growing more obviously indignant with each word she spoke, and Diana expected some sort of explosion to occur the moment she stopped speaking. Instead, his attention suddenly drawn by something behind her, the marquess gave what seemed, most oddly, to be a sigh of relief. Even as she wondered at this strange reaction, the hairs on the back of her neck seemed to stand on end, warning her as the marquess's oblique glance had not, that split second before Simon spoke from the doorway.

"Will you excuse us for a few moments, Father? There is a small matter requiring Diana's immediate attention upstairs."

"To be sure," the marquess replied politely, his eyelids drooping, hooding the expression in his eyes. But Diana was almost certain she had seen a glint of sympathy, and the sight did nothing to reassure her as she got slowly to her feet and turned to face her husband.

He stood in the doorway, dressed for dinner in creamy knee breeches and a dark coat. His neckcloth was neatly but not ornately tied, and he wore a simple watchchain across his plain, green silk waistcoat, as well as white unclocked stockings, and ordinary neat black shoes. His appearance, compared with that of many other men of his time, was unremarkable, but Diana would no doubt have thought he looked very handsome had her attention not been caught by the look in his eyes. His general expression was bland, but his eyes told her all she needed to know. He had overheard her conversation with the marquess, and he was not at all pleased. In fact, if she got out of the forthcoming interview with a whole skin, Diana told herself, meekly passing Simon and moving toward the grand staircase, it would be a miracle.

Even meeting Lydia and Ethelmoor on the stairway did nothing to help her, though Diana made a feeble attempt to persuade Simon that whatever task awaited her upstairs could just as well wait until after dinner, since their primary task was to see to the well-being of their guests.

"Aunt Ophelia and Father will do the honors," he said quietly, too quietly, she thought. "My father is in the new hall, Ethelmoor. Madeira and sherry have been laid on there, as well. We'll join you shortly."

"As you wish," Ethelmoor replied with a sharp glance at Diana. She met his look directly and was not particularly pleased to note dawning amusement in his expression. "Come, Lydia," he said then.

They met several other guests on the way, but Simon, albeit polite, was determined and, willy-nilly, Diana soon found herself in her own bedchamber, alone with him. She turned toward him as he shut the door, but the defiance in her expression faded quickly in the face of his open anger. "Simon . . . my lord, please . . ." she said hesitantly. "I know you said I must not interfere, but I could not help myself. His lordship, your father, was in such an amiable frame of mind that I simply had to do my possible."

"You *had* to, Diana?"

"Yes," she insisted. "You must try to understand, sir. I was not merely defying you. Truly, I was not."

"Then, I should like to know just what you were doing, since I warned you most specifically only this morning that you are not to meddle in affairs that do not concern you."

His calm fury was more unnerving than his usual blustering anger, and Diana was not at all sure she knew how to deal with it. The loudly scolding, fiery-tempered Simon was more familiar to her, and she had long since learned that however much she might dislike his scolds, they were generally harmless. In his present mood, she was not at all sure she could trust him not to become physically violent. Lord knew, even gentle husbands had been known to beat their wives for defying them, and Simon was not a man one would generally describe as gentle. Moreover, she could scarcely go on pretending, even to herself, that she had not defied his express order.

"All right," she said after a long pause. "I did defy you, sir, and I'm very much afraid that no matter what you choose to do about it, I shall probably defy you again."

She could scarcely believe she was saying the words. They seemed to come from someone else entirely. Was she crazy? She watched Simon closely. If she was still reading the golden eyes correctly, his fury was unabated, but the calm expression on his face did not change by so much as the twitch of a muscle. He merely waited for her to continue, and she was not by any means certain she could do so. This calmness of his frightened her as his rages had never done.

"I cannot stand by, it seems," she said, biting her lower lip. "I would obey you, sir, an I could. But my feelings with regard to the way your brother is treated seem to get in the way of my good sense. Just now, below, I knew I was doing him no good with your father. I could see that in the marquess's expression. I was merely annoying him, as I seem to annoy you. But I could not help myself. It is the injustice of it, Simon, nothing more. Please, you must believe that if you believe nothing else."

"You may thank the Fates that you were not subjected to the words my father must have itched to say to you," Simon said coldly. "The only reason he held his tongue is that he deems it improper to reprimand my wife when I am at hand to attend to the matter myself. But he expects me to say a good many things to you, Diana, and I can think of no acceptable reason why you should not hear them. You deserve more than a scold for this little incident, my girl. You went to my father when you could not get what you wanted from me. How am I to take that, do you suppose?"

His cold anger sent a shiver up her spine, and she could not think how to answer him. She had not realized he would see the matter in such a light and was uncomfortably reminded of a time when, having failed to gain permission from her mother for something she particularly wished to do, she had applied to her father, assuring him that Mama had said his decision would prevail. The subsequent confrontation had resulted in one of the very few times during her childhood that her father had been moved to punish her. Remembering the incident now, she eyed her husband more warily than ever.

"I did not think, sir. To speak to your father in such a way was indeed wrong of me, but I truly did not think of defying you, merely of helping Rory." She touched his arm. "Please, Simon, do not be angry. I won't do it again."

He looked down at her, still stern and apparently unmoved by her gesture. "You will not seek to reopen the subject?"

She hesitated. "I cannot promise that, sir. However," she added quickly when his jaw tightened, "I will promise to discuss the matter with no one but you."

His attitude relaxed slightly, though his expression and tone remained stern. "You are determined not to let this matter rest, Diana, no matter how angry you make me? You are not being wise, you know."

"I cannot help it, sir, I must make you see how unfair the situation is for your brother."

He looked for a moment as though he wished to shake her, but Diana stood her ground, meeting his look with one just as determined, and at last Simon gave a small sigh. "I will promise to give the matter more thought. But that is all. And in the meantime, you are to keep your tongue civilly between your teeth and to behave in a circumspect manner where my brother is concerned. I will not allow the two of you to provide further substance for gossip in this house."

His anger was gone, but there was another expression in his eyes now, one that she could not read. He looked tired, even a little sad, but Diana decided she was merely seeing things that were not there in her relief at having disarmed his anger. She was pleased, too, that he had agreed to consider the possibility of taking his brother's side with the marquess. Marimorse must listen to Simon, and she was quite certain that having moved Simon so far, she would soon convince him to go the extra step.

When they returned to the new hall they found the others assembled there, waiting for Figmore to announce that dinner had been served. It was a small but merry company, and after dinner the men soon joined the ladies in the hall again, where Lydia was persuaded to sing and Susanna was prompted to play a brief sonata on the pianoforte. Since she knew herself to be very well taught, and since she enjoyed playing, she acquitted herself well, and Diana could see her confidence growing as the others begged for just one more piece. Thus the evening passed off well, and the following day a number of other guests arrived, including the Earl and Countess of Jersey, the handsome Viscount Villiers, Sir Richard Colt Hoare, the Earl and Countess of Westmorland, the Lady Sarah Fane, and the Earl and Countess of Trent. Diana practically threw herself into her father's arms.

"Papa, how I have missed you!" she cried. "And Mama, how delightfully that bonnet becomes you! Oh, how glad I am to see you both. Do, do come in and meet everyone!"

"Diana, love," begged the countess with a fond smile, "do try for a little conduct. You are a grand lady now, and no longer a madcap little girl."

"Oh, now, my lady," said the earl, chuckling as he put his arm firmly around his daughter's waist, "no need to scold the little puss just because she's glad to see her papa and mama. Be a dashed sight worse if she greeted us by looking down her nose, y' know. Good day, Andover, pleased to see you again, lad. You're looking mighty well."

"I'm stout enough, sir," Simon replied, smiling. "Won't you take a glass of madeira?"

"Don't mind if I do," replied the earl, following him with a casual recommendation thrown over his shoulder to his wife to find out where their rooms were and to let him know.

Diana laughed. "Here, Mama, I'll take you up myself. The house is already as full as it can hold, I think, and we've more guests arriving every day. I cannot think when I've had so much to do!"

"The activity agrees with you, my dear," said her mother, following her up the wide stair. "You're looking very well indeed. Do we seek out the platitudinous Lady Ophelia, or may I simply find my bedchamber and take off my stays?"

"You may do precisely as you please," said Diana. "I must leave you almost at once, because Simon promised the children he would take them all riding this afternoon, so I must be sure he and Papa do not get to talking or Simon will forget. And Rory cannot do it, because he has gone into Bath for the afternoon. I don't know precisely what errand he had there," she added, when Lady Trent made a querying noise, "but I daresay he thought it of utmost importance. Either that, or he merely wished to avoid attending to any more host duties than absolutely necessary. From one cause or another, he has been like a cat on hot bricks these past days and more."

She was babbling, and Lady Trent would notice, Diana realized, but she could not stay to be cross-questioned, and for once she was grateful not to have the time for a comfortable coze with her beloved mother. Leaving her to recuperate after her journey, Diana hurried toward the stairs again, only to discover her young nephew lurking in the gallery attempting to peer over the railing.

"John, whatever are you about? Simon will come for you when it is time to ride out, you know."

"Oh, it ain't that, Aunt Diana," the boy assured her, grinning. "I was wanting to see the heiress. I have never had an opportunity to see one before, you know."

8

Diana laughed at her young nephew, but she could scarcely blame the boy for wanting to catch a glimpse of Lady Sarah Sophia Fane. The slender, dark-haired beauty, taller than Diana by at least three inches, had stirred everyone's interest from the moment of her arrival with her parents, first because her father, the tenth Earl of Westmorland, had chosen, in Lady

Ophelia's words, "to inflict his presence upon the house party," and secondly because Lady Sarah's inheritance was so great that it must command interest in any company.

However, as the days passed, Lady Sarah's light began to dim, and despite her magnificent fortune, she was discerned to be not entirely above reproach. "A tiresome schoolgirl," said Lady Ophelia predictably late Wednesday morning when Diana chanced to find her alone for a moment in the blue parlor. "Young Sarah—for call her Sally after her mama I will not, and she no longer wishes to be styled Sophie, as I'm given to understand she was during her childhood—young Sarah carries delusions of her worth beyond all limits. She talks too much and too often and has a coarseness of manner that I cannot like. In point of fact, she puts herself forward in a most unbecoming fashion. I trust that Susanna will not be so mistaken in judgment as to imitate such improper behavior."

Diana reassured her ladyship on that score and then had to hide a smile a moment later when Lady Ophelia wondered aloud where Lord Roderick might have taken himself off to. "For I cannot but think that Lady Sarah might appreciate his company for a walk through the shrubbery, you know. The house grows close with such a great company."

It had been rapidly borne in upon the members of her family that Lady Ophelia did not wish them to believe that such trifling circumstances as Lady Sarah's manner and conversation, both of which might easily have been improved, ought to blind anyone of sense to the very real advantages of a fortune of forty thousand pounds per year. During the two days following Lady Sarah's arrival, it had become clear that Lady Ophelia had decided that Lord Roderick should be encouraged to cut out Lord Villiers in his pursuit of the heiress. Diana, believing that Simon, too, would see nothing amiss in adding forty thousand pounds per annum to the Warrington fortune, had taken the first opportunity to tease her brother-in-law about his excellent prospects for a prosperous future. To her astonishment, Rory had not seen anything funny in the situation.

"Dashed if I'll let them push me into making a cake of myself," he had said in response. "In the first place, I love Sophie and I mean to marry her. In the second place, dashed if I can see any way they might expect me to cut Villiers out of the picture. I can scarcely expect Simon to slip his wind merely to oblige me, and if you think Sally Fane has any intention of giving herself over to a younger son when she might have the heir to an earldom, you're mighty mistaken, my girl. Furthermore, I'll be damned if I'll let myself be leg-shackled to a self-centered chit who sings till after midnight with the voice of a corn crake and who precedes every one of her inane observations on the state of the world or anything else with 'my goodness me.' No one of sense could expect a fellow to wish for such a thing."

"Not even for forty thousand pounds a year?" Diana had asked him, one eyebrow cocked in disbelief.

"Not if she were King Midas's sole heir," he replied uncompromisingly.

His attitude had not deterred his aunt in the slightest, however, and so Diana could not be amazed now to be sent in search of her brother-in-law with orders to "suggest" that he find Lady Sarah Fane and offer to show her over the gardens. She knew that Lady Sarah was sitting in the first-floor drawing room with her mama, as well as with the Countess of Trent, Lady Jersey, Lydia, Susanna, and several other women, engaged upon needlework and conversation. No doubt either of the younger ladies would appreciate any suggestion that would enable them to escape the atmosphere of barbed compliments and wicked gossip that was common to any group of which Lady Jersey was a part. For that matter, Diana thought with a grin, there was little chance that Lydia or Lady Trent would turn down such an opportunity.

The gentlemen had, for the most part, spent their mornings and part of each afternoon out hunting and shooting, and she knew that Simon, her brother, and Lord Villiers had gone with them this particular morning, but she knew also that Lord Roderick had not accompanied them. Not that she had seen him yet today, but she knew he had promised to take young

John Sterling into the home wood for a shooting lesson. Accordingly, she decided to walk toward the stables in hopes either of encountering them upon their return or of gaining some information as to their whereabouts.

Leaving the house was no simple matter, for she encountered first one guest, then another. But after assuring one stout dame that a luncheon would be set out in the morning room at half past twelve and then informing a dour, gray-headed gentleman that the marquess and Lord Jersey could be found with their heads together over a backgammon board in the new hall, she did manage to make her escape.

The day was crisp and chilly, but the skies overhead were clear and blue with light, fluffy clouds drifting along as though they little cared how far they traveled or how long their journey took them. Diana breathed deeply of the fresh cold air, gathered her shawl more tightly around her shoulders, and set out through the hedge garden toward the stables at a brisk pace. The hedges on either side of her were much too tall for her to see over them, and as she rounded a turn in the path, she nearly collided with her breathless nephew.

"John!"

John had indeed been hurrying, head bent, one hand stuffed in his jacket pocket for warmth, the other resting upon the barrel of the shotgun he carried under his arm, as though to ensure that the barrel pointed properly toward the ground. He pulled up short when she spoke his name, clearly startled and none too pleased at having met her there. But when he spoke, his attitude was one of studied carelessness.

"Oh, sorry, Aunt Diana, I was in a bit of a rush."

Diana's eyes narrowed as she looked down at him, noting the flush beginning to creep up his neck and into his cheeks. "Well, then, my friend, where are you bound in such a hurry?"

"Oh, just to put this gun up," he said. "Doesn't appear that his lordship means to take me out, after all."

"John, you haven't been out shooting alone, have you?" Diana demanded suspiciously. "Your father would never—"

" 'Course I haven't been shooting," the boy replied stoutly. "Don't you think I know better than that? But the fact is, Aunt Diana, that his lordship promised to take me out, so when I saw him from my window heading for the stables, I thought like as not he was looking for me. Only . . . only he wasn't," he finished lamely, shooting her an oblique glance from under dark lashes.

"What did Lord Roderick say when you found him?" Diana asked, thinking it odd that Rory would not honor a promise she knew he had made.

John's complexion grew a shade redder. "Well, the fact is I—I didn't speak to him."

"Didn't speak to him?"

"No, he was engaged in conversation with someone else, you see, 'n I didn't like to interrupt. It was clear as anything that he'd forgotten he meant to take me out."

"But you should have reminded him, John. Where is he? I'll speak with him myself."

"No, please, I'd rather you didn't. He's . . . well, he's a trifle out of sorts at the moment." The boy seemed more flustered than ever.

"Out of sorts? I wish you will be plain with me, John, for I begin to think you are merely cutting a wheedle in order to avoid punishment for taking a gun out when you know that you are not to do so. Just what do you mean by all this? Out with it, young man. What have you done?"

John was indignant. "I? I haven't done anything. Well, leastways," he amended conscientiously, "nothing but take this gun out without a grownup by. And I'd as lief you didn't tell Papa I did, for I promise I'd never have loaded it or fired it without Lord Roderick's permission. But like as not, Papa wouldn't care about that, 'n he might cut up stiff on account of my having it out at all."

Diana could well believe it. Nothing was more likely to rouse her brother's usually placid temper than one of his dependents doing something foolish or dangerous. She felt like cutting up a bit stiff herself. "I won't tell him if you promise never to do it again," she said quietly, "but what happened with Lord Roderick, John?"

"He was talking with an old man," said the boy, "a

pretty fat old man, leaning on a cane, with gray hair all round the edge of his head when he took off his hat, which he did to wipe off his forehead, though how a fella could sweat so much when it's as cold as be dam— As cold as this, I meant to say," he added quickly. "Well, I don't know how he could, is all."

At first Diana could think of no one among their many guests who answered such a description, but even as she began to say as much, sternly, to young John, she realized who the gentleman must be.

"I daresay the Comte de Vieillard has arrived, then," she said. "Did you hear him speak? Did he sound French?"

"He certainly did," replied the boy with a chuckle. "Half his words were French, like *mon dieu* and *merde* and—"

"Yes, I see," she said dryly, "but do you mean to say you eavesdropped upon their conversation?"

"N-not precisely." John looked at his boots, well aware that a gentleman did not listen to the conversations of others. "I daresay I ought to have come away at once, but I didn't immediately perceive that it was a private conversation. Then, I heard the old gentleman say he thought someone had most likely been arrested, so I knew at once that I mustn't listen. Only then . . . well—"

"I understand perfectly," Diana interjected quickly. "But arrested! Who was arrested?"

" '*Madame la comtesse, mon fils, et ma chère* Sophie,' whoever they may be," John informed her with a promptitude that belied his earlier casual unconcern. "He mentioned *l'empereur*, Auntie. Isn't that Napoleon Bonaparte of France? Isn't that how he chooses to style himself? Is he the one who arrested them? Who are they, anyway?"

"Mr. Bonaparte is not an emperor yet, John, but he has said he means to be, so he is no doubt the person to whom the comte referred, but for heaven's sake don't go gibbering of this to anyone else unless you wish also to explain how you came by the information. We cannot ask what was meant without explaining that you overheard them speaking, which would then lead to a discussion of the gun, I fear."

John's eyes widened, and his voice was touched by dismay. "I should say I'll keep mum then, but if someone has been arrested who ought not to have been, oughtn't Uncle Simon to be told? I daresay he could effect their release quick as a cat could lick her ear."

"No doubt he could if they have indeed been arrested, and no doubt Lord Roderick will apply to him for assistance if such is the case," Diana told him, trying without much success to achieve a normal smile. "But you know, my dear, the countess, her daughter, and her son are all guests at Versailles just now for Christmas, so an arrest is most unlikely. I daresay that with the comte mixing his French and English, as you say he did, you merely misunderstood him."

"Perhaps." But John sounded doubtful, and Diana could scarcely blame him. He would not be so unmannerly as to contradict her, but she knew Ethelmoor's French, like her own, was nearly flawless, and he had made a point of seeing that his son had excellent training. She had no doubt that John had heard exactly what he said he'd heard. But she wanted to defuse what might prove to be an awkward situation. It would be much more difficult to explain that the comte himself, no doubt senile as well as gout-afflicted, had simply overstated his alarms. Not having heard from his family with the regularity that he had hoped for, he was no doubt worrying before it was necessary to do so. She would certainly give the matter more thought and make an opportunity to discuss it with Lord Roderick before approaching Simon with the tale.

Just then young John's head came up alertly, his face the picture of dismay, and she heard at the same time the voices of several men approaching through the shrubbery. The sound drew steadily nearer.

"Papa! Oh, Aunt Diana, may I go? I promise I'll not repeat what I heard to a soul, but please don't let Papa find me here like this. Though he hasn't thrashed me but twice in my life, this"—he patted the shotgun—"would take the devil of a lot of explaining."

"Run along then, you little wretch. I'll hold them at bay till you're safe. But mind you put that gun up at

once and don't take it out again unless one of the
gentlemen says you may do so. Your word, John."

The voices were closer, just around the bend. The
boy glanced anxiously over his shoulder, then said,
"Word of a Sterling, ma'am. Now, *please!*"

She nodded, and he was gone, his feet fairly flying
over the gravel path. Diana moved quickly toward the
sound of masculine voices. She had heard Simon's as
well as her brother's and assumed the men had finished their hunt. A scant few seconds later, she encountered Ethelmoor, Simon, Lord Villiers, and Sir Richard
Colt Hoare. The last, a gentleman with some fifty-five
summers in his dish, who was generally as much at
home in the hunting field as in his exquisitely decorated drawing room, was limping slightly. Upon meeting Diana, he appeared to be somewhat embarrassed.

"You're back early," she said smiling.

"My fault, Lady Andover," said Sir Richard with a
grimace. His voice was gravelly, and his manner was
often curt, but she liked him and knew he meant no
harm to anyone. He seemed now to be trying to sound
at least amiable as he explained, "Took the deuce of a
tumble, and my mount came up lame. So did I, as you
see—my leg though, not my head, as these young fools
seemed to think. Feared I'd muddled my senses and
insisted upon showing me the road home."

"No such thing," declared Villiers, grinning. "Not so
much as a pigeon to be seen this morning, don't you
know. Westmorland and some of the others stayed out,
but it's my belief they won't bag a thing. I say, m'lady,"
he added more consciously, "you wouldn't know where
a fellow might find the Lady Sally, would you?"

"Indeed, sir, she is in the drawing room with your
mama and some of the other ladies." Villiers looked
anxious to be off but loath to leave Sir Richard, so
Diana turned to the older gentleman and said kindly,
"Lady Ophelia was going to speak to her housekeeper
when I left her some moments ago, Sir Richard, and I
know she will want to order a poultice for your leg to
keep the swelling down. She is quite knowledgeable
about such things, I assure you. We all go to her with
our injuries. Do you take him straight along, my lord."

"Aye, like a pony for quacking," agreed the older man. "She'll more than likely treat me just as the fellas in the stable will treat my poor old Dutchman. Well, we both need a touch of cosseting, I daresay. Take me to her ladyship, Villiers, and fling me upon her mercies before you go off in search of your young heiress."

Diana chuckled, and her eyes were still twinkling when she met Simon's gaze. She could see her amusement reflected in the golden-hazel eyes, and the expression caused a sudden, unexpected stirring in her midsection. Over the past few days she had had an opportunity to see him in a different light. He had seemed at times to be everywhere, playing at spillikins with the children one moment, dancing the next, then taking a hand at whist with his father and Lord Jersey, or even exchanging charming pleasantries with Lady Jersey while she flirted outrageously with him. Each morning he rode out shooting with several gentlemen, but in the afternoons he could often be found in the billiards room or in the library, and in the evenings he seemed to be part of every activity. When a problem arose or a servant wasn't where he was supposed to be or a meal was delayed, it was Simon, who with a quiet word in the right ear, saw that things were put to rights. The marquess scarcely noted what went on around him, devoting his attention to those guests like Lord Jersey or Sir Richard whom he personally found to be interesting. He ignored Lady Jersey, albeit with great politeness, paid little heed to the children or the younger women, and spoke to the younger gentlemen only when it was necessary.

Simon was undeniably the host, and he was carrying the burden easily and with flair. He had even managed to steal a moment or two of privacy with his wife from time to time, and he didn't seem the least bit flustered, Diana realized with a small pang of envy, by the knowledge that royalty was about to descend upon them.

The Prince of Wales, the Duke of York, and Mr. Brummell were to arrive the following day. And really, she mused now, one might think from the way Lady Jersey and some of the others went on that Mr. Brummell was the one who was bestowing the greatest honor upon Alderwood Abbey, and the one who must be best pleased.

Thanks to a friendship with the prince that had grown steadily over a period of years, as well as to his own nimble wit and acid tongue, George Bryan Brummell had risen over the past three years to become a powerful arbiter of fashion among the members of the *beau monde*. His strictures upon dress had been known to make more than one duke cringe and rush back to his tailor, but it was also said of the Beau, as he was known to most of the world, that he had been endowed with such imperturbable amiability that he could maintain a simultaneous friendship with people who were bitterly at odds with each other. Diana found herself hoping now that that particular description of Mr. Brummell was an accurate one.

"Diana, have your wits gone wandering?" demanded her brother. "I have twice asked you if Lydia is likewise in the drawing room."

"Oh, I beg your pardon, Bruce. I was thinking of Mr. Brummell."

"What, that fellow? Why on earth think of him? He ain't even a ladies' man, and you've no business, moreover, to be thinking of any man but your lord here, my girl." Ethelmoor chucked Diana gently under the chin, but his smile grew rueful when she glared at him. "Forgive me, Di. Where is Lydia?"

"She was indeed in the drawing room with the others," Diana told him, "but Lady Jersey and Lady Westmorland were being so out of reason polite to each other that Lyddy may well have taken flight by now. She will certainly have done so if Lady Ophelia has joined the drawing-room party. Oh, dear," she added with a comic grimace, "I was supposed to find Rory and send him out walking in the garden with Lady Sarah Fane, only I don't know where he is, and Lord Villiers has very likely walked off with the prize by now, any way."

"For which you will undoubtedly be blamed," said Simon, grinning at her. "Do you go away, Ethelmoor, and find your beautiful lady. I've a mind to enjoy a few brief moments of privacy with mine."

"I'll bid you both good luck, then, for someone will no doubt be coming in search of you before you've enjoyed much time alone." He waved amiably and wandered off down the path.

"Why Brummell, sweetheart? Are you worried?"

"Should I not be, Simon? The prince has made it clear that he has given up Lady Jersey in favor of Mrs. Fitz, only her ladyship refuses to be given up. If she has mentioned his name with sickening sweetness once, she has done so a thousand times. What if Mr. Brummell allows his wit to run free? We could find ourselves in the midst of a shocking bumble broth."

"Would that be so new to us?" Simon's tone reflected bitterness as he drew her hand through the crook of his elbow and rested it upon his forearm.

Diana caught her breath at the tone. They had been getting along well these past days and she found she had no wish at all to quarrel with him. She was afraid to speak, not knowing what to say and fearing to spark his temper.

Simon looked down at her. "Well, sweetheart?"

She looked away. "Simon, please, I only worried because such a thing would distress Lady Ophelia and your father. If Mr. Brummell doesn't cause a scene between the prince and Lady Jersey, he may still stir something between the prince and the Duke of York. There is naught but envy and bile between the two of them, as you know perfectly well."

"Don't fret, sweetheart," Simon said then, gently. "Brummell would never do anything so tasteless. Prinny is a martyr to insecurity, and George defers to him and amuses him. His air of supreme confidence seems to support Prinny's spirits as nothing else can. And George makes Lady Jersey believe that no one understands her as well as he does, so that disposes of her. He has known her well, after all, since the prince first married Princess Caroline. George was as much in evidence in royal circles then as her ladyship was, only I daresay his presence was much less distressing to her highness."

"Oh, Simon, if even half the stories about Lady Jersey are true, the princess must have wished herself back in the middle ages when she might have shouted 'off with her head' and been done with it. Is it true that Lady Jersey actually poured some evil-smelling stuff in the princess's hair on her wedding night and dosed her wine with a purgative and the prince's with a sleeping potion?"

"From what I've been given to understand, there was little need to put him off. The princess was not what he had been led to expect his wife to be. But, according to George, the princess was surely sick and the prince was more than a little worse for drink on their wedding night. The rest of what one hears about Lady Jersey's tricks is best forgotten, I think. And as for your worries about York, you may also trust Brummell to bring out the best in him, rather than the worst. George calls him a 'jolly, cursing, courageous man,' says he's noble to a fault and other such muck, and York laps it up like one of his wife's damned poodles lapping cream. Believe me, we will have cause to be grateful to George if the New Year comes in quietly. No one else could ride the waves of this particular flood of guests with his skill."

They had begun walking toward the house as they talked, and Diana gave his arm an impulsive squeeze as she glanced up at him. "No doubt you are right, sir."

"I am. Did you not say, by the by, that you were searching for my brother? If you want him, we are moving in the wrong direction. He's at the stables talking with the Comte de Vieillard. Said he had a horse to show the old gentleman. Don't believe it myself. The comte scarcely has the look of a Melton man."

"Maybe he is looking for something for the Vidame de Lâche," Diana said pacifically. "But it doesn't matter in the slightest, I'm afraid, for your aunt will think I've shirked my duty by not bringing Rory up to scratch. I cannot think, however, that he can be persuaded to make much of a push to engage Lady Sarah's affections."

"Good Lord, no." Simon laughed.

"You don't favor such a match?"

"With that tedious child? I should think not. She shows not the slightest sign of generosity, kindness, grace, integrity, or even dignity. She's just a foolish chit who has been allowed to think entirely too much of the importance of her fortune. Westmorland would have done better to teach her manners and deportment, but I daresay his nose was put out by old Mr. Child's will, so he never did a thing for the girl. And she lacked the benefit of a mother. I may have my differences with my twin, Diana mine, but I'd never serve him such a trick as to push him into a match like that one."

"But forty thousand pounds, Simon. Every year!"

"So what?" Simon retorted rudely. "Rory wasn't born without a shirt, whatever he says. He'll not starve if he doesn't marry a great heiress. I think all the better of him for not attempting to free himself from Father's authority in such a way." He paused, seeming oddly reluctant to continue, but when Diana didn't speak, he said, "I did speak to Father, by the way, as you asked me to do, but he remains adamant. Says he has no wish to allow Rory to play at ducks and drakes with any Warrington property before he has first shown us that he can behave responsibly."

"Oh, dear." Diana wondered if her father-in-law would deem it responsible of Lord Roderick to have fallen in love with an émigré's daughter. She was glad that Simon didn't want his brother to marry Lady Sarah for her fortune, but she was nearly certain that he wouldn't be impressed by Rory's choice for a wife. Lord Roderick might have expectations, but Mademoiselle Sophie had none unless there was some truth to the improbable Beléchappé treasure. Even that would more likely go to her brother. And whether there was treasure or not, and even if the marquess did not share his sister's great distrust of foreigners, she doubted whether either he or Simon would regard Rory's hopes with much favor. Her thoughts were interrupted at this point by the sound of a high-pitched, giggling voice from just around the next bend in the path.

"Oh, my goodness me, Lord Villiers, but we have come so far from the house! I know my papa and my stepmama—though I oughtn't to have to call her so when she is so few years older than I am, myself— would not think it proper I should come so far without a footman, you know, just because you met me on the point of stepping outside for a breath of air. Oh, my goodness me!"

With a startled look at one another, Simon and Diana turned right about and fled down the nearest turning. They emerged at last, safely, in the courtyard near the entrance to the cloister, and Simon guided her through the doorway into the chilled recesses of the magnificent cloister itself. At the moment there was no one about, though a good many servants' rooms were located just off the long, fan-vaulted chamber and the kitchens and laundry rooms were close by. But the cloister was empty. It was also cold. Simon turned Diana to face him and tucked her shawl more securely about her shoulders.

"You'll catch your death with only that thing to protect you," he said gruffly, looking down at her. The expression in his eyes changed noticeably, and Diana was not the least surprised when the firm grip on her shoulders relaxed and his arms went around her. His lips found hers quickly, and she was soon feeling anything but chilled. She responded eagerly to his caresses, her cheeks glowing now as much with passion as from the cold air outside, and when Simon suggested they might slip into a servant's unused bedchamber, she chuckled, the twinkle in her eyes daring him to follow through on the suggestion. With a sigh he set her back upon her heels. "I suppose not," he said. "Not here and not now, but someday, Diana mine, when I am not host to two or three dozen assorted people who would like nothing better than to spread a tale about finding the Earl and Countess of Andover making love on a servant's bed, then I'll accept the challenge I see in your eyes."

"And I, Simon? Do you think for a moment that I would stand for such a thing?"

"You'll do as you're told, wench," he said, raising his fist in mock threat. "This place gives me the sort of medieval notions you say the princess must feel from time to time. Only it's not 'off with her head' for me. I can think of much better stuff than that."

"I'll not venture to dispute that fact, my lord," she returned demurely.

Delighted, Simon laughed, gave her another hug, then pushed her along toward the stairs leading to the back hall. Within minutes, they were the well-behaved host and hostess again, speaking politely with one guest and then another and seeing to it that everyone had some activity to occupy his time until the hour appointed to prepare for dinner.

At six o'clock Diana and Lydia were descending the grand staircase together, preparing to join the others in the new hall for a congenial glass of sherry or ratafia before dinner was announced, when Diana spied Lord Roderick crossing the great hall below them.

"Good evening, sir," she said, loudly enough for him to hear her. He glanced up, and she noted that he looked disturbed. Her curiosity aroused, she excused herself to her sister-in-law. "And pray, make my excused to Lady Ophelia, as well, Lyddy. There is something I wish particularly to discuss with Rory."

"Diana, do you think that is wise?"

"Oh, pish tush, 'tis nothing of consequence. I shall be with you again in the twinkling of a bedpost."

"In the— Diana, for heaven's sake, of all the things to say!" But Lydia went away chuckling, and Lord Roderick, who had overheard the exchange, shook his head in exasperation.

"I wish you will have a care, Diana," he said when she approached near enough that his words would not be overheard by the footmen in the hall. "You will have us both in the briars again, and I've no wish to annoy Simon just now, if it's all the same to you."

"Just now, Rory? Do you wish to annoy him at other times, then?"

9

Lord Roderick had the grace to look ashamed of himself. "From time to time, I confess to an unquenchable urge to stir his temper," he said, speaking low. "Come into the library if you wish to speak with me privately. No one will be in there just now."

"That's what we thought in the Double Cube room, Rory."

"Oh, the devil take Simon and his jealousies! I have had a surfeit of them."

"Then tell him about your Sophie," she suggested quietly, "or allow me to do so."

"No, Diana." He closed the door of the library after first assuring himself that no one had been near enough to overhear their last exchange. "You don't understand." He sounded weary. "*They* wouldn't understand. Sophie is as well-born as we are—I met her at the Duchess of Devonshire's ball at the end of the Season, after all—but Papa and Simon both think I should set my sights on someone like the Fane wench. I tell you, I can't do it. I wish George Villiers joy of her, but she would drive me to Bedlam in a week. On the other hand, I've no wish to have Papa or Simon ringing a peal over me."

"Simon won't," Diana told him, "at least not about Sarah Fane. He likes her as little as you do, and he told me that he thinks the better of you for not showing an interest in that quarter."

"Did he, indeed?"

"He's your twin, Rory. I should think you would understand a little better than you do how his mind works."

"Do you understand him?" he countered. "You're his wife."

"That isn't fair. I've not known him a full year yet, whilst you've known him all your life."

He turned away from her. "I guess I've never tried to figure him out," he said quietly. "I've always felt like his shadow, you know, never really like his brother."

"Do you now expect me to wring my hands with pity for you, Rory?" she asked calmly. "Because I won't. I know exactly the sort of nonsense you've had to stand, first from your mother and later, though less blatantly, from Lady Ophelia. Simon is the good twin, and you are the bad twin. Nor shall I deny that the marquess treats you in a like manner. But what have you ever done to alter their opinions? Nothing that I can see. And I refuse to feel sorry for someone who has spent a great deal too much of his life doing the thing better than I could ever hope to."

He turned back to stare at her, and hearing the echo of her words, Diana was aghast at what she had said. Would she never learn to keep her thoughts to herself? Why must they spill out as though she had no control over them at all? Lord Roderick's face was suffused with anger, and she could scarcely blame him. Who was she to take him to task? She searched her mind rapidly for words that might unsay those that had gone before. There was nothing. She bit her lip, trying to make herself tell him she hadn't meant such a flat rebuke.

Lord Roderick drew a long breath, visibly making every effort to stifle his temper. "Lord," he said at last, looking directly at her, "no wonder Simon has such a time of it with you. What a vixen you can be."

"I-I—"

"No, don't apologize. You might undo the good you've done. You're right, you know. I'm a past master at the art of self-pity." He shook his head sadly. "I suppose the time has come to do something, at that."

His words startled her, but no more so than his attitude. There was a strength of purpose emanating from him just then that was frightening. She remembered what John had told her earlier. "Rory, what is it you plan to do? Is it true that Sophie and the others have been arrested?"

"Good God, Diana, where did you get such a tale?"

"Someone told me he overheard you talking with the Comte de Vieillard this afternoon," she admitted warily. "I had not even known he had arrived."

"He leaves tomorrow. Look here, Diana, I must know who repeated that story to you. I cannot risk having such an exaggerated statement of the case reach the wrong ears."

"Whose ears, Rory? I don't wish to tell you who it was, but I can promise you he won't say anything. Keeping mum is in his own best interests, I assure you."

"Keeping mum? That phrase comes straight from young John or I miss my guess. What the devil was he doing? Hiding in the bushes?" He gazed at her, but Diana said nothing, and suddenly his expression changed to one of near-boyish guilt. "Oh, Lord, I'd promised to take him out, hadn't I? Completely slipped my mind. But that young man wants manners. Imagine slipping up on a fellow to overhear his private conversation! You may tell him for me that I'll dust his jacket if I find he's repeated anything he heard to anyone else."

"But why, Rory? If they have been arrested, Simon can help. He has connections in France, you know, and in London, too."

"If there has been an arrest, which is still in great doubt, the possibility exists that the precious Vidame de Lâche is a party to it, and if he is, you may take your oath that games are afoot that even Simon could do nothing to prevent."

"But I thought they had all been arrested."

"De Vieillard merely suspects that to be the case," he said, "so there is no reason to bring Simon into it. At this point, he has no particular reason to become involved, and if I were to tell him of my feelings for Sophie, he would merely advise me to have nothing further to do with her. You can't deny that."

She couldn't. She agreed with him. But she was afraid he would do something foolish if no one stopped him, so she was greatly relieved when he told her it was all very likely a hum anyway. That followed her own line of thinking, particularly when he said he thought the comte was growing a bit senile, causing his fantasies and fears to overcome his good sense.

"He hates Bonaparte and fears him as well, you know. Thinks he's nothing but a petty upstart. He and Aunt Ophelia have more in common on that head than she knows," Rory said with a bitter laugh. "I don't doubt that de Lâche is attempting to exploit Sophie's beauty and innocence, damn him, and I wouldn't put it past the man to offer his sister in exchange for his properties, but I cannot think how an arrest would benefit him. Nor can I think of a single reason for Bonaparte to clap them all up. I've told the comte the best thing is to give the post another few days or so, at least, before he really begins to worry. He's sent a letter to Versailles, too, and should have a reply within a week or two. No doubt, they will all be safe at home by then."

"I am persuaded you have advised him well," Diana said, "and I hope you will also have the good sense not to scold young John. A reprimand from you would only draw his attention more narrowly to the matter, and I can safely promise he will say nothing of what he overheard to anyone else."

"You said it was in his own interest to keep mum."

She grinned. "He had a shotgun under his arm when I ran across him."

"Good Lord, the young scamp! He'll keep mum, all right. He won't want word of that to come to Ethelmoor's ears. Gentle chap, your brother, but I daresay if he knew his enterprising son had taken out a weapon without adult supervision, he'd give the lad a trimming that would leave him reeling."

"He would."

"That's all right, then, but mind you say nothing to Simon, either, Diana. He may not care for the Fane, but he'll care even less for poor Sophie. I mean to make all right and tight in that direction, somehow, before I say a word about it to Simon or Papa."

"I won't say anything, Rory, though I cannot think how you mean to convince the comte that you can support Sophie unless you make an arrangement with your father that will allow you to do so."

"I'll come about," he said. "You are right in saying I've spent my time in wasted self-pity. Now, you'll see a changed man. See if you don't."

"What I'll see is a man late for dinner," she said with a laugh when the little clock on the library mantel chimed the hour. "You won't impress either Simon or the marquess with bad manners, sir."

He grinned at her, then pointedly held the door for her to precede him into the hall. Diana laughed again but obeyed the gesture, walking out of the library just as Lady Jersey and Lady Westmorland descended the grand stair.

Although she would mark her fiftieth year in little more than a month and was, thanks to her three prolific daughters if not to either of her sons, a grandmother several times over, no one would deny Lady Jersey's beauty. Her features were delicate, although her nose had been accounted too large for some tastes and more than one ill-wisher had remarked that her upper teeth protruded too much for beauty's sake. Still, her light brown hair showed more golden highlights than gray, and although she was a trifle plumper than it was currently the fashion to be, only the most critical persons would deny that she had a most pleasing figure.

That figure was set off tonight by a petticoat of pink crepe, tufted with frosted silver. Her high-waisted tunic was of matching material, crossed with silver embroidery and foil stones on black velvet, and was also tufted with silver and variegated to correspond with the petticoat. The dress was fastened up with elegant silver rouleaus and tassels.

To be sure, her ladyship did not appear to full advantage beside the youthfully blond, artlessly vivacious Countess of Westmorland, who had chosen to wear a white satin dress, superbly embroidered in gold thread and covered with gold netting. Lady Westmorland's movements were quick but graceful, and good humor showed in every expression of her mobile features. Some said she was eccentric, but Diana, who had been acquainted with Jane Saunders before she ever became the Earl of Westmorland's second wife, attributed this so-called eccentricity to the fact that Jane never rested or allowed anyone else to rest in her presence. Indeed, what with Lady Sarah Fane's constant chatter and her stepmama's restlessness, Diana had begun to wonder if the earl's critics had not been a trifle unfair to the man when they accused him of not being at home so often as they thought he ought to be. Perhaps he had good reason.

The two ladies broke off an animated conversation as Diana emerged from the library, and two pairs of blue eyes turned toward her, one pair merely curious, the other very nearly malicious.

Behind her, Lord Roderick muttered under his breath, "Oh, damn, that tears it. Word of our *tête à tête* will be all over the abbey in a trice."

Diana ignored him, moving forward to greet the two ladies, then catching her breath when she noted her husband with Lady Ophelia and Sir Richard Colt Hoare approaching the half-landing from the left upper branch of the stair. But perhaps, she told herself, Simon's appearance might be put to good use.

"Ah, Andover, there you are," she said, summoning up a bright smile. "I have been searching for you this age, sir, but no one knew where you were. And your hopeless twin, whom I found dozing in the library, could not be of the slightest assistance."

Lord Roderick promptly accepted his cue, adopting the demeanor of a gentleman but recently awakened from his nap. He let his eyelids droop and drew a hand across his mouth as though he would stifle a yawn. "Must beg pardon, ladies. A dashed nuisance, I know, Simon, Aunt Ophelia, but I daresay I shall be a few minutes late."

"I'll tell them to put dinner back fifteen minutes or so, if you think you can manage to dress that quickly," Simon said obligingly, though his eyes were fixed upon his wife, who kept her smile carefully pinned in place.

"I cannot think what has kept you from your valet, Roderick," pronounced Lady Ophelia.

"Can't dress in only fifteen minutes," put in Sir Richard, surveying Rory over the banister through his quizzing glass. "No man could."

"Lord, yes, I can," Rory said cheerfully. "I dress well, but I'm no cursed fop who takes two or three hours to make himself presentable. I'll just nip upstairs if the ladies will excuse me, and be back before anyone notices I've gone."

He suited action to words, slipping past the two women still standing on the bottom stair. Neither one had said a word, but Diana held her breath when both nodded a greeting to Simon, now descending the lower stairs with his companions. Lady Westmorland's eyes danced with merriment, but Lady Jersey's expression was one of haughty displeasure.

"Good evening, ladies," Simon said smoothly. "Won't you allow my aunt to take you into the drawing room with the others? I am persuaded you would all enjoy a glass of wine before that scapegrace brother of mine returns."

"An excellent suggestion," said Lady Jersey, relaxing at once in response to Simon's charming smile. "You will join us, of course."

"Delighted," he agreed. "Come along, sweetheart. I'll pour you a small glass of sherry. You look wonderful, by the way."

Her smile felt more natural now. She could not deny feeling pleasure in his approval of her appearance. The gown was one of her favorites, made of white and silver satin, embroidered along the top edge of the bodice and the lower half of the slim skirt with tiny purple flowers. Her hair had been styled in a soft twist of ringlets fastened at the back of her head with a spray of artificial violets. Other, shorter ringlets framed her face, and her eardrops were amethysts so dark as to appear more nearly like sapphires. She placed her hand obediently upon Simon's forearm when he held it out to her, and let him take her into the crowded drawing room behind the others. Once inside, however, Simon steered a course to one side, a little withdrawn from the chattering throng. When he stopped and turned to look down at Diana, the smile had gone from his eyes.

"What was that little charade in aid of, if you please?"

She met his gaze directly, intending to ask him with limpid innocence to explain his meaning, but the stern look she encountered deterred her at once. Simon meant to have a straight answer, and he would not be put off by prevarication. She decided to tell him nothing that was not perfectly true.

"I wanted to stop Lady Jersey from making a piece of gossip out of what she saw," she said.

"We will hope you have succeeded in that endeavor, but I should like to know, all the same, what you were discussing with my brother. Since I was in my dressing room, where anyone might expect to find me at this hour, do not hope to fob me off with the tale you invented out there."

"No, of course not. I wish you will believe I have no improper feelings for your twin, Simon. I merely wished to tell him that you had attempted to plead his case with your father. I met him as I came down the steps with Lydia, and since we could scarcely discuss the matter in the hall, we stepped into the library. I assure you, we were not inside that room together above five or ten minutes at the most."

She had spoken earnestly, and noted now with relief that he relaxed, that his expression was not nearly as grim as it had been moments before. She smiled, saying demurely, "I also told him that I am as tired of his self-pity as I am of your ridiculous jealousy."

There was an answering smile in the golden eyes now. "A home thrust, sweetheart. I must confess, you've certainly given me no just cause for jealousy since we've been here at Alderwood. You accused me once of jumping to unfair conclusions, and perhaps you had reason. I shall attempt to mend my ways."

Slightly more than fifteen minutes had passed before Lord Roderick reappeared, but no one noticed his tardiness, and Figmore announced directly thereafter that dinner was served. Throughout the meal, then afterward in the drawing room with the ladies, and later when the men joined them and tables were set up for cards, Diana found her thoughts continually drifting back to her discussion with Simon. He had already mended a good many of his ways, she thought. Or had he? Certainly, they had argued a deal less during the past week. But he clearly believed the reason for that was that she was behaving better, and that was ridiculous. She was behaving as she always did. Or was she? As busy as she had been, preparing for guests and then providing for their needs as they arrived and afterward, she had certainly had little time to stir Simon's temper. Indeed, she was more often moved to thank him for his efforts to assist her, for he had also been busy, carrying more than his share of the hosting duties.

Later that night when he came to her, she snuggled into his arms, meeting his overtures with an eagerness that delighted him, and afterward, as she lay with her head on his shoulder, she felt a contentment that she had nearly forgotten it was possible for her to feel.

"Simon," she said drowsily, "would you like to have a child?"

His muscles tensed beneath her. "Are you trying to tell me something?" Without giving her a chance to answer, he sat up, turning to grip her shoulders tightly. "Are you . . . good God, Diana, you shouldn't be doing so much! I daresay you ought to be spending your days with your feet up or something. Why didn't you tell me? By heaven, I ought to—"

Her soft chuckle interrupted the string of sharp words. "To think you promised only a few hours since to stop jumping to unwarranted conclusions," she said teasingly.

He expelled a long breath. "I ought to spank you. How did you expect me to react to such a question?"

"I just wanted to know," she said.

He leaned back against his pillow, pulling her back into the shelter of his arm. "Of course I'd like a child," he said. "I'd like a dozen children."

"Not all at once, Simon, surely!"

"Oh, I'm willing to wait six years or so," he said with a chuckle.

"Six?"

"Twins do run in the family, Diana mine."

"Not in *my* family, they don't," she retorted. "I think we should begin with one child and see how we do as parents."

He was silent for a moment. Then he said, "My

relationship with Rory distresses you, doesn't it, even more than yours with him annoys me?"

She nodded, knowing that although he could not see the gesture in the darkness, he could feel it. "He has been bitter so long, Simon, and it is so easy to understand why he should feel as he does. But he is trying now—I know he is—not to give in to his feelings anymore. I wish you would help him, instead of always believing the worst of him."

To her surprise he did not argue with her. Instead, he murmured something about doing his best. Diana knew her words were slightly unfair in view of the fact that he had already attempted to plead Rory's case with the marquess, but she decided against retracting them. Perhaps if both brothers gave the matter their best efforts, they would come to be good friends.

"Brothers should like each other," she said quietly, putting her thoughts into words.

"I do like him," Simon protested. "If you don't see that now, perhaps you will when you can compare us to Prinny and York—or Prinny and any one of his charming brothers, for that matter."

A gurgle of laughter escaped her at the notion that the Warringtons could be compared in any way with the royal brothers, and the serious mood was broken.

When Diana awoke the following morning, Simon was already up and gone, and she regarded the clock on the mantelpiece with dismay. Though it was not customary for guests to arise before ten or eleven during a houseparty, it was certainly customary for any hostess to be up before that time, particularly when the family was about to be descended upon by royalty. Accordingly, she jumped out of bed and yanked the bellcord, summoning Marlie to her assistance and scarcely heeding that young woman's assurance that the master had said she was to let Diana sleep.

"Never mind that, Marlie. No doubt he has forgotten that the prince meant to stay in Bath with his grace of York overnight and to come straight on to Alderwood this morning. He will very likely arrive before noon, and I must be ready. Lady Ophelia would never forgive me if I left her to manage alone."

She had plenty of time, however, for the Prince of Wales and his party did not arrive until shortly after midday. There were no ladies with them, and they were a small company, merely the royal brothers and their attendants and Mr. Brummell.

Though the royal brothers were both rather fat and had been described as kin to whitebait because of their jowly faces, protruding eyes, and small, pursed mouths, nature had been a deal kinder to Mr. Brummell. He was slightly above medium height and the proportions of his form were remarkable. His hands, in Diana's opinion, were particularly well shaped and his voice particularly pleasing. His face was rather long with a high, well-shaped forehead. His complexion was fair, his hair light brown, and his countenance showed a good deal of intelligence, though his mouth was wont to twitch unexpectedly with sardonic humor. His eyebrows were expressive, as were the gray eyes beneath them, and he used both to full effect when he wished to give additional point to one of the humorous or satirical remarks for which he was well known.

Lady Ophelia, greeting the new arrivals, gave no hint by her expression or behavior that she thought they, rather than the Warrington family, ought to be more gratified by their presence at the abbey. Indeed, although she looked down her long nose at them all after making her curtsy to the prince, her tone when she spoke was perfectly gracious.

"You will no doubt wish for refreshment after your journey, sir," she said. "A nice luncheon will be set out in the blue parlor for you when you have seen your chambers."

The prince winked at Brummell, then smiled at her ladyship. Since his smile was one of his best assets, Diana was not at all surprised when Lady Ophelia returned it, but the older lady's expression changed ludicrously when his highness said, "We must hope, ma'am, that you have not planned to serve many green vegetables. George, here, don't like 'em."

"Good gracious, I've not the slightest notion if there are too many or not," said Lady Ophelia, regarding the

Beau in awed dismay. "Surely, you eat *some* green vegetables, sir."

"Yes, madam," returned the Beau with a twinkle. "I
once ate a pea."

"His highness is merely roasting you, Aunt Ophelia,"
said Simon, putting his arm around her, "and no doubt
is attempting to get his own back with Mr. Brummell
for something that gentleman said to him earlier."

"Damme, Andover," said the prince, chuckling, "but
you're a sharp one. That's it, exactly. Damn fellow
refuses to say he likes this coat. And York, there, says it
don't become me. Well, I say it does, Weston says it
does, and George here, if he knows what's good for
him, will also say it does." His highness turned for
them then, modeling the dark blue coat he wore over a
green-striped satin waistcoat and cream-colored breeches
that did little to conceal his plump figure.

The Beau's lips twitched, and his eyelids drooped.
"The fit is excellent, sir," he murmured, "a masterpiece
of Weston's clearly considerable skills."

Simon turned quickly as though to speak to one of
the footmen, but Diana noted that the prince was well
pleased by Brummell's remark, and she was too grateful
to the Beau for not indulging his sense of the ridiculous any further to worry overmuch about exposing
her own smiles. Brummell said something to York just
then, forestalling that gentleman's entrance into the
discussion, and a moment later they were all safely
upstairs in their own bedchambers.

Realizing that Simon had judged Mr. Brummell more
accurately than she had herself, Diana went about her
business with a lighter step, believing the royal visit
would indeed pass off without incident. And so it might
well have done, had it not been for Lady Jersey, but
when the Prince of Wales came downstairs that evening
for dinner, he chanced to meet her ladyship making
her way up the upper righthand wing of the grand
staircase.

Diana, above them, talking with her mother, Susanna,
and Lydia by the gallery rail, turned when she realized
the prince had emerged from his bedchamber and saw
Lady Jersey curtsy, right there on the narrow stairway,

effectively blocking the royal passage. The curtsy was a deep one, and still bent, her ladyship looked coyly up at the prince from beneath her lashes. "Good evening, your highness."

The prince said nothing, his attitude making it clear that he was merely waiting for her to move. People stood behind him on the stairway, and there were others along the gallery and below in the hall. Until the prince's arrival on the scene there had been a babble of friendly chatter, punctuated now and again by a burst of laughter. There was no laughter now. There was stillness and a tension that spread quickly throughout the company. At last, her countenance darkened with mortification, Lady Jersey rose, lifted her chin, and stood aside to let him pass.

As he moved past her, the prince turned to his aide, Colonel McMahon, behind him on the stair, and said in a voice loud enough to carry to everyone in the hall, "Pray, McMahon, tell that woman she is not to speak to me again."

Joining in the general gasp of dismay, Diana turned instinctively toward her mother, only to find Lady Trent stifling a smile of unholy glee. "Mama, really!" she exclaimed under her breath. "What on earth are we to do?"

"Nothing, love," replied the countess, her eyes still dancing. "That little scene is nothing to do with us, but it has been in the making these six months and more. We may all relax now and go about our business, knowing it no longer hovers over us, waiting to take place. Is that not so, Simon?"

Diana had realized even as her mother was speaking that Simon had come up behind her from the other side of the gallery. She searched his face now to see if he would agree with her mother. Apparently, he did. He, too, seemed to be laboring under the difficult task of controlling his mirth. "What a pity George missed it," he said. "Or, did he?"

Mr. Brummell, his countenance for once betraying no expression, could be seen now at the top of the right branch of the stairway. Lady Jersey, her face still scarlet, passed right by him without so much as a glance, and disappeared in the direction of her own bedchamber.

Lady Ophelia soon received word that Lady Jersey, suffering from a migraine headache, would be unable to join them for dinner, but Diana had learned even sooner that her mother and Simon were right not to worry about the effect of the scene upon the rest of the company. Lord Jersey, as was his custom, had been in the new hall with the marquess, and neither Lord Villiers nor Lady Sarah Fane had been among the witnesses to the confrontation, so the others were able to go on with their evening very much as if nothing had happened at all.

The New Year came in merrily without her ladyship's assistance, heralded by the pealing of bells and the blowing of whistles, and accompanied by a new snowstorm as well as much laughter and singing. Toasts were drunk and good wishes exchanged.

Shortly after midnight there was a clamor at the front door of the abbey, and the porter opened the doors to a snow-covered Simon, who entered amidst more whistling and laughter, as well as offers of food and drink—particularly drink—since custom had it that the First Foot, or the first visitor to the house during the morning hours of the first day of January was the luck-bringer for the entire year. Since the luck would be good only if the first visitor was a man and not a woman, the Warringtons, like most families, took no chances. The oldest son played the important role each year.

Simon carried with him a piece of bread, a lump of coal, salt, and a half-dozen coins, symbolic gifts which he promptly handed to his father, thus ensuring that the marquess and all his family would have food, warmth, and prosperity all through the year. After the ceremony, Simon strode to his wife, picked her up in his arms, and carried her into the new hall to stand beneath the kissing bough, still hanging from the ceiling there. To the huge delight of all, he proceeded to kiss Diana thoroughly, setting an example that many of the other young gentlemen hastened to follow with their own ladies.

By the time they finally went to bed, Diana was so exhausted that she thought later she must have fallen asleep even before Marlie had helped her to undress, but early the next morning Simon shook her awake.

"Go away," she muttered, turning over again and burrowing into her pillows.

"Up you get," he said cheerfully, hauling her out of the bed without ceremony. "I promised the brats we'd wassail the apple trees this morning, and if I must brave the snow, so must you."

"Wassailing is for Twelfth Night," she protested.

"But the children won't be here for Twelfth Night, and no one amongst their families grows apples," he explained patiently. "I doubt six days will make any difference to the trees."

Fully awake now, she grinned at him and shook her head, unable to decide who would be more disappointed to miss the wassailing, the children or Simon, who would also be gone from Alderwood before Twelfth Night. Less than an hour later, bundled up from top to toe, she stood beside Lord Thomas Warrington's daughters and watched as Simon, Rory, Ethelmoor, and several other hardy gentlemen, as well as her nephew John, approached the favored tree. Simon carried a shotgun and a pail of cider. The others, including young John, all carried shotguns.

Everyone dipped pieces of toast in the cider and laid them in the fork of the tree. Then Simon poured the remaining cider onto its roots, the shotguns were fired through the tree's branches, and a traditional wassailing song was sung, with Diana and the girls joining in. Afterward, content in the knowledge that they had done what was necessary to make the trees bear an abundance of fruit in the coming year, they piled into sleighs to return to the abbey, looking forward to a hearty breakfast.

In the sleigh, Simon put his arm around Diana. "Warm enough, sweetheart?"

She snuggled against him, nodding, aware once again of that feeling of contentment. But as she savored the feeling, she remembered the scene the previous night between Lady Jersey and the Prince of Wales. Supposedly, like Diana and Simon, the two had once been madly in love with each other. For some months Lady Jersey had been seeking to rekindle that love, but last night's confrontation proved that she had failed miserably.

Just then Simon laughed at something Ethelmoor said to him, and Diana looked up at her husband. Men, she thought, were prodigiously unpredictable.

10

The royal party took their leave by late afternoon, not wishing to remain until Monday, which they would otherwise be forced to do, since the prince did not travel on Sundays. A number of people, including Diana's parents, her brother and his family, and Lord Thomas Warrington and his, followed their example, if not from religious scruples then because they feared the New Year's snowstorm might be a warning of harsher weather to come.

Once the prince had gone, Lady Jersey emerged from her bedchamber, haughtier than ever. Diana could not see that her ladyship was at all cast down by his highness's snub, nor (aside from a few knowing glances, quickly hooded) did it seem that the remaining guests treated her ladyship any differently than before. Nevertheless, Diana expressed her relief quite as frankly as Lady Ophelia did when Lord Jersey and his family departed before noon on Monday, followed soon afterward by the Earl and Countess of Westmorland and his daughter. As the farewells were being exchanged, the countess turned to Simon.

"Do not forget, Andover, that you are promised to us

at the end of the month. You, also, my lord," she added with a twinkling smile to Lord Roderick.

"Oh, my goodness me, yes, you must come," added Lady Sarah, giving Rory's arm a squeeze. "You have never seen Osterley Park, and I promise you, it is something to be seen, indeed. So opulent, so magnificent—quite a fairy-tale palace. I am only sorry that dearest Susanna will be unable to come with you."

"Never mind that," said Lady Ophelia, looking down her nose. "Next winter Susanna may enjoy as many house parties as she likes. She is several months younger than you are, Lady Sarah, so I cannot approve of allowing her any more freedom in such matters than what she's had. My nephews will represent the Warringtons at Osterley. And Lady Andover, of course. And you will have Ethelmoor and his wife, as well, you know."

Lady Sarah looked pleased to be reminded of her superiority in age, and when the Warringtons returned to the abbey, Diana laughingly said she had not expected to hear Lady Ophelia adding to that young woman's sense of her own consequence.

"That's as may be," said Lady Ophelia. "Only let her get a few more years in her dish and then see if she likes being reminded that Susanna is younger. When do you and Simon leave us?"

"In just a few hours. We are promised to Lady Tyson in Bath for her ball this evening, and then we go on to Bellwood for a Twelfth-Night houseparty."

Lord Roderick was not going to Bellwood with them but was promised instead to friends in London, and Diana had only a moment to exchange a word with him later by the chaise before she and Simon left for Lady Tyson's house in Bath.

"Do not outrun the constable, Rory," she said, grinning.

"Never fear. I've reformed, remember?" He glanced at Simon, standing beside her. "I have, truly, you'll see." A flush stole up into his cheeks. "You won't be sorry this time. Thanks, Simon." He reached out and gripped his brother's hand. "See you both at Osterley."

And with that, he turned and hurried back up to the house.

"What did he mean, thanking you like that?" Diana asked as the chaise rolled down the broad avenue toward the Bath-Bristol Road, followed by their attendants in another carriage, their extra horses, and Simon's phaeton.

"Can't imagine," Simon said, his eyes twinkling as he made himself comfortable against the squabs.

She regarded him pensively. "I know for a fact that he didn't have a sou at Wilton House, and I know you were furious with him for those debts he had run up whilst you were in France, so you didn't give him anything to speak of then. But if he is going to join friends in London now and planning to meet us at Osterley . . . and he is in a very good mood— Simon, you gave him money, didn't you?"

"You are becoming very wifely, are you not? Do you mean to demand an explanation of every groat I spend?"

"No, of course not." She tucked her hand in his. "I wish your father would change his mind and do something sensible by Rory, but since he will not, I'm very pleased with you, sir."

Her pleasure lasted less than twenty-four hours. The ball at Lady Tyson's was a squeeze, and with no responsibilities to worry her, Diana threw herself into the festivities, never lacking for a partner. She caught Simon's eye upon her from time to time and noted the sardonic twist to his mouth, but she was enjoying herself and feeling far too carefree to worry about his jealousy. Because of the crush of guests, she found herself sharing a bedchamber that night with two other ladies instead of with her husband; however, in the face of Simon's curt good night, she could not be sorry for it.

The period of good feeling between them had ended. Indeed, it seemed almost as though the pleasant time at Alderwood had never been, for their relationship deteriorated further at Bellwood and during the weeks following, as they continued from house to house in the last flurry of parties before members of the *beau monde* would begin to remove to London for the social Season.

If Simon was not criticizing her dress or her behavior, he ignored her entirely while he engaged in discussions with other gentlemen, generally concerning the ominous behavior of Napoleon Bonaparte. Diana had not hitherto paid much heed to such conversations or to the continual rumors assailing her ears. But since they had had no word from Lord Roderick since leaving Alderwood, and since she had heard nothing further from anyone about the Beléchappé family, she found herself listening more carefully to what was said in her presence.

Many people were beginning to express a belief that the Peace of Amiens would prove to be no more than a brief truce, for despite his agreement to its provisions, Bonaparte's aggressions had not ceased. He had already annexed Elba and a large portion of northern Italy, and the French army now occupied Switzerland. Then, too, his attitude of late toward England had scarcely been conciliatory.

According to the information Diana overheard, particular difficulties had arisen over the island of Malta, for although the English had agreed to restore the island to France, they now refused to do so. She sought further enlightenment in the matter from Simon, demanding to know how the English negotiators could quibble over such a matter. "To renege on our part of the agreement cannot be honorable," she pointed out.

"Honor has little to do with it at this juncture," he returned curtly. They were in the midst of a large, before-dinner company in the drawing room at Foley Castle, and he was annoyed with her again, partly because she was wearing a very becoming but gossamer-thin gown of which he disapproved, but mostly because she had not been feeling quite the thing that day and had ignored his command to stay in bed, insisting upon joining the others for dinner. "The French," he went on, "have virtually ignored the treaty, and Malta is our last hole card. We have—thanks to that weak-kneed Addington—nothing else left with which to bargain."

Diana personally thought the prime minister was a

dull but well-intentioned man. She knew, however, that Simon's opinion was a deal harsher. He could not approve of the immediate disbanding of the navy that had followed the signing of the peace, nor of the vast reduction of manpower in the English army. And Diana, listening to the uneasy talk that had become more and more common in drawing rooms and at dining tables as the days marched by, could not help but think that if England were to go to war with France again, as indeed everyone now seemed to believe would be the case, it would be most difficult to effect a victory without benefit of a proper military force.

By the time they climbed into their chaise that last week of January to make the short journey from Denham Place to Osterley Park, winter seemed to have passed its peak, while Diana's relationship with Simon had reached its lowest point. With the exception of a few brief days that he had spent on business in London without her, Simon had continued, or so it seemed to Diana, to carp and correct or to ignore her entirely for nearly a month, and she had reacted as she always did by lifting her pointed chin and doing precisely as she pleased, practically daring him to stop her. Simon had only grown grimmer and more censorious. Even their nights together provided little respite in the cold war between them, for Diana continued to feel unwell. The long days of partying following so closely upon the festivities at Alderwood seemed to be taking an unwarranted toll of her energies, for she was extremely tired and found herself falling into bed each night with relief, scarcely closing her eyes before she was fast asleep.

She was grateful now that their journey to Osterley would be a short one, for not only was Simon in a particularly surly mood, but she was feeling distinctly unwell. The chaise was well sprung, but it rocked, and thanks to a break in the weather, the roads were clear of snow and ice, so the pace was rapid, increasing that motion. She had said little to Simon about her continued indisposition, knowing that he would behave as he had at Foley Castle, demanding that she quack herself, issuing orders and counterorders. And if he began to suspect, as indeed she had herself, the cause of her indisposition, he would have her back at Andover Court or even Alderwood, wrapped in cotton wool with her feet up on a stool. So, instead of requesting that he order the postilions to slow their pace, she merely placed one hand over her stomach, willing it to calm itself, praying that she would reach Osterley without disgracing herself.

At last, however, followed by their usual cavalcade of servants and extra horses, they turned off the Bath Road onto a tan-graveled drive, leading through a thickly wooded area, and proceeded at a slower, more comfortable pace into Osterley Park. Diana's first view of the house was little more than an impression of turrets soaring above the trees of the park, but minutes later they emerged from the woods to see the great house in all its splendor, its corner turrets giving it the look of a red-brick Elizabethan palace.

The house had indeed been built in Elizabethan times, by Sir Thomas Gresham, but Lady Sarah Fane's grandfather, Robert Child, had hired Robert Adam, the famous Scottish architect, to transform it into its present appearance, and it was considered by many to be one of his greatest masterpieces.

The Warrington chaise drew up in front of the great double hexastyle portico, built to resemble an open classical temple, through which, once one had mounted the broad, high, sweeping stairway, the central courtyard could be seen. Diana, feeling much recovered once her feet touched solid ground, expressed approval of the airy sense of space one felt between the great columns of the portico. Inside, as they followed the butler through a series of magnificent state rooms, she saw that no expense had been spared by Lady Sarah's trustees to keep the house as Robert Adam had intended it to be kept.

The ornaments in each room were in beautiful taste. The deep crimson frieze in the pale green damask drawing room produced a particularly admirable effect, and all the designs in the next and principal drawing room were excellent, though a trifle too profusely distributed to suit Diana's taste. In consequence, the rich Gobelin tapestries adorning the walls seemed busy rather than magnificent.

As they passed through the unoccupied state bed-chamber, hung with green velvet, Simon murmured that he had heard the bed there had cost Robert Child over two thousand pounds. Diana was sorry to hear it had cost so much, for the ornate wooden dome looked overheavy, as though it might crush the occupants at any moment, and the curtains were mere trumpery, festooned with artificial silk flowers. But the greatest shock came when they passed out of this gaudy chamber into a smaller room wainscoted with deal and painted with little figures that must have been copied from an Etruscan vase. The wooden chairs scattered about the chamber were decorated in a like manner, and the whole effect seemed out of place after the grandeur of previous apartments.

They found Lady Westmorland at last in the long gallery with its view of a broad lawn edged by enormous cedar trees. Dressed becomingly in an orange crepe afternoon frock with a low-scooped bodice, tiny puffed sleeves, and a white satin sash, she turned away from a large vase of dried flowers which she was attempting to rearrange and stepped forward lightly and quickly to greet them.

"I had nearly despaired of the Warringtons," she said in her musical voice, ending on a trill of laughter. "You were invited to provide leavening to an otherwise dull group, you know. I feared you had all failed me."

"Why, I had thought my brother must be here," said Simon with a smile.

"No, indeed, Andover, and never a word from that wretch to excuse himself, either, if you please. And you and Diana a full two days late, though you did indeed write to say you would be."

Simon smiled. "I explained that the delay at Denham was unavoidable," he said.

"*I* was delayed," Diana corrected, shooting him a barbed glance. "Simon rode into London to attend to some diplomatic business or other and left me well nigh stranded with Lord and Lady Hill, whether they wanted me or not."

"Well, you are here now, and that is all that matters," said Lady Westmorland quickly when Simon looked ready to debate the issue. The laughter was still in her eyes as she explained that the younger members of the party, approving of the change in the unpredictable weather, had ridden down to the chain of lakes beyond the cedars they could see in the distance, hoping to find ice there thick enough for skating. "Your brother and his wife are somewhere about, of course, and *dear* Lady Jersey, and a good many others, as well," she added, "but Westmorland and Jersey have deserted us, saying they had no choice but to attend a levee for the king at St. James's. Since I do not feel her majesty will miss my presence at her drawing room—the January and February presentations are always too thin of company for my taste—I cannot help but think they might have sent regrets to the King. But they will both return for the ball on Wednesday, so you will not miss seeing them."

Diana did not particularly care whether either earl honored them with his presence or not, but she was disturbed to hear that Lord Roderick had neither arrived nor sent his excuses. He had promised to meet them at Osterley. Moreover, whatever were his shortcomings, he was by nature too polite to accept an invitation and then forget about it. That sort of behavior was unfortunately becoming only too common among the younger men, but Rory had never to her knowledge left a hostess in the lurch.

Though she asked both Lydia and Ethelmoor as soon as she encountered them, neither had heard from Rory, and when she attempted to broach the matter to Simon sometime later in their own bedchamber, a charming room with a high, blue-curtained bed and curtains of a darker shade of blue framing the window, he dismissed her worries with a shrug.

"No doubt he is under the hatches again and doesn't wish me to know of it. Certainly, his rudeness in not informing her ladyship of his change of plans does not auger well for his supposed reformed ways." Simon peered at her searchingly. "You have dark smudges under your eyes, Diana. I think you would be well advised to lie down until dinnertime."

"Really, Simon, I am not such a poor honey as that," she protested. "What would Lady Westmorland think if after a journey of scarcely ten miles I were forced to take to my bed?"

"I don't give a cracked groat for what she will think. You have been going the pace too strongly, and I want you to rest."

"Simon, please," she said coaxingly, laying a hand upon his arm, "I am fine, really."

He looked down at her, and the look in his eyes softened. "You've not been looking at all well, sweetheart. Since I don't want you to make yourself truly ill, I won't argue any further, but if you go downstairs, I will insist that you take a good thick shawl with you. No discussion," he added sternly, when she opened her mouth to protest again. "Either you obey me or you don't leave this room."

Diana shut her mouth, unsure for once of the feelings rushing through her. Usually the sort of highhandedness he was presently displaying filled her with resentment, but now she felt as if she needed his strength instead. She didn't want to fight with him. If he regarded her submission with uncertainty, she was unaware of it, but she did feel confident enough of his mellow temper to suggest that something might have happened to prevent Lord Roderick from communicating with Lady Westmorland.

"Nonsense. What could have happened?" His words were brusque, informing her that his mood was still volatile. "I tell you, he's merely off on one of his starts again, and I wash my hands of him. I don't wish to hear any more about it."

So Diana kept her worries to herself and managed for two days to pretend to be amused, as the other guests were, by Lady Jersey's efforts to solidify her son's matrimonial interests. Her ladyship's antics were many and varied, and since Lady Sarah had more than once tactlessly made it plain that she thought the Princess of Wales had been treated shabbily ever since her arrival in England and that, furthermore, she thought the princess would make a delightful friend, it was generally agreed that great forebearance was required on Lady Jersey's part even to speak to the chit. Clearly, Lady Jersey put the advantage of a great fortune ahead of more personal feelings, and the resulting scenes between the self-centered young girl and the woman of the world bent upon securing a fairy-tale fortune for her son must have provided vast entertainment had Diana not been too concerned about her brother-in-law to be truly amused by them.

By the third day she was convinced that something dreadful had happened to keep Rory from coming to Osterley, and was sorely tempted to confide what she knew about the Beléchappé family to Simon, but she dreaded his reaction one moment and feared the next that he would not take the matter seriously enough to do anything. Then, too, she was by now quite certain of the cause for her lack of energy and for the nausea she had been suffering from time to time and was afraid that somehow or other, during any argument they might have over Rory, she might blurt out the information to Simon.

They had planned to go from Osterley to London, in order to open Warrington House for the upcoming Season. February was early for the remove to the metropolis, but Lady Ophelia, planning to bring Susanna out in the spring, wanted everything prepared well in advance, so that she could devote her attention to the details necessary to present her niece properly to the *beau monde*. Once Simon discovered he was to become a father, Diana was certain he would not only forbid her going to London but would put an end to their stay at Osterley, and would thus effectively prevent her from discovering what had become of Rory. She had no doubt that Simon would clap her into bed at Andover until further notice, convinced that such treatment was necessary to ensure the health and well-being of their future child. Better that she wait at least until they were safely settled in London at Warrington House, where she could argue that the best doctors were near at hand, before she mentioned a word to Simon about the baby.

She considered confiding in Lydia, but the notion occurred only to be dismissed. Even if Lydia agreed that Simon would overreact to the news, she would insist that it was his right to know. And if she did not tell Simon, she would certainly tell Ethelmoor, which would be much the same thing, for he would not stand for Diana's keeping such news from her husband. If anyone was to find out what had happened to Lord Roderick, it must be Diana herself.

She remembered Rory's mentioning that the comte had hired a house near Langley Marsh for the winter. That village, she knew, could not be more than eight miles or so along the Bath Road from Osterley. She could ride there and back in two or three hours. She paused for a moment, wondering if riding would present a danger to the baby, but she dismissed any worry on that head when she remembered her mother telling her she had ridden during both her pregnancies until she could no longer clamber onto the back of her horse. So long as she did not ride neck-or-nothing and did not fall off her horse, the baby would be fine. Therefore, suiting thought to action, she called Marlie to help her into her riding habit and sent orders to the stable to saddle the dapple gray. Marlie eyed her askance when she gave her orders, and Diana, knowing the maid had ample reason to wonder about her condition, merely snapped at her not to stand staring like a fish but to fetch the habit.

"And, Marlie, do not worry about me, and if you have any odd suspicions, keep them under your tongue. Please, Marlie."

"As you say, Miss Diana, but if the master suspicions what I do myself, he won't like you riding that gray, and that's a fact."

"The gray is as gentle as can be, and I intend to ride only along the main road, you know, with Ned Tredegar beside me, so I shall be perfectly safe. Mind now, Marlie, not a word."

"Aye, m'lady," Marlie agreed. But she frowned and Diana was not by any means certain she could trust her. Still, Marlie was her servant, not Simon's, so she could hope the young woman would keep her counsel.

She met several people on her way to the stables, but she managed to evade any attempts to bear her company on her ride, and found Ned Tredegar awaiting her, the gray saddled and ready to go. The journey to Langley Marsh took just over an hour, and they soon found the tall, elegant mellow-brick house that had been hired for the winter by the Comte de Vieillard. As she allowed Tredegar to help her dismount, she hoped the comte would not think her ill-mannered to visit him in such a fashion. After all, it could not be so dreadful when he was an elderly man. She could not have visited his son, she thought with a grimace, without a female companion at her side. And even so, such a visit would have been highly improper. But for Rory's sake, she might even have ventured that far beyond the line.

She gave her name to the French servant who answered the door and begged audience with the comte. The servant spoke fair English, but when he presented her to his master in a small, book-lined library, he did so in French. Diana greeted her host in the same language.

"Forgive me, monseigneur," she said, taking a seat near him, "but I have come to you because I am worried about Lord Roderick Warrington. We expected him, my husband and I, to meet us at Osterley Park House several days ago, but he was not there, nor has he sent word to explain his absence. I know, though my husband does not, of his close acquaintance with your family, so I was hoping you might be able to assist me with information of his whereabouts."

"Ah, *mon dieu*," said the comte in a near moan, "you echo my own worries, madame, for the good Roderick left for France more than two weeks ago, and barring the brief note I received from him informing me that he had safely stepped off the boat onto French soil, I have heard nothing. Since he was bound directly for Versailles, I can only fear that he, like my to-be-pitied wife and my so-beautiful daughter, has been arrested."

11

The Comte de Vieillard was white-faced. His breath came in short, rasping gasps, causing Diana to fear for his health. Clasping her hands together in her lap, she made every effort to keep her voice calm.

"Then, you have had word of your family? They have indeed been arrested?"

"Ah, this we still do not know, madame." The comte spread plump-veined, liver-spotted hands. "I posted a letter, no? But there was no reply. The good Roderick became most impatient. An English trait, I believe."

"Yes, he was impatient during Christmas," Diana said. "He visited you again?"

"But yes, madame. Will you take refreshment?" he added when the servant slipped silently into the room with a tea tray.

"Some tea would be delightful," Diana told him, her thoughts racing. "Please, monseigneur, tell me why my brother-in-law decided to go to France. What was his purpose, exactly?"

"Why, to discover the truth, no?" the comte said, raising his bushy eyebrows. "He carries a tenderness for my beautiful Sophie, and he feared that my son would . . ." He shrugged expressively. "I do not know if you have made the acquaintance of my son, madame."

"I have met the Vidame de Lâche," Diana said evenly.

"Then, you know he is not as he should be. I do not know how he came to be as he is. The Terror, you know, and all that has passed. But although he has not been raised in penury, as have many, still he lusts after what is no longer obtainable."

"My brother-in-law has told me much, monseigneur.

I am in his confidence. But, quite honestly, we have not known what to believe. Your son spoke of a treasure. Emeralds."

To her surprise, the comte nodded. "The Beléchappé emeralds are quite well known in France, madame. When we came away, my family and I, my Sophie was just four years old, but Bertrand was nearly ten and quite old enough to have some understanding of what had come to pass. Only enough, however, to understand that his birthright had been taken from him. My wife and I have been unable, over the years, to make him understand how lucky he is to have his life. The emeralds stayed behind. We had enough money hidden about us for our needs, and other, less known pieces of jewelry, but the emeralds were too dangerous. If we had been discovered while still on French soil, we might have been able, successfully, to plead our fear without revealing our true identities, to say we wanted to get away from so much horror. Others were fleeing who were no more than royalist in belief, without being of the nobility. Some were spared. But the emeralds would have identified us too easily. To have carried them with us might have been fatal."

"So the emeralds do exist, and they were left behind," Diana said, almost to herself.

"Indeed, madame. It was safer for us."

"Where are they now?"

"With a trusted servant, my dear Milice, who will release them to no one who does not present my signet. My son does not know where they are, nor could he obtain them if he did. I have entrusted my signet to the good Roderick."

"Lord Roderick is going in search of the jewels?"

The comte nodded. "To be sure, madame, for if my son has informed the First Consul that the jewels are indeed still in France, then my people at the château are in danger. But the good Roderick will go first to Versailles, or to Paris if the Consul has removed to the Tuileries, to discover what has become of my wife and daughter. That was his intent, you know, and I believe him to be an honorable man. He will discover the emeralds only if the doing will not endanger Sophie or Vivienne."

"Would your son truly put them in danger, monseigneur?"

The comte sighed deeply. "Alas, Bertrand cares for naught but the reclamation of his estates. That is why I could not trust him with the signet. He would attempt to use the emeralds to bribe Napoleon Bonaparte and, me, I know that would be the action of a fool. Bonaparte would take the emeralds and keep Beléchappé, and Bertrand would decorate a dungeon for his trouble. And Sophie and Vivienne would still be in peril."

"Why did your wife and daughter go to France if the danger was so great for them?" Diana asked gently.

"They do not know Bertrand as I do," he replied. "My wife adores both her children, but her firstborn . . . I believe it is so with all mothers, madame. They dislike believing ill of that firstborn child."

Diana's hand went of its own accord to rest upon her stomach. No doubt that was true enough, she thought. She would probably believe only the best of her children, all twelve of them. The thought made her smile. "I understand, monseigneur. The Vidame de Lâche begged their assistance, and they went, thinking the danger over."

"That is so. England is at peace with France, they said. It is safe. But, me, I know this is not so. Still, when Vivienne makes up her mind, she is not always obedient to my will." He smiled as though he were remembering incidents from the past, then gave himself a little shake, and frowned. "Vivienne is a practical woman, madame. It is that which makes me fear for her. She would repudiate our son if it became clear to her that he meant to betray the family altogether."

They talked for some time longer. The comte, eating Bath buns and sipping tea, seemed glad to confide in Diana, and she realized he was extraordinarily worried. She remembered thinking he was probably senile. The thought brought a grimace to her lips now. He was not senile at all. He was a shrewd old gentleman who cursed his own infirmities and who worried as much about the young man who had set out to rescue the Beléchappé family as he did about his wife and daughter. At last he leaned back in his chair and gestured ruefully toward the last bun on the plate. "Will you not eat something, madame?"

"No, thank you," Diana said, rising. "I must go back. My husband will not approve of my having come to you like this, but I was worried. I shall have to reveal to him all that you have told me, monseigneur, but he has friends both in London and in Paris who may be able to help. If Lord Roderick has indeed come to grief, perhaps Andover can help them all."

The comte nodded. "I do not say that the diplomacy will avail us much, but you will please to thank your husband for his assistance." He rang for his servant. "Forgive me if I do not rise, madame. Too many Bath buns and too much port."

The farewells were formal but speedy, and Diana was soon mounted and racing along the London Road toward Osterley again, a disapproving Ned Tredegar at her side. Only after fifteen minutes of hard riding did she remember the precious burden she carried and slow to a safer pace. Thus, it was midafternoon before they rode up the gravel drive to the main entrance of the great house. Flinging her reins to Tredegar, Diana dismounted unaided and ran up the broad sweeping steps to the portico, skirting the giant columns to enter the stair hall.

Without pausing to speak to anyone other than the porter, who informed her that he believed my lord of Andover could be found in his bedchamber preparing to ride out, since his horses had been put to only moments before, Diana hurried up the carpeted stairs, scarcely laying a hand to the exquisite handrail in her hurry. As she sped along the gallery toward their bedchamber, she heard Lydia's voice calling her name from behind, but she merely waved a hand and hurried on .

The door to the bedchamber opened as she approached and Pettyjohn emerged, his face creased in worry lines. "Ah, my lady," he said on a note of vast relief. "His lordship has been—"

Diana pushed past him into the room. "Simon, I must—"

"Where the devil have you been?" He turned to face her, dressed for travel. "If you've got into some scrape or other through one of your escapades, Diana, so help me—"

"Simon, it's Rory. He's—"

"Oh, you've heard, have you? Good. Saves me a deal of explaining. I want you to pack your—"

"Heard? Then you know he's in France?"

"In France, indeed. He's under arrest in Paris, the idiotic fool. I should have known he'd be up to no good the minute my back was turned. What the devil he hoped to accomplish by getting himself involved in mischief over there, I hope he can tell me when I next lay hands upon him."

"How did you hear about it?" Diana asked, feeling as if the wind had gone out of her.

"Diplomatic channels, of course, a message from London. Bonaparte will scarcely wish to make more of this than necessary. They've charged Rory with crimes against the state, but I daresay they'll listen to reason. They won't want to stir the Warringtons any more than necessary. If we're reading the signs correctly, there will be war again soon, but Bonaparte won't want the English preparing for it any sooner than he can help. He knows damn well that my father still carries influence with a significant number of men, men who can stir even that fool Addington if they are pushed hard enough. This arrest is a damned nuisance, but it may be more of a nuisance to the French than it is to us. That's no doubt why they've let it be known. No way for them to know who over here knew he was going to Paris, after all. Did you know, by the by?" he demanded suddenly. "You were mighty thick with him at Christmas."

"N-not exactly," she hedged. "I certainly didn't know he'd gone to Paris, but, Simon, you should know—"

"I haven't time to discuss this, Diana," he said brusquely. "I want you to get your things packed."

"Of course," she agreed. "I'll tell Marlie to pack only the necessities. You'll be wanting to leave immediately." There would be time to explain everything on the way. She moved quickly to pull the bellcord.

Simon stared at her. "Why wouldn't you pack everything? You're going back to Alderwood, my girl."

"Alderwood? Don't be silly, Simon. I shall go with you. I know a good deal about the matter that you don't, things you need to know."

"All I need to know, Diana mine, is that my fool brother has got into a scrape again through his own fault. I can deal with the people in Paris through normal diplomatic channels. And you are not going with me. You are going to Alderwood, where you can help Aunt Ophelia and Susanna prepare to leave for London next month. You can tell Aunt I'm sorry about the alteration in plans, but there was an emergency. I've already sent a message to London to have the house opened and to attend to any details she may think of later. She can trust Pennyworth and his wife to see to everything. They've been butler and housekeeper there longer than I can remember. They'll attend to things far better than I could do."

"Simon, will you listen? I'm going with you. You may not be able to achieve all you wish to achieve through diplomatic channels. You do not know the whole. And if you cannot, it will look a deal less suspicious if you are traveling with your wife, particularly when your wife speaks fluent French. I can help, I know I can. You must not leave me behind!"

"Don't be nonsensical, Diana. My command of the French language may not be as complete as your own, but I speak it well enough. And I have no time now to discuss your theories about my brother's misadventure. You should be thanking the Fates at the moment that I do not, since it is not his actions for which I should be demanding explanations, but yours. Where the devil have you been all day? Clearly, you've been riding, but if you took anyone with you but Tredegar, I've been unable to discover it. Did you have some sort of assignation you'd as soon not discuss with me?"

"No, of course not!" she snapped, her temper soaring beyond control. "I had no intention before of telling you where I went, but—"

"That I don't doubt, and if I were not in a great hurry, I can tell you, my girl, that we would discuss that business thoroughly whether you wanted to tell me about it or not. But since I haven't time, you will have a week or so at Alderwood to think up a convincing tale to tell me that will keep me from turning you across my knee this time. Now, I've already sent ahead to Portsmouth to have the *Sea Maiden* prepared for immediate departure with the first tide tonight, so I must make haste."

"Simon, if you would only stop being so idiotish, perhaps you might realize that there are other capable people in this world besides yourself! No doubt you have no wish to encumber yourself with a wife when you may enjoy yourself a good deal more without one, but—"

"Enough, Diana." He snatched up his driving cape from the bed and turned toward the door. "You will obey me this time and without further argument. You go to Alderwood. I'll speak with Tredegar before I depart, and I daresay that for once you will find him strenuously opposed to following your orders instead of mine. We will talk about all this when I return."

He was gone on the words, leaving her to stare in stupefaction at the door as it banged behind him. Angrily, she turned away, flinging her hat at the wall. The door opened again behind her.

"You rang, my lady?" It was Miss Floodlind, her dresser, and as Diana turned she saw the thin woman's long face going properly blank. "Marlie is indisposed, my lady, nor did she expect you to need her until later. Is there something I can do for you?"

"Yes, Floodlind, you may begin to pack my things. My lord wishes me to return to Alderwood at once. He has been called away to France on business."

"Yes, my lady, the news has already reached the hall." She referred to the servants' hall, of course, though Diana doubted that Miss Floodlind spent much of her time consorting with common servants. Still, at such a time and place as this, there were a number of her peers in residence. Miss Floodlind quite liked the house party season. She said now in highly cultured tones through her long nose, "We were sorry to hear that

Lord Roderick has met with difficulties in Paris, but no doubt my lord will soon see things right."

"No doubt," Diana said bitterly. But she smiled when Lydia entered the room a moment later. "Hallo, Lyddy, you find me in one of my tantrums again."

"I saw Simon," Lydia said with a sympathetic smile. "He's in the devil's own temper. What on earth did you say to him?"

"I wanted to go with him," Diana said. "He flew into the boughs and ordered me off to Alderwood at once." She sat down, gesturing to a nearby chair. "I'm so tired of being ordered about, Lyddy. I could help him in France. I know I could."

"Well, there's no point pursuing the matter now," Lydia pointed out practically. "Simon has gone. Is there anything I can do to help you here?"

Miss Floodlind was efficiently removing Diana's clothing from the wardrobe. "What do you wish to wear, my lady?"

Diana stared at her. "Wear? I don't know. Surely, Simon does not expect me to leave immediately." She glanced at Lydia. "It is nearly one hundred miles to Alderwood from here. He cannot have intended for me to leave before morning."

"No, nor to travel alone," Lydia reassured her. "He has already spoken to Ethelmoor. We miss the children, you know, and had planned to return to the hall within a day or two, so it will be no inconvenience to us to leave in the morning. I daresay, your brother will wish to be at least the one night on the road. The weather has improved, but at this time of year, of course, it could snow before morning."

"He planned it all," Diana muttered. "But he said nothing to me of the details. He just assumed I would do whatever he commanded."

Lydia eyed her warily. "I don't like the way you are looking, Diana. Surely, you will not be so foolish as to disobey Simon's orders. Why, where would you go instead? Moreover, I daresay Ethelmoor will have something to say about that."

"Everyone has a say, except me," Diana said bitterly. Then she looked at her sister-in-law and smiled ruefully. "I sound like the spoiled brat everyone thinks me to be, do I not? 'Tis just my mood, Lyddy. Pay me no heed. I am a little tired, I think."

"You look very tired, indeed, Diana. I cannot think it was wise of you to take so long a ride this morning. We have all been going the pace rather strongly. Perhaps you should rest before dinner."

Diana agreed to the suggestion immediately, not so much because she needed to rest as because Lydia's reference to her morning's ride brought back all that the comte had said to her. She was dismayed to think that because of her own private war with Simon, she had let him leave without putting him in possession of the information she had gleaned from de Vieillard.

Ruthlessly dismissing Miss Floodlind, she plumped down upon the high bed to collect her thoughts. Simon had no notion of what lay before him. Possibly he was right in thinking that Bonaparte would wish to rid himself of the burden of Lord Roderick Warrington as quickly and simply as possible. However, Simon would not be prepared to meet with resistance from his twin, and Diana was certain that Rory would refuse to leave France without Mademoiselle Sophie and her mother. Possibly he would refuse to leave without the emeralds. If, as she suspected from what the comte had told her, de Vieillard had promised him Sophie's hand in return for her rescue and the retrieval of the treasure, Rory would never consider leaving France without them.

Such an attitude on Rory's part could endanger them all, particularly if Simon were not forewarned. How could she have been such a ninnyhammer as to let him leave without telling him what she knew? The question made her squirm. If she had not leapt into battle with him, if she had merely remained calm and insisted upon telling him what she had learned from the comte, Simon would be much better prepared to meet whatever lay ahead of him. As it was, he had no idea of what was at stake. Indeed, if the Vidame de Lâche had already informed Bonaparte that the emeralds were still in France, Bonaparte would already have begun to search for them. Thus, if Rory insisted upon initiating his own search, despite Simon's efforts to stop him, he would be putting Simon in as much danger as himself and the Beléchappé family.

With such thoughts as these for company, it was not long before Diana knew what she had to do. She would go after Simon, catch him before he boarded the *Sea Maiden* at Portsmouth, and tell him all she knew about Lord Roderick and the Beléchappé family. He would be furious with her, of course. Heaven knew what he would do to her, but perhaps the fact that he was in a great hurry would save her for a time. He would send her back to Alderwood, probably under guard, but at least he would know what he was getting into.

She still wore her habit, and she had money. She tipped out the contents of her reticule onto the bed. Simon had given her a generous amount not a week since, for there were always vails to be paid and impromptu visits to nearby villages for shopping expeditions wherever one visited, and she had spent very little. Having no notion of how much it would cost her to hire a chaise, for she would certainly never convince Ned Tredegar to drive her, she found herself hoping that thirty-seven guineas and odd change would prove to be sufficient.

Taking a warm cloak from the wardrobe where Miss Floodlind had left it, she left a note for Lydia, then made her way down a back stair, avoiding the long gallery, and slipped out of the house by way of a servants' door. Most of the guests had retired to their rooms to begin dressing for dinner, but she had no wish to take the chance of running into anyone who might try to stop her.

The stables were empty except for a pair of young stableboys in Osterley livery. One was in the hay mow, pitching down hay, which the other was methodically transferring to each of the inhabited stalls. The latter smiled at Diana's approach.

"Mr. Tredegar be gorn t' 'ave 'is supper, m'lady. Ought I ter fetch 'im?"

"No, no, that won't be necessary," Diana assured him, hoping her relief at Tredegar's absence didn't show too clearly. "I merely want my bay hunter saddled. I wish to ride out to meet some friends who are driving over from Maidenhead."

The stable lad agreed that like as not he could saddle her bay for her and proceeded to do so. He was a chatty young man, and it was not at all difficult for Diana to turn the subject to her husband's journey. "He had to leave so quickly," she said, "and I believe he must have taken his phaeton. I hope he doesn't come to grief."

" 'Is lordship drives like 'e be born to it, me lady," the boy said, chuckling. "Ye'll not need t' worry over the like o' 'im."

"No, very likely not, but if one of his horses should come up lame or if something should go wrong with the phaeton, I don't know what he would do. He is in a dreadful hurry to reach Portsmouth, you know."

"Well, like as not he'd just up and 'ire a chaise, like all the nobs does when they dassn't 'ave their own." He screwed up his forehead as he thought over what he'd said. "If 'e be in an all-fired 'urry, like as not that's why 'e wanted t' know the quickest way from 'ere t' the Portsmouth Road."

"What did you tell him?" Diana asked quietly.

"Why, the quickest'd be t' go cross country, south across the heath t' the river, but 'e'd be wantin' a road wi' that get-up o' is, 'n there ain't but a track across the heath, 'n dangerous rutted it be this time o' year. Your Tredegar tol' 'im t' take the Staines Road. 'E kin get from Staines right enough to Esher. 'N if 'is rig breaks down afore then, why, I guess 'e could get sumpin' in Esher t' git 'im to Guildford."

"Oh, Guildford," said Diana. "Yes, of course, he could find whatever he needed there, could he not? And that's right on the Portsmouth Road."

"Well, o' course," agreed the stable boy, proud to show off his geographical knowledge.

Diana took a chance. " 'Tis a pity he took the phaeton at all if it would have been quicker to ride directly across the heath. But how would he know he was going in the right direction?"

"Said there was a track, didn't I? Easy as kiss yer 'and if 'e keeps the sun on 'is right 'n don't mistake some sideway fer the real thing. It's only 'bout four, mebbe five, miles t' the river, atter all, 'n there be folks'd put 'im right, if'n 'e got lorst."

"How would he cross the river?" Diana asked, hoping she sounded merely curious.

"Hampton Court crossing's 'bout a mile east o' where 'e'd come upon the river. Road there goes straight into the Portsmouth Road. Meets it 'bout a mile 'r so above Esher."

Having thus acquired a great deal of useful knowledge, Diana chatted with him a few moments more, then accepted his help in mounting her horse. "I shan't be gone long," she said then, casually. "I daresay I shall be back before Ned Tredegar returns from his supper."

His directions were not at all difficult to follow, and she reached the banks of the Thames less than half an hour later. Crossing Hounslow Heath on the rutted, muddy, and at times, snow-banked track had been a little frightening, for she had heard the heath teemed with highwaymen, but she had seen no one but an occasional pedestrian, no doubt wending his way home looking forward to his supper. Turning east, she found the crossing less than ten minutes later, and the road after that was well kept and completely clear of melting snow.

It was dark by the time she reached the village of Esher, so although she would have preferred to ride as far as Guildford before she attempted to find another means of transportation, she knew she didn't dare. It would be too dangerous. Moreover, she had ridden hard, her worry over Simon outweighing any concern she may have felt for the baby she carried. She was very tired, and so was the bay hunter. Seeing an inn sign, she drew up, sliding down from the saddle, and giving orders to the approaching ostler to attend to her horse and see the animal was returned to Osterley the following morning.

"Aye, mistress," he returned eyeing her appreciatively.

His reaction to her solitary state warned her to expect difficulties from mine host. Consequently, she drew on all she had learned from Lady Ophelia and Lady

Jersey and hoped he would not realize she was quaking inwardly.

The innkeeper was a stout fellow with red cheeks and bristling sidewhiskers. He frowned as he moved to greet her, looking over her shoulder as though he expected her companions to show themselves at any moment.

"Well, madam?"

Diana drew herself to her full height and looked down her nose at him, although she had to tilt her chin a bit to accomplish that feat. "I beg your pardon, my good man," she said haughtily. "I require a decent carriage to convey me to Guildford where I can hire a proper post chaise and four. I am in a great hurry. I trust you can accommodate my needs."

His attitude changed almost ludicrously at the mention of a post chaise and four, quite the most expensive form of transportation one might consider. He rubbed his fat hands together. "Well, as to that, ma'am, I daresay my lad could drive ye t' Guildford in our gig. 'Tis likely it ain't what you be accustomed to—"

"That will be suitable," Diana said calmly. "I believe I mentioned I am in a great hurry."

He looked her over again as though he were trying to judge whether she might be a schoolgirl running away from home, but when she met his look without losing a jot of her poise, he turned and shouted over his shoulder for Lem to shake a leg, there was a customer wantin' to go to Guildford.

Diana paid the innkeeper as liberally as she dared, knowing it would cost a great deal for the chaise in Guildford, but hoping a little largesse in Esher would pave her way later. She was glad she had done it when she discovered a cloth-covered basket at her feet in the gig, containing cold roast chicken, bread, cheese, and a jug of wine. There was even an apple. Conscious of hunger for the first time, she whiled away the thirteen miles from Esher through Cobham and Ripley to Guildford by sharing the meal with the taciturn Lem. The journey took longer than she had hoped, and it was after eight o'clock when they reached the Angel in Guildford.

Using her experience at Esher to guide her, Diana had less difficulty than she had anticipated hiring the post chaise and four. With two armed postilions mounted ahead of her, she had little fear that she would be molested on the way. It was all of thirty-two miles further to Portsmouth, and since she had demanded all speed, it was necessary to stop in Petersfield for a change of horses. Even so, it was after midnight when the chaise finally reached Portsmouth. She had hoped to overtake Simon on the road, and at every posting house or decent-looking inn she had looked into the yard to see if she could recognize his phaeton, but she had seen nothing that looked remotely like that sleekly lined carriage. Frightened that he might already have left for France, she had the postboys take her directly to the wharf where the *Sea Maiden* was berthed. Once they drew near the sea, they encountered no difficulty in obtaining necessary directions from first one and then another sailor until, arriving at dockside, Diana was gratified to discover that the yacht still rested in her berth. Surprisingly, there seemed to be no one on board. There were no lights, and no one was keeping guard at the gangplank. In fact, it did not look at all as though Simon could be aboard or as though anyone were expecting him.

She hesitated only briefly, however, before paying off the postboys and ordering them to leave her there. She certainly did not want to put up at a hotel, and if she could find at least one of Simon's crew and convince him to let her remain in the master cabin until Simon arrived, then her husband could decide what to do with her.

By the time she was aboard the yacht, she had changed her mind. Simon would send her back to Alderwood under guard with a polite request that his father keep her there. She would be in disgrace. If he was going to be angry with her anyway, why not give him good reason? She smiled as she made her way across the dark deck of the yacht. She had never been aboard before, but she knew enough to realize that there must be some way of getting below. Even as the thought crossed her mind, she heard whistling and realized someone was approaching. She ducked down behind a huge coil of thick rope.

A man carrying a lantern came alongside the ship's bulkhead, walking with a rolling gait to the head of the gangway, where he set the lantern down and settled himself onto a folding stool. Evidently, Diana thought, she had arrived during a changing of the guard or while the guard had had to attend to a call of nature. Either way, she had been lucky, but there was no point now in calling attention to herself. The light of the lantern had flickered across an open hatch leading down into a companionway. The guard's attention was focused upon the wharfside. If she were quiet, she could slip into the companionway without being seen.

The deed was accomplished almost as easily as the thought, but once below it was even darker. No candles or lanterns had been left lit, and she had no notion what she would find. For all she knew there were men sleeping down here. She felt her way carefully, listening hard for the slightest indication that there were other humans nearby. She could hear nothing.

A few moments later, her nerves at breaking point, she felt a latch beneath her fingers. Moving with the greatest care, she turned the latch, feeling satisfaction when a door opened silently toward her. Groping about in the darkness beyond the door, she realized she had come across some sort of storage locker. The floor was bare, but there were shelves along the walls, made with high lips so that things stored would not go crashing about whenever the ship moved. Slipping inside, Diana discovered that if she curled up, using her cloak as a cover and a bundle of cord discovered on the first shelf as a pillow, she could be perfectly warm and comfortable. As she settled down, she realized she was exhausted. The day had been long and arduous, and she had ridden a great distance. Her eyes would scarcely stay open. Her last conscious thought was that surely no ship of Simon's would dare to be rat-infested.

She was awakened by a change from darkness to halflight and a roughly muttered curse. "God's life, what 'ave we here? A bleedin' wench. And won't 'is lordship be pleased, bein' in such a fine mood, as 'e is?"

12

The burly young sailor reached down and grabbed Diana by her arm, hauling her upright without ceremony. "Come along, wench. There'll be the devil t' pay, and no pitch hot. His lordship be in no frame o' mind fer romantical shenanigans."

Diana straightened her shoulders, glaring at him. "I am Lady Andover," she said, attempting to gather her dignity.

The sailor glanced at her, looked pointedly back into the storage locker, then brought his gaze back to examine her more carefully. No doubt she looked like an owl dragged out of an ivy bush, Diana thought, restraining the temptation to smooth her hair and skirts. The man's eyes lost their insolent look as his gaze drifted from her tousled hair down her dusty bodice to her wrinkled but undeniably expensive velvet skirts. His glance moved to her hat, lying beside her crumpled cloak on the floor, and he grimaced expressively, shaking his head.

"M'lady, methinks yer in the soup, right enough."

Diana bit her lower lip. "I don't suppose you could contrive to go about your business and simply forget that you ever opened that door." When the man, looking uncomfortable, said nothing, she sighed. "No, of course not. 'Tis most unfair of me even to suggest such a thing. Is his lordship up there?" She gestured toward the open hatch leading to the main deck.

The sailor shook his head. "He's still in his cabin, ma'am. Lost a wheel off that phaeton of his, and had the devil's own time finding a wheelwright in Petersfield. Well nigh didn't make it afore the morning tide. What with enjoyin' the company o' that pernickety Pettyjohn 'n the added weight of 'is groom up behind, 'tis no wonder 'e lost the wheel, or that he be in such a temper now."

Diana knew now how she had passed Simon up without seeing the phaeton, but she asked no questions about the accident, for she had realized by then that the deck was moving beneath her feet. "We've sailed," she said, not without satisfaction.

"Aye, that we have." He released his hold on her arm and made a gesture toward the end of the companionway, adding affably, "That way, ma'am. Door at the end." She stumbled, catching herself against the bulkhead, and the sailor chuckled. "Not got yer sea legs yet, but they'll come quick. Good thing we ain't 'avin' a true winter, though. Some winds I seen would toss this little craft about somethin' fierce. Nobbut she's a seaworthy lass. No need t' fret. Only light winds these days, any gate. This 'as been the mildest winter since I can remember. Growin' roses already, they are in Southampton. Saw it m'self, but it don't seem natural. Usually, January 'n February, these waters ain't fit fer fish, but if we make Le Havre afore sundown t'day, I'll be that amazed. Here we be, ma'am. Ye'll be needin' a stiff upper, I'm thinkin'," he added in a lower tone as he brushed dust from the shoulders of her habit. "Beg pardon fer the liberty, I'm sure, ma'am, but 'is lordship's been in a fearsome temper. Best ye tread lightly, ma'am." With these encouraging words he knocked on the door at the end of the companionway, and Diana's knees began to tremble.

A gruff voice bade them enter, and the young seaman pulled open the door. "Party t' see ye, me lord," he said hastily. "Doubt ye'll be wishin' fer me t' hang about. Be topside, an ye want me." With that he fairly pushed Diana through the door, shutting it behind her.

The wood-paneled cabin was small, containing only a narrow bed under a porthole, two chairs, a small chart table, a brass fitted trunk, and the desk where Simon sat writing. He had not looked up until Diana's somewhat precipitous entry, but just as the sailor shut off any hope of escape behind her, Simon turned. At first his expression was disbelieving, but no more than seconds passed before anger took over and, scraping his chair back, he leapt to his feet.

"By God, this time you've gone too far, Diana." Two strides brought him to face her, his strong hands bruising her arms as he pulled her up onto her tiptoes and peered down into her face. "You look a mess. What the devil have you been doing to yourself?"

"I fell asleep in some sort of storage closet," she said. "Please, Simon, you're hurting me."

"I intend to hurt you. I've warned you not to flaunt your defiance of my wishes before the world. I told you the next time would be your last, that I'd put you across my knee, and by God—" He broke off, bewildered, when she swayed in his arms. "What is it? Diana, are you all right?"

The deck persisted in rolling about under her feet, and even with Simon holding her, Diana still felt dizzy and a little sick. Fear of what he promised to do to her only augmented the other feelings. She swayed again, her face going white.

"Simon," she whispered, "let me sit down."

He half carried her to the nearest chair. "What's wrong, Diana? Are you hurt? You look dreadful. Are you ill?" His questions shot at her one after the other, but his tone was anxious now rather than angry.

Her stomach was churning, and the walls of the little cabin seemed to be going up and down, up and down.

"Diana!"

She took a deep breath. "I'm all right, Simon, just tired. I rode so hard, and I've been so worried, and I've had nothing to eat since breakfast yesterday except for a bit of cold chicken last night." The thought of food unsettled her stomach again, and she closed her eyes.

"Worried, why worried?"

She looked at him. "Because I didn't tell you something you need to know. I went to the Comte de Vieillard yesterday and he told me why Rory went to France, and Rory means to marry Mademoiselle Beléchappé, and you made me so angry that I never told you, and I was afraid that awful Mr. Bonaparte would arrest you, too."

Tears welled into her eyes as the words tumbled over themselves, and Simon gave her another small shake, though he spoke more gently. "Whoa, sweetheart. I think you'd better begin at the beginning. What the devil do you mean, you rode to visit the old Frenchman? Alone, too, I'll wager."

"Ned went with me. Not inside, of course, but I was quite safe, Simon."

"No doubt. Tell me the whole, right up until Darby found you in that locker, and mind you don't leave anything out," he said sternly.

She told him everything, and the more she talked, the grimmer Simon looked. He interrupted with sharp questions more than once, and several times she thought he would shake her again. When she described her journey to Portsmouth his expression grew black.

"By God," he muttered wrathfully when she had done, "I will beat you. Of all the totty-headed things to do! Why, anything might have happened to you, if not on the road, then certainly once you reached dockside. What had you planned to do if the *Sea Maiden* had sailed?"

Swallowing carefully, Diana willed her heaving stomach to calm itself. "I didn't think about it," she said in a small voice. "I was so worried about what might happen if you went after Rory without knowing what you ought to know that I just told myself the *Sea Maiden* must be here. I had to tell you. Oh, Simon, are you going to take me back now?"

"I can't. There's so little wind, it would take all day, assuming we could manage it at all. We've all we can do to get to Le Havre. But don't get it into your head that you'll go with me to Paris. You'll stay right here aboard the *Maiden*, where I'll know you're safe."

She opened her mouth to protest, but just then after a perfunctory knock, the cabin door swung open and the sailor she had met earlier entered, a tray balanced over one shoulder. "Beggin' yer pardon, me lord, but I remembered ye'd ordered a bite afore the interruption,

so t' speak, and thinkin' the lady would like a bit o'
refreshment, I took the liberty . . ."

As he talked, he lowered the tray, pushing charts
aside to make room on the table near Diana's chair. The
smell of food reached her, and she glanced at the tray.
The first thing that met her gaze was a pile of juicy,
pink slivered ham. With a strangled yelp, she turned
away, clapping one hand to her mouth, the other to
her rebellious stomach. "Simon," she gasped, "a basin!"

He stared at her in amazement but quickly recognized her predicament and snatched up a wash basin
from under the table with little care for the empty
pitcher inside it. The pitcher rolled back and forth on
the floor as Simon pushed the basin into Diana's hands.
He glanced back over his shoulder.

"Get out, Darby."

The sailor fled, snapping the door shut behind him.

Simon was grim but efficient. He held her head
while she rid herself of what little remained in her
stomach of the cold chicken, bread, and wine from the
evening before, then handed her a towel and took the
basin to the door. Since he didn't shout for anyone or
leave the cabin, she assumed that Darby had not gone
far, but she was too weak to worry about embarrass-
ment. She wiped her face, watching her husband. He
spoke quietly to someone in the companionway, then
turned back, shutting the door again.

"Are you wearing stays?" he asked.

She shook her head, surprised by the question.

He regarded her through narrowed eyes. "I think
you'd better come out of that habit, anyway," he said.

"Really, Simon," she said, "I'm not ill. It is only—"

"I know you've merely succumbed to a case of *mal de
mer*, my dear, but I think you can trust me to know
more about what will help under the circumstances
than you do. And I wish you to become well soon, so
that I may deal with you as you deserve. Now, get out
of those clothes. Here," he added quickly when she
swayed in her chair, "I'll help."

That made her smile. "Simon," she said softly, "it was
the motion of the ship that made me lose my balance
just then, but I am not seasick. Furthermore, my lord,

you cannot scold me one moment and then leap forward to help me the next. It quite ruins the image of the stern lord and master. You will have to learn to manage better before our son is born."

He was unfastening her spencer, but her words stopped his fingers. For a moment he looked down at her, puzzled, but when she smiled at him again, he shook his head a little as though to clear it, and his hands tightened on the lapels of her jacket. "Our son? Are you trying to tell me—"

"That you cannot beat me, Simon. You might injure the baby."

There was a moment of silence before Simon looked her straight in the eye and said, "If your mad journey on horseback and in a rented, probably poorly sprung, chaise did not harm the child, I doubt that my taking a strap to your backside right now would come at all amiss. He'd probably side with me if he were asked for an opinion in the matter after being bounced about like that."

"My mother rode every day when she was carrying her children," Diana said defensively.

"I doubt if she rode the way you must have today," Simon retorted, applying his fingers once more to the fastenings of her jacket.

She could see that he was still angry, and she felt a surge of disappointment. She had thought to disarm him entirely by telling him of her condition. Instead, the news had merely made him angrier. He pulled her spencer off, then reached to unfasten her bodice and skirt.

"Surely, I needn't take all my clothes off," she protested. "What if that sailor comes back?"

"Don't fret about Darby. I'm going to put you to bed. You can wear one of my shirts."

He helped her to the side of the bed, then moved to take a soft white shirt from the brassbound trunk. It was too large for her, but its softness seemed to caress her skin. In the huge shirt and with Simon standing over her, she felt particularly small and vulnerable, so she did not attempt to speak until she was in the bed, but once she had the dark wool blanket over her, she said, "Simon, I'm not sick, truly I'm not. Aren't . . . aren't you glad about the baby?"

He bent over her, his lips just touching her forehead. "I'm glad, sweetheart," he said softly, "but I'm also angry with you, and the emotions get a bit mixed. I'm going to leave you to rest for a while, then Darby will bring you a little food and some brandy to settle your stomach. No," he said, putting a finger to her lips, "don't argue with me. You put both yourself and our child in danger last night, and I don't think I can trust my temper. We'll talk later."

When he was gone, Diana lay in the narrow bed staring at the cabin door until the tears came. Simon had never been too angry to talk to her before. Whenever he was angry he bellowed at her and shouted like he had earlier, scolding and threatening, but he had never simply walked away. His last three words had sent chills racing through her. Three words, spoken calmly, yet they had sounded more ominous than all that had gone before. She wanted to go after him, but she knew that to do so would be most unwise. Besides, he had taken her habit with him, no doubt hoping to shake the worst of the dust out of it. The more she thought about his anger, the faster the tears fell, until she had cried herself into exhaustion and sleep.

It was dark in the little cabin when she awoke, but someone was lighting candles on the chart table. She recognized the young sailor, Darby.

"What time is it, Darby?" she asked, stretching in the little bed.

"Just after six, my lady."

"Gracious, have I slept all day, then?"

"Guess you was a mite tired."

"Where is his lordship?"

"Gone ashore."

Diana sat up, clutching the blanket about her. "Ashore! Have we landed in Le Havre? Has he gone on to Paris already?"

"No, no, my lady, not to Paris. He's only gone to bespeak dinner at an inn. He thought you would be more comfortable dining on solid ground."

With a sigh of relief, Diana sank back against the pillows. "Are you his only crew, Darby?"

"No, m'lady, there be three others topside, but I takes care of my lord when we sails, bein' as that pernickety Pettyjohn prefers to go by the packet. Forsham, too. He'll be gettin' transportation all laid on fer 'is lordship, 'cause the packet landed only shortly after we did ourselves. I've no doubt Mr. Pettyjohn 'as arranged fer 'is lordship's supper, but bein' as 'ow he went straight into town and didn't know you was meanin' t' accompany 'is lordship—"

"I see, Darby. Have I time for a wash?"

"Brung the water, meself, m'lady. In that pitcher, there. An' yer clothes be on the hook yonder. Don't be in a worry about wearin' yer habit. Them Frenchies won't know but that it's the fashionable thing t' do."

He winked at her as he slipped out through the door again, and Diana knew she had found a friend. She wondered now if his interruption with the ham earlier had been intended to spare her further scolding. If it had, she ought to find some way to thank him, even if his efforts had been unsuccessful.

Her eyes were puffy from crying, but cold water helped, and her hair was easily dealt with. She simply stuffed it back into its net and tied the ribbon at the nape of her neck, deciding the strands and curls that escaped the net were becoming and kept the style from being too severe. She dressed slowly. It seemed odd to be donning her riding habit to have dinner with her husband at an inn. No doubt he had come prepared for anything, since he intended to mix socially in Paris, while she had nothing but the clothes on her back. He would probably have something to say about that, too, she decided. She wondered what else he would say to her when they talked.

Simon entered the cabin without ceremony fifteen minutes later. He was wearing buckskins and a dark jacket. He looked very handsome, but he would scarcely outshine her at the inn. She picked up her hat, facing him with her shoulders square.

He looked her over appraisingly. "Ready?"

"Yes."

"You look a good deal better," he said with a little smile. "Come along, then. Our dinner is waiting."

The inn was a small one off the main street in Le Havre, but the parlor to which Simon led her was cozy with a beamed ceiling and a crackling fire. Pettyjohn served them.

Diana contained her surprise admirably until he had gone, leaving them alone. Then she asked, "Does your valet always serve you in this fashion when you travel alone, Simon?"

"He does when I travel abroad. There are often things to be discussed that are not for every ear to hear. I can trust him. Is that beef done to your liking?"

"Yes, thank you." She cut a piece, speared it with her fork, then hesitated. "Simon, I'm sorry I made you so angry, but I wish you will believe me when I say that neither I nor the baby was ever in real danger. I rode as fast as I dared, but I had a very good horse under me and I took no chances."

"Eat your dinner, Diana. We'll talk afterward."

"Simon, please!"

"I'm not angry now. I do know you would not purposely harm our child, but I cannot agree that you used good judgment. And that's all I wish to say about the matter until after we eat. You may, if you wish to talk, tell me more about what the comte said. Are there truly emeralds at Beléchappé?"

"Yes, and Simon, I'm sure Rory won't agree to go back to England without them. The comte promised him Sophie in return."

"Rory will do as I tell him to do," Simon said flatly. "He won't be given a choice in the matter."

"But the comte gave him his signet ring, after he refused to entrust it to his son. Rory will think himself duty-bound to retrieve the emeralds. And he won't leave Paris without Mademoiselle Beléchappé and her mother. I'm sure of that."

"I have barely met mademoiselle, but her parents are well-connected and perfectly respectable, although they are no longer as powerful as they were in France, of course. The Vidame de Lâche is another matter. A nastier piece of work I hope never to meet. I have no duty toward that family, Diana, nor does Roderick."

"He won't agree with you," Diana said flatly.

"The very fact that he has not so much as mentioned her to me or to my father tells me he cannot care for her as much as you seem to think he does, my dear. For the treasure, perhaps."

"I cannot believe you said that," she told him, putting down her fork. "You of all people must know how strongly Rory feels things. His emotions rule him, Simon. They always have. Love has now replaced the bitterness and envy he felt before, and he is determined to take control of his life, but that does not mean he doesn't realize that neither you nor the marquess will take kindly to the notion of a French émigré wife. Her parents may be well-connected and respectable, but without the emeralds they have only sufficient money to make themselves comfortable. You may not wish for him to marry Lady Sarah Fane, but you do want him to marry money, to add to the Warrington fortunes."

He was silent for a moment, but she doubted he was really listening to her. He seemed to be applying most of his attention to his dinner. At last, however, he said, "I would not wish to leave anyone in Bonaparte's clutches. That last meeting in London served to convince me that there is little time left before he will make his true colors known, so if I am able to effect a release for the comtesse and her daughter, I will do so. But nothing can be done about the emeralds, Diana. They cannot be worth all that much, whatever you may have heard, and the risk is too great. First, as you admit yourself, there is every reason to believe that de Lâche has already informed the First Consul of their presence in France. The chances are very great that Bonaparte already has them in his possession. If he does not, it would certainly be foolhardy beyond belief to lead him directly to them, which is exactly what we should be doing if we set foot next or nigh Château Beléchappé after convincing him to release the family."

She could not argue with his logic. The comte had said very much the same thing, and she knew that Lord

Roderick would put Sophie's safety above everything else. Nonetheless, she could not doubt that once Sophie was safe in Simon's care, Rory would insist upon taking a stab at retrieving the emeralds. When she attempted to convince Simon of this, however, he merely glared at her and repeated his earlier statement. "Rory will do as he's told. Just as you will, Diana mine. I will leave at first light, but you will stay with Darby and the others on the *Sea Maiden* until I return. I will not tolerate disobedience this time. Do not even attempt to persuade me to allow you to accompany me to Paris, and do not think for a moment that by following me on the road, you will force me to take you along. If you do such a thing, I promise you, you will regret it—painfully. Do you take my meaning?"

She nodded, unable for once to meet his gaze. He had spoken softly, his words as ominous as they had been earlier in the cabin on board the *Sea Maiden*. She swallowed carefully, then forced a smile. "I'll obey you, Simon. I haven't much choice. This riding habit is all I brought with me. I can scarcely appear at Bonaparte's court in such a rig."

He relaxed. "I wouldn't present you to that man, whatever you chose to wear."

She asked him to tell her more about the man who ruled France, and Simon complied, relaxing more and more as he talked and sipped his wine. Their meal was long finished and the covers cleared away before he stopped, wiping a hand across his forehead with a rueful grin.

"I must be boring you by now, sweetheart."

"No, I like to listen when you talk."

"But not when I shout, right?"

She dimpled. "I'm afraid you think I do not listen at all then, sir."

He shook his head in mock exasperation. "If I were not awash with wine and more tired than I can remember being in my life, I'd accept that challenge, Diana mine, and we would continue our earlier conversation. But I have decided to delay that discussion until we have ample time and privacy to pursue it. There will be some changes made, my wife, but I do not intend to discuss them tonight."

Diana sighed. "I doubt you will discuss them at all, sir. You will merely issue orders and commands as you always do."

He stood up. "Perhaps, but you have made it very clear that more is needed than orders, my girl. That's the part I intend to think about on the road to Paris. But right now, I'm for bed. Come along."

He led her into the corridor, but instead of turning toward the front of the inn, he turned toward the stairway. Diana looked at him questioningly. "Are we not going back to the *Sea Maiden*, Simon?"

"We are not. In case you didn't notice, my bed there is sadly lacking in size, and I've no intention of spending my night in a smaller cabin or a hammock on deck. You came after me. You may warm my bed, little wife."

She chuckled, making no objection when he put his arm around her, but later in bed, as she lay with her head in the curve of his shoulder, she said solemnly, "I do not mean to defy you, Simon. I wish you will believe that."

"You are a stubborn, willful chit who wants taming," he said softly against her hair. "Defiance comes as naturally to you as breathing does."

She snuggled against him, rubbing her hand across his broad chest. "Lydia says our problem is that I am as accustomed to having my own way as you are to having yours. Do you suppose there might be some truth in that viewpoint?"

He caught her hand, bringing it up so that he might nibble at her fingertips. She could feel his lips moving when he said, "Nonsense. You cannot always have had your own way. I have met your mama, remember?"

"But she does not go against Papa's wishes, and he always had the final say. And he, my lord, always let me do as I pleased. Even Mama said I should learn better from the consequences of my actions than I should if people were always preaching at me. Consider that, my lord."

"I believe you might better consider what you said

about your mama always submitting to your papa. You should follow her excellent example, Diana mine."

She sighed, then gave a little gasp when his fingers touched her breast. After that she found it difficult to concentrate upon anything other than the movements of Simon's hands and body. When he settled over her at last, preparing to consummate their union once more, he paused for a moment, holding both her hands over her head and looking down into her eyes.

She smiled at him. "I am utterly helpless, my lord. Is this how you would keep me?"

He chuckled. "I like the idea."

"Do you, Simon?" she asked gently. "Do you, really? Would you truly prefer a wife who said always, 'Oh, Simon, how strong you are!' or perhaps 'Dear Simon, how wise you are!' and who never had so much as a thought to call her own? You know a good many women like that, Simon. We both do. Why did you not choose one of them instead of me when you went looking for a wife?"

His only response to that question was a growl, low in his throat, before he claimed her, and Diana, wrapped up in her own passions, had no wish to pursue the matter.

He woke her when there was little but soft gray light at the window. Indeed, for a moment she thought it must have snowed, so dim was the daylight. But she soon discovered that the sun had not yet arisen, that the day had scarcely wakened, itself. Simon, however, was in a hurry. He bustled her into her clothes and scarcely allowed her enough time to swallow a cup of coffee and a few morsels of beef and bread in the taproom before he conveyed her back to the *Sea Maiden.*

His groom and Pettyjohn were to accompany him to Paris, and Diana wondered as she saw them drive off together how he would manage to bring Rory, madame la comtesse, and Mademoiselle Sophie all back safely. But she told herself that Simon would manage, and turned her mind to other things. The first of these concerned her clothing. She could not wear her riding habit for the week or more that it might take Simon to accomplish his mission.

But even as she considered the problem, her thoughts turned again, almost of their own accord, to Lord Roderick and the question of the emeralds. She did not for one moment believe that Rory, so near his goal, would agree to leave France without them. No matter what Simon thought, she knew he underestimated his twin's feelings for Sophie and his desire to prove himself to the Comte de Vieillard. Simon might think all he need do was to order his brother home to England. Diana was quite certain Rory would refuse to go.

The results would undoubtedly be violent, but even assuming Simon could best his brother in a contest between them—an assumption that, under the circumstances, she was not prepared to make—Rory would not be easily balked of an attempt to retrieve the emeralds, and would very likely do something rash enough to endanger them all. Clearly, something must be done before then to ensure that he would board the *Sea Maiden* when Simon demanded it. And since there was no other recourse, Diana would have to contrive by herself. But she could not do the thing entirely alone. Glancing about her, she spied the burly young sailor, Darby, near the offshore railing. Calling to him, she sat down upon a bench nailed next to the bulkhead and invited him to join her there.

Darby flushed to his eyebrows at her request, but Diana merely laughed at him. "I'm hoping you can help me solve a problem," she said cheerfully. "I've nothing at all to wear beyond what I've got on my back. Do you think that if I were to give you my measurements and what money I've got left, you might contrive to find something in the town? Even peasants' clothing would be preferable to living in this habit."

He looked her over appraisingly. "I've a young sister at home, m'lady, and I've brung her things from France afore what fit well enough. I don't speak the lingo, mind, but likely I'll manage."

Pleased by this small success, she moved ahead to the next hurdle. "Is there perhaps an inn or a livery stable where one might hire a horse or two? I confess, I don't look forward to staying on board the *Sea Maiden* for so long without any exercise."

He looked doubtful. "His lordship said you was to stay put, m'lady. I'd not like to cross 'im, if it be all the same to you."

Diana bit her lip. "I know you would not want to make him angry, Darby, but . . . oh, dear, I see I must trust you. I had hoped perhaps to ease you into my plan quite slowly, but that will not do. You see, Darby, I need your help quite desperately."

13

The skies were overcast and the wind had risen the following day when Diana and Darby set out for Château Beléchappé, located some four miles west of the village of Deauville. The *Sea Maiden* rested uneasily at anchor outside the small harbor, its skiff tied to the outermost of the narrow timber piers pointing inward from the stone breakwater that protected the harbor from the rougher waters of the Baie de la Seine. The two sailors from the yacht who had come ashore with them and who would await their return carried weapons, as much because they had little belief in the trustworthiness of the French as to protect Diana and Darby, should they require such protection upon their return.

The task of convincing Darby to help her had not been an easy one, but Diana had not spent more than twenty years cozening her doting father into bowing to her will for naught. By emphasizing, indeed exaggerating, the danger to Simon, she had finally begun to turn the young sailor from his stolid insistence that he could not disobey his master's orders. Even then, particularly since she had no wish to reveal all she knew about the Beléchappé emeralds, it had taken patience and all her wiles to make him listen to her. At last, faced by his seemingly unyielding determination to follow orders, Diana had had no hesitation in resorting to outright prevarication.

"My lord is on a very dangerous mission," she had said, glancing about and keeping her voice very low. "I should say nothing at all about it, of course, but I see there is naught to be gained by keeping you in ignorance. When he returns from Paris, there is every likelihood that there will be French soldiers on his heels and that he will be in a great hurry. If he has to flee without all he came to get, he will believe he has failed. Indeed, he *will* have failed. His very honor is at stake, Darby. I am persuaded you must understand what his lordship's honor means to him."

The young sailor nodded, watching her with much the same fascination as a cobra watches a mongoose. "He be a proud man, right enough."

"Yes, very. Too proud sometimes," Diana said, shaking her head. "He would protect me when I am the best person to accomplish this one task for him. I speak French fluently, Darby. I know the person to seek and the right words to use in the seeking. I can do the thing faster and with greater efficiency than my lord himself. But though he has confided in me," she added, with a shrewd glance at the burly man beside her, "he still thinks a woman too soft to deal with such stuff as this when, in fact, I shall do better because of my sex. No one will suspect that I have business at Beléchappé. Therefore, I shall be able to accomplish the matter quickly and without suspicion."

"What be this matter ye speak of?"

" 'Tis confidential. I am to present certain credentials and to receive certain important materials in exchange," Diana said.

"Sounds t' me like some sort o' spying," Darby said.

Diana nearly denied the suggestion indignantly before she realized that the lad's eyes had lit up and that there was a sudden sense of suppressed tension in his demeanor. He was excited at the thought of being involved in a spy mission against France. Diana glanced around again. "Indeed, I should not have revealed so much. But I must tell you, Darby, that the fate of a

good many people hangs by the thread of Beléchappé.
If we can reach the château before anyone suspects
that my lord has the slightest interest in the place, we
can retrieve the . . . uh, the material and be back here
before he returns. Otherwise, he may insist upon putting us all in danger by going to Beléchappé himself
when he gets back from Paris. Now, will you help me?"
She held her breath, watching him for further sign of
doubt, but she needn't have worried.

"Aye," he said.

Diana had left him to explain as much as he thought
necessary to the other three sailors and to arrange for
proper clothing for herself and horses for both of
them. At the same time she requested that he learn, as
subtly as possible, the exact location of the Château
Beléchappé. When Darby had returned from Le Havre
without horses but with the information that the château
lay nearly fifteen miles to the west of the city, Diana
had been appalled. Neither of them knew the countryside, which would mean stopping frequently to ask
questions. And even with her command of the language, she had no wish to draw that much attention to
herself. She had a notion that even dressed in the
peasant clothing Darby had procured for her she would
have a difficult time convincing any French peasant
that she was merely another like himself. No doubt her
accent would be wrong, for one thing. She spoke the
French of the nobility, not that of the peasantry. Darby,
too, had been worried.

"I doubt we can do it, m'lady. It be too far."

" 'Tis on the coast, you say?"

"Aye, or as near as makes no difference."

"Then the captain must sail us there. That is the
answer. We will drop anchor offshore, and you and I
will take the skiff, beach it, and go in search of Monsieur Milice, the man I am to meet. Once we have the
material his lordship needs, we shall simply return to
the *Sea Maiden,* and the captain can sail us back to Le
Havre to meet his lordship and the others."

"Aye," Darby said, mulling the notion over in his
head, "it might work that way, but the cap'n be a mite
thick-headed 'bout going counter to 'is lordship's com-

mand, 'n so far I only told 'im ye wanted a bit o' exercise, like what ye said t' me afore ye explained the lot. I'll 'ave t' tell 'im a bit more like, I'm thinkin'."

"Tell him whatever you must, only get him to do what I need done," Diana said fervently.

Darby had returned sometime later with the information that the captain flatly refused to drop anchor anywhere close to Beléchappé. "He says the shoals there be right dangerous, my lady, 'n 'e won't take the responsibility fer either the yacht nor yet the skiff, fer the shore along that bit o' the coast be all rocks and such like. Best 'e can do be t' take us into Deauville, which be 'bout four miles this side, as I reckon."

"Four miles is nothing," Diana had said cheerfully, quickly recovering from the lurching feeling in the pit of her stomach at the thought that the captain would fail them just when her goal seemed within reach. By then the tide was out and on the turn, the captain said, and even if the wind had not been in the wrong quarter, which it was, it would have required a far more foolish seaman than himself to consider taking the yacht out of the harbor and along the unknown shoreline with dusk rapidly coming on.

Diana chafed at the delay, but there was nothing to be done other than to await the morning light. At least by dawn the wind had risen, and the *Sea Maiden,* once her sails had been set, fairly skimmed across the bay, accomplishing the ten-mile journey in little over an hour. The captain had kept the yacht outside the harbor in order to avoid being at the mercy of the tides, and Darby had rowed ashore at once to arrange for horses. Although such arrangements were not so easily accomplished in the smaller village as in Le Havre, he had been successful and now, at last, they were on their way to the chateau.

Riding along the rutted, muddy road at a distance-eating lope, enjoying the caress of the cool breeze against her cheeks, her golden hair breaking free of the bun in which she had tried to confine it, Diana nearly forgot the importance of her journey. It seemed ages since she had felt this sense of freedom. It was possible almost to forget the burly sailor riding behind her, clinging to his saddle.

"Oh, aye," Darby had assured her when she'd asked if he rode. "Brung up on a farm, I was. 'Course, it be a time since I last sat a horse, me lady, but I expect ye don't be fergittin' once ye know how."

When he had clambered awkwardly into his saddle, glaring at his mount with undisguised suspicion as though he expected to be bitten or tossed into the nearest pig sty, Diana had nearly laughed. She controlled her mirth, however, knowing that laughter would humiliate the sailor. Now, she only hoped he wouldn't fall off and that he wouldn't be so sore when they reached Beléchappé as to be useless to her.

Remembering the comte's words about his signet ring, she wondered now how she would convince his erstwhile major domo, Monsieur Milice, to part with the emeralds. For Milice must agree to part with them. Only by returning safely to Le Havre with the emeralds in her possession could she hope to mitigate Simon's fury when he discovered, as he inevitably would, what she had done. By then, surely he would have come to recognize the truth of her warning that Rory would not leave France without the Beléchappé treasure. But even so, she knew him well enough to realize that he was not likely to welcome her assistance with open arms. Indeed, he would be beside himself with fury. But that mattered little if by retrieving the emeralds she had managed to spare them all a difficult time with Lord Roderick. Heaven alone knew what that gentleman might be capable of if pushed far enough. She had seen that look of purpose in his eyes at Alderwood. He would not be swayed from his intended task, certainly not by the brother he had fought one way or another all his life. She knew that under the bitterness and envy he loved Simon, but she was as certain as she could be that he loved Sophie more. And to win her, he needed to retrieve the treasure. To win her he would fight Simon.

She could not let them fight. Such a course would put them all at risk. Indeed, she was assuming, was she not, that Simon would manage to effect a release for Sophie and her mama as well as for Rory in Paris.

What if he failed? But Simon would not fail, she told herself firmly. He had agreed to do what he could. Moreover, Rory would not let him leave Paris without the others. She would spare Simon further confrontation with his brother by getting the emeralds. He would not thank her. Her thoughts had gone full circle again. She caressed her stomach, wondering if the precious burden she carried would protect her against the full force of his wrath, then remembering that Simon himself had said it would not. At least the baby seemed calm this morning. She had not felt at all sick, either on board the *Sea Maiden* or since mounting her horse.

At last the outline of the château appeared on the horizon ahead. They had ridden past fields and an occasional peasant's cottage, but there had been little sign of any real habitation since they had left Deauville. There were open fields, hedgerows as high as her shoulders, and gray alder and oak thickets that would be green and shady in spring. But now the fields were barren, the hedgerows ragged, the trees and shrubbery bare of leaves. Despite the roses Darby had seen growing in Southampton, there was still the look of winter here on these wild, windblown cliffs. Everything seemed drab and gray under the overcast sky, and the château, as they approached nearer, reminded Diana of nothing so much as Maria Edgworth's *Castle Rackrent*. All it lacked were black clouds looming about its graystone turrets, with lightning flashing and thunder booming in the background. She grinned at her fancies and glanced back over her shoulder to assure herself that she still had an escort.

Darby was there, although his face was set and his muscles taut. As she slowed the pace to a trot, she saw him grab his horse's mane in an attempt to stop the jarring of his bones. Taking pity on him, she slowed more till they were walking. He heaved a sigh of relief loud enough for her to hear.

"There is the château," she said cheerfully.

"Aye," he said on a long breath. "Do we just ride up to the front door? Don't look t' me as if there be anybody t' home."

Diana scanned the entryway with a sinking heart. A

dirt road clogged with strawlike weeds led from two huge stone pillars straight to the main entrance of the château. Windows on either side of the entry were covered with weathered boards. Nobody had been home for a long time. No doubt Monsieur Milice lived somewhere else, even perhaps in Deauville. Why had she not thought of the possibility before?

But, no, she told herself firmly. He would know that eventually someone from the family would come to claim the treasure. The comte had called him devoted. Surely he would do nothing to put difficulties in the way of whoever came for the emeralds. She touched her mount's flank with her spur and gestured for Darby to follow. There must be a way to find the old servant. They would start at the château.

From all she could discover, it was entirely deserted. A pathway of sorts led off toward the cliffs from a rear entrance. Following it as it wound through one of the alder thickets, she came upon a stable, long disused. But beyond the stable there was a cottage with smoke drifting from its chimney. Diana gestured for Darby to remain where he was and slipped down from her saddle.

She found it necessary to pound upon the door before she heard any sound from within, but finally there was a creaking and a shuffling of footsteps and the door opened to reveal a tiny, ancient woman wearing a shapeless black dress with a once-white kerchief wrapped around gray hair above a face that looked like a withered apple. Diana quickly explained that she was looking for Monsieur Milice, who had once been major domo at the château. The woman continued to stare at her through faded blue eyes, and Diana wondered if the dialect in this part of France was totally different from the French she was so proud of. Then the woman put a hand up to cup her ear.

"Eh?"

Breathing a sigh of relief, Diana shouted, "Monsieur Milice!"

"*Il est mort,*" said the old woman, shutting the door.

Diana felt the wind go out of her. Standing on the little stone stoop, she looked back at Darby. "She says he's dead."

"Well, then, that be it, 'n there'll be the devil t' pay."

The muscles in her jaw tightened. She couldn't simply go back. Rory wouldn't accept Monsieur Milice's death as the end to everything, and neither could she. Diana turned back to the cottage door and pounded on it again, this time in anger and frustration as much as to draw attention. The shuffling noise sounded again, and the little old woman opened the door. She stared at Diana as she had done before.

"*Sa famille!*" Diana shouted. "*Où est la famille de Milice?*"

After a small hesitation during which the old woman continued to stare at Diana, she gestured to the right. "*Là-bas.*" She shut the door again.

"Talkative sort, ain't she?" Darby said, smiling when Diana returned to her horse.

"She said enough, I hope," Diana replied, leading her horse to a nearby stump so that she could mount. Darby hadn't offered to assist her, and she wasn't at all sure he would be able to get back on his own horse if he did. He looked every inch a battered man. Once in the saddle again, she said, "Down there. It looks as if there's a path through the thicket, and it leads downhill. Come along, Darby."

She led the way, and found the thicket overgrown but not enough to impede their progress. The pathway had the appearance of having been used by foot travelers rather than those on horseback, but it was passable. Ten minutes later they emerged into a clearing. In the center was another cottage that might have been cast from the same mold as the old woman's. The thatch was moldy, black in patches, and the ground around the tiny cottage was hard-packed dirt with puddles of assorted sizes and patches of bent straw that looked as if snow had lain upon it fairly recently. Again, just as at the old woman's, smoke came from the chimney, but here the smoke was thicker as if the fire inside burned more heartily.

Diana slid down from her saddle, but this time Darby followed suit, coming to stand beside her.

"I don't like this place, m'lady," he said quietly.

"Nonsense," Diana replied, but she spoke in the same tone. There was a feeling about the clearing, about the cottage for that matter, that she could not place. She was near the treasure. That must be what she felt. "This is only a peasant's cottage, Darby," she said, hoping she sounded more confident that she felt. "I daresay the best we can hope to come by here is information. Surely, you don't fear a French peasant or two."

"Seems to me them French peasants was what begun that there Revolution hereabouts, m'lady," Darby said, frowning. "Don't hurt t' keep a weather eye peeled. Didn't think rightly back there, bein' glad to make journey's end, so t' speak, 'r I'd a paid more heed. Lucky it were just one old crone."

"I'm sure that's all we'll find here, too. Probably Milice's wife and maybe a child or two, is all. That old crone, as you call her, didn't precisely give me a full description of his family when I asked her about them."

Darby chuckled. "She were a one, right enough, but I'll jest come along o' ye now, mistress."

She didn't argue with him but turned to approach the stone stoop. Hearing someone singing inside, she knocked on the door with less fervor than she had knocked on the old woman's. The singing stopped, and a moment later a young woman near Diana's own age opened the door. She wore an apron over a laced bodice and full skirt very like the ones Diana wore under her cloak. The young woman's hands were dusty with flour. She wiped them carefully on her apron.

"*Oui, madame?*"

"Good day," said Diana in the same language. "I seek the family of Monsieur Milice."

"I am Pétrie Milice," said the young woman, frowning slightly. "My father, he is dead for a long time. Also, my mother," she added conscientiously.

"I am sorry your father is dead," Diana said, "for I have come a great distance to speak with him. I come from the Comte de Vieillard."

The young woman frowned. Her lips formed a tight, straight line. "Do you indeed, madame?"

Diana grimaced. This was not going to be easy. Still, she was safe enough. Looking past Pétrie Milice, she noticed dough on a floured board sitting upon a long wooden table. "You are making bread," she said conversationally. "I do not wish to inconvenience you. Perhaps, if my man remains outside, you would allow me to come in and speak with you while you work. There is much to explain, and I hope you will agree to help me."

Pétrie Milice looked at Darby. The sailor's cheeks turned rosy and he looked away. The young woman's lips twitched. "You may come inside, madame. It is true, the bread must be kneaded. My brother is away to Deauville, but he will return tomorrow and he will want his bread."

Diana nodded to Darby, who moved away, patting the dagger in his belt as if to say he would protect them both. Then she followed Pétrie Milice inside, glancing around with interest. The cottage consisted of the one room only, but it was neat and tidy, the furnishings plain but serviceable. The young woman was not an ordinary peasant girl, for her accent was cultured. She had been trained to speak her language well, no doubt, Diana decided, by her father. The news of a brother alarmed her, for she had been hoping that the girl would be able to tell her what she needed to know. It was quite possible, however, that she would not know the answers to Diana's questions. The information might have been passed on only to the son. Nonetheless, Diana had to try. She watched, fascinated, as Pétrie Milice turned her attention to the thick lump of brown dough on the long table. The muscles in her forearms rippled with each turn and push, as she kneaded with a practiced rhythm.

"Talk, madame. I am listening."

"Very well. I come from the comte, as I said. I do not know how to convince you of that fact," Diana added honestly, "nor how to make you trust me. All I ask is that you listen to what I say. It is of prodigious importance that you help me. Mademoiselle Sophie's life and that of madame la comtesse may well depend upon your helping me." She paused, regarding the young woman carefully to see if she was making any impression.

Pétrie continued to knead her bread.

"I know you expect someone who carries the comte's signet," Diana said frankly.

There was expression in the girl's gray-green eyes now. They widened slightly. But she was cautious. "I do not know of what you speak, madame. Of what concern to me would be monseigneur's signet ring?"

Diana took a step toward her, but when a flicker of fear crossed the other's face, she backed away again, taking a seat upon one of the room's straight-backed chairs. Its woven straw seat gave comfortably beneath her. She leaned forward intently. "Please Mademoiselle Milice, you must trust me. Other lives, possibly even your own, depend upon it. Monsieur le comte told me about the emeralds. He explained to me that they had been entrusted to your father, who was his major domo, that your father was to surrender them only to one who came for them bearing monsieur le comte's signet. My husband's brother, who is in love with Mademoiselle Sophie, carries the signet. Unfortunately, he, mademoiselle, and madame la comtesse have all been arrested. My husband goes now to effect their release."

The young woman continued her kneading, but Diana was certain now that she was listening. More than that, she had been shocked by the news of the arrest. Diana built upon that shock, insisting that no matter how successful Simon was in his endeavors, the danger remained to them all because of the emeralds.

"My husband discounts their importance," she said. "He does not intend to allow my brother-in-law or Mademoiselle Sophie to come for them. But others will come if they do not," she added quickly. "The Vidame de Lâche"—Pétrie Milice winced—"knows of them, but he does not have his father's trust."

"I remember him, that one," said Petrie. "A hateful little boy, cruel and deceitful. One who tells not the truth. My father said he would come."

Diana expelled a breath of relief. Pétrie Milice knew about the emeralds. She had not been certain before, but she was now. The girl had merely gone on with her kneading, reacting little, as though she were only hearing an interesting fairy tale, until Diana had mentioned the vidame. But now Pétrie admitted she had expected someone to come.

"The comte," Diana said carefully, "does not trust his

son. He is afraid he will give the emeralds to Napoleon Bonaparte in exchange for Château Beléchappé. The comte believes Bonaparte will agree to the trade, but that he will then take the emeralds and de Lâche will be heard from no more."

Pétrie nodded. "Not a bad thing, that."

Diana had made an error. She recognized the fact immediately, but nothing she said seemed to make any impression. She continued, nonetheless, while Pétrie wiped lard around the inside of an iron pot, then set her dough inside it to rise, covering it with a damp cloth. Diana continued to argue, calmly, matter-of-factly, and to no avail. Pétrie offered her a cup of coffee, and she accepted, hoping to build trust by simple things. She talked of her childhood, of her husband—making him sound even to her own ears like a knight from a fairy tale—and of her long journey after hearing all the comte had had to tell her.

"You are English," Pétrie said at one point, as though the phrase explained many things.

"And you are French," said Diana with a smile. "Our countries have warred with one another, but now they are at peace."

"My brother says the peace will not last."

"My husband says the same thing," Diana acknowledged, "but you and I, we are not at war. We want peace, not violence. But the emeralds will lead to violence, Pétrie."

Darby knocked on the door some moments after that, asking how much longer she intended to be. "Cap'n will git t' worryin', m'lady."

"I cannot go without what I came for," she said in English. "I cannot come so far for nothing. A little more time, Darby, I beg you."

"Right enough, m'lady. I'll jest take a turn o' the watch, as they say. The birds 'ave gorn all silent. Mebbe a storm brewin'." He glanced at the sky. "I'd 'a thought them clouds was a mite too high fer it, but ye never know wi' the weather. Best we git back soon."

She nodded, shutting the door on him and returning to her chair. Pétrie was bent over the fire, banking it so that only coals were left. She lifted the cover from the iron pot, poked an exploratory finger into the round mound of dough peeking over the rim, and nodded her satisfaction.

"*Bien.*"

Diana watched as the young woman carefully set the pot, covered now with an iron lid, into a clear space she had made among the coals. The coals were stacked in hills surrounding the pot, but there was an airspace. None actually touched the pot. So that was how one made bread without an oven, Diana thought. Not, she admitted silently, that she knew how to bake bread *with* an oven, but all the same . . .

"Pétrie, I beg of you," she said when the woman turned from completing her task, "you must help me. Where are the emeralds?"

Pétrie Milice straightened her shoulders, letting her gaze meet Diana's directly. "I regret to have to say, madame, that I cannot be of assistance. I know of no emeralds."

"But you said—"

"I regret, madame," she repeated, finality in her tone. "I will tell my brother of your visit to me when he returns. I will tell him all you have said to me. More than this I cannot do." She took off her apron and shook her dark blue skirts. Then her gaze returned to Diana's face. "You will return, madame. Perhaps you will conduct to this cottage your good brother with the so important ring," she added softly, suggestively.

Diana, feeling victory sliding away before she had even touched it, nearly groaned in dismay. "You cannot have been attending," she said desperately. Lord, she thought, Simon would kill her. She couldn't go back empty-handed. The captain would never dare conceal this escapade from his master. She didn't even have any money left with which to bribe him. She had given her last groat to Darby to purchase her clothes. For that matter, she couldn't even expect Darby to keep silent, although he would very likely reap disaster from his assistance to her. She had to make Pétrie Milice understand the urgency of the situation. "Please, Pétrie—"

"I regret, madame," was all the young woman would say. Her face had closed in, as though she feared to give information by her very expression. Her features now were stony. She averted her eyes.

"My brother cannot come here. It would be to risk his life. Others want the treasure. Can't you understand that?"

"I very much hope," said a smooth voice behind Diana, "that Mademoiselle Milice understands that fact very well, else it will perhaps be her own life that is at risk."

Pétrie Milice gave a cry of dismay and clapped a hand to her mouth, and Diana whirled, coming face to face with a tall, narrow-faced man wearing a black chapeau bras, a dark green jacket, buckskin breeches, tan gloves, and black topboots with a long, golden velvet, double-caped cloak over all. He stood in the open doorway, and beyond him, senseless on the hard ground, lay Darby.

The man turned, his gaze following Diana's, and when he turned back, he drew a lace-edged handkerchief from his jacket pocket and dabbed at his lips with it. "I regret the inconvenience to your servant," he said, still in that thick-liquid tone. He lifted the quizzing glass that hung on a black ribbon about his neck and surveyed her insolently from head to toe. "Very beautiful. I confess that although I have heard a great deal about you, *madame des frédaines*, which made me long for closer acquaintance, I cannot for the moment recall whether or not we have been formally introduced." The quizzing glass shifted toward Pétrie, and the voice went on, "I am certain, however, from the expression on her lovely face that Mademoiselle Milice retains pleasant memories of my younger self. Do you not, my dear little cabbage?" He paused, then shook his head in mock sadness. "You do not answer, Pétrie? Never mind, you will answer all my questions presently, will you not?" He turned away from the wide-eyed, trembling girl and bowed elaborately to Diana. "Bertrand Beléchappé, Vidame de Lâche, at your service, Lady Andover."

14

Diana had recognized de Lâche at once, but shock held her speechless. As she collected her wits, her first thought was for Simon. Where was he? Did he know that de Lâche was no longer either at Versailles or in Paris? For that matter, would he even think about de Lâche, or consider his disappearance important? Simon had discounted the importance of the Beléchappé treasure, had he not? Not that any of that mattered now. He was not really, after all, the knight on a white charger that she envisioned from time to time. He couldn't help them now.

She faced the tall, thin man squarely, noting for the first time that he wore a sword beneath his golden cloak. The expression in her eyes was one of glacial contempt.

"You waste your time, Monsieur de Lâche," she said, hoping she sounded more like the haughty Lady Jersey than like the twittering Lady Sarah Fane. "Mademoiselle Milice does not possess the knowledge you seek. Her brother holds the key to your fortune, and he does not return from Deauville until tomorrow."

Pétrie's eyes widened a little at Diana's tone, and she licked her lips nervously, but she did not take her gaze from de Lâche.

He was watching Diana. "You were most foolish to come to this place, madame," he said smoothly. "Indeed, I cannot think why you have come, unless perhaps my father entrusted his ring to your keeping. I had thought the so charming Lord Roderick Warrington carried it, but my friends could not find it when they searched him, so perhaps I was wrong."

Diana's face blanched. "Lord Roderick? You have seen him?"

"Indeed, he came to Paris demanding madame, my mother's, release. Also, that of my sister. The First Consul ordered him clapped up for his insolence."

"But he lives," Diana said tightly. "Tell me he lives, monsieur."

De Lâche hesitated, and she felt her stomach knot in fear that he would tell her Rory had been killed by the dreadful Bonaparte. But then the man smiled. His upper teeth were crooked, she noted absently before giving herself a shake and demanding that he answer her question.

"He lives, madame. At least, I trust he does. I lost sight of him on the road just before reaching Louviers. I had thought perchance to find him here."

"Here! On the road? Then Bonaparte has released him?"

"He escaped," de Lâche said with an odd look. "Was that not so very clever of him?"

Something in his tone, as well as the strange expression, warned Diana. "He would not have left your mother and sister," she said slowly.

"Oh, indeed not. Did I neglect to mention that the so clever Lord Roderick effected an escape for all of them? Most brilliant, it was, I am sure, though I myself was not privileged to be a witness to his cleverness. I, too, was a prisoner, you see. I was not released until it was reported that the three of them were quite outside the city of Paris on the Le Havre road." He smirked.

"I see how it was," Diana said, regarding him with disgust. "The French know all about the emeralds, do they not? Your father was right to mistrust you, monsieur. You do not know where the treasure lies hidden, but your mother does, so it was arranged for her to escape in hopes that she would lead you to it. But if you were following them, how is it that you happened upon this cottage? We have seen no one."

"Ah, bah," he said, "I know this country well, madame, for I rode all over it in my childhood before the terrors began. Though it was possible until now that the emeralds rested elsewhere than at Beléchappé, it was obvious when the good Roderick and the others disappeared in Louviers that they were indeed heading for the château and not to Le Havre, which is the nearest port and the most likely place for them to seek passage to England, or to any other city. My mother knows the country well, also, but she is merely a woman, and therefore weak. It was no great accomplishment, once I had lost sight of them, to ride cross country to the château."

"But why to this cottage?" she demanded. If Rory and the two women were on their way, they could not be far behind this despicable creature. The longer she could keep him talking, the better chance she and Pétrie had for rescue. "Did you go to the château first?"

"It is boarded up, as you must have seen for yourself," he replied, "however, his lordship is not the only clever one in this world. I found our old cook living behind the stables, and once she had told me who among our old retainers had chosen to remain here on the estate, it was no great mental feat to deduce that my parents must have entrusted the emeralds to the so estimable Milice. And I do not believe for a moment," he added, turning now to face the trembling Pétrie, "that mademoiselle there does not know precisely where they are to be found."

"I do not!" she cried. "I swear I do not."

"Swearing to a falsehood will do naught but ensure you a place in hell, my dear," he said in that same smooth voice. "Times have been troubled hereabouts and are likely to become more so. I doubt your respected parent would have entrusted his knowledge to only one of his children." He stepped toward her, the look on his face menacing enough to make her draw back toward the hearth.

"Leave her, monsieur," Diana said, attempting to maintain her calm. "I have talked with this poor girl for some time, and I am convinced that she knows nothing about the treasure. You will simply have to await her brother's coming."

De Lâche glanced over his shoulder, but Diana realized he was paying no heed to her. He was looking out the open door to where Darby still lay, unmoving. De

Lâche closed the door, then moved again toward Pétrie. When she tried to elude him, he grabbed her arm, shrugging his cloak back over his right shoulder as he did so.

"We waste time," he said. "Precious time. The others may be slow, but they will come. It will be more convenient for me if I am gone before that time. I'm sure you comprehend the matter, mademoiselle." He pulled Pétrie toward him, and when she merely turned her face away, his expression changed to one of rage so quickly that the transformation startled Diana. His other hand shot out to grab the girl's shoulder, and he shook her cruelly. "You will tell me. At once!"

"I cannot!" she cried. "The ring! You do not bring the ring, nor does madame. Monsieur le comte said only to him who brings the ring!" She struggled in his grasp, and Diana could see by her expression that de Lâche was hurting her.

"Let her go!" She rushed forward, grabbing de Lâche's arm and attempting to pull him away from the struggling girl. He shrugged her off, and in doing so, flipped his cloak back from his other shoulder, revealing his sword. Diana lunged, managing to get her fingertips on the hilt before he let go of Pétrie long enough to slam the back of his left hand against her cheek, knocking her away. Stumbling, trying to catch herself, Diana grabbed for the back of a chair, but her knees threatened to give way beneath her, and her breath came in ragged sobs.

De Lâche now had his hand entangled in Pétrie's hair and was forcing her to her knees. "You are at my mercy," he growled, all trace of the smooth facade gone now, leaving only a mask of fury. "Consider that fact carefully before you continue in your foolish stubbornness. You gave yourself away by admitting you await the ring." Tears welled in her eyes, and when he gave a harsh twist with the hand holding her hair, she cried out sharply. "Remember when we were children, Pétrie? Remember?" When she only sobbed, he jerked her head back and slapped her.

Gathering herself together, Diana leapt forward again, determined to put a stop to de Lâche's cruelty. She

grabbed his cloak this time, yanking hard, but the strings
holding it at his throat, instead of choking him as she
had hoped, broke free. The cloak fell to the floor in a
swirl of golden velvet, landing with a muffled thump.

De Lâche hardly seemed to have noticed the interruption. After he'd slapped her, Pétrie had begun to
struggle in earnest, and he was having all he could do
to control her. When he slapped her again, Diana moved
past them to the hearth, catching up the cloth with
which Pétrie had covered her rising dough and reaching in over the coals to the iron pot. With swift, sure
motions, using the cloth to protect her hand, she snatched
up the heavy iron lid and turned, scarcely taking the
time to aim properly before she launched it at him.
The hot, heavy lid caught him just beneath his ear,
where the folds of his neckcloth provided protection.
But the force of the blow staggered him nonetheless
and when he automatically reached up to catch hold of
the thing that had assaulted him, he yelped in pain and
let it fall to the floor, releasing Pétrie and turning on
Diana.

Looking swiftly about for another weapon, she noticed for the first time the slim iron poker resting in a
crevice to the left of the fireplace where the stones met
the wall of the cottage. Seconds later, with the weapon
in hand, she faced de Lâche.

"Do not attempt to touch me, monsieur. I should not
hesitate to use this."

He shook his head. "You are no match for me, madame. That weapon is but a child's toy. Put it down."
He moved closer, keeping one eye on Pétrie as she
staggered to her feet, the other on the poker, as though
he would judge the exact moment of Diana's swing.

Instead, she stepped backward, shouting, "Darby, *à
moi, à moi!*" then, "Help me!" when she realized she
had shouted in French to a man who spoke only the
King's English. A gasp of relief leapt to her throat
when she heard the sounds of someone coming toward
the cottage, and she heard de Lâche mutter a curse
even as he lunged toward her and jerked the poker
from her hand. Tossing it to his left hand, he reached
for the hilt of his sword with his right as he turned

toward the opening door. The man who burst through it was not Darby, however, but Lord Roderick Warrington, and not the dapper figure Diana was accustomed to seeing, but a man who looked as though he could well do with a night's sleep and a change of clothes.

"Diana!" he shouted. "Are you all right?"

"Look out, Rory!" she screamed.

But he had already seen the menace confronting him, and before de Lâche's sword could clear its scabbard, Lord Roderick had flung himself on the man, knocking the poker away. It rattled across the floor, coming to rest against the far wall. But de Lâche was quick. Having lost the poker, he likewise abandoned his attempt to free his sword, and met the larger man's attack head on, taking a step backward, and falling to the floor, letting Lord Roderick's momentum carry him in an awkward somersault across the floor to career into the table upon which Pétrie had kneaded her bread. Rory turned like a cat, getting his feet under him again just as de Lâche, who had been scrabbling among the folds of his velvet cloak, brought his right hand up, holding a pistol.

Pétrie screamed, and Diana's breath caught painfully in her throat.

"I think you must cede this little game to me now," de Lâche said in English.

"When pigs fly," snarled Lord Roderick, launching himself again. This time he brought de Lâche down and the two men struggled desperately. Rory's elbow shot forward with a crack of flesh against bone, but there was a muffled explosion at the same time. He gave a cry of pain and slumped to one side, holding his left hand against his right shoulder and breathing heavily. "My God, the devil shot me," he gasped before his muscles relaxed and he collapsed.

With a grunt de Lâche extricated himself from under his unconscious victim. He rubbed his reddening jaw briefly, then leaned back down to turn Rory over, searching swiftly through the pockets of his jacket. "So he did have it, after all," he said, seconds later, as he peered at the gold, carved ring resting in the palm of his hand. He held it out to Pétrie. "Here you are, my dear. Get the emeralds, if you please, unless you wish to watch me dispatch madame, the Countess of Andover, to her Maker. I have no wish to waste my time further over this matter."

Rory groaned, and without a thought for her own danger, Diana rushed to kneel beside him. Blood oozed from between his fingers, and she knew the bullet was still lodged within his shoulder. She could smell burnt powder as she leaned nearer to him. "Rory! My lord, do you hear me?"

He groaned again. His eyelids flickered, then opened, and she breathed a sigh of relief. He grinned. "Did you think me sped?"

"Aye." She looked about for something to stanch the seepage of blood.

"Leave him," de Lâche ordered. "Where is my respected mother, monsieur?"

"Outside," Rory told him bitterly. "In the thicket. You'll find them easily enough, I daresay. Do you mean to kill us?"

"There is no need for that," de Lâche said, not meeting his steady gaze. "I'm for Paris once I have the emeralds." They had been speaking English, but now he turned to a bewildered, frightened Pétrie, adding in French, "Get them, damn you!"

She glanced at the wounded Rory, and he nodded, grimacing. "Get them," he said in the same language. "Too many lives at risk. Thank you, Diana," he added with a small gasp as she attempted to stanch the oozing blood with the same cloth she had earlier used to hold the pot lid. She had ignored de Lâche's order to leave Rory, vowing silently that he would have to kill her to keep her from doing what she could to help her brother-in-law. She looked up now as Pétrie took a step away from de Lâche.

"It is no use threatening me, monsieur," the girl said slowly. "I cannot give you the emeralds at once."

"What the devil do you mean by that?" he demanded fiercely. "Where are they?"

"There," she replied simply, pointing to the hearth. They all stared at the fireplace, filled with red hot coals, emanating heat that could be felt throughout the little room. De Lâche gave a sound like an angry growl.

"Beneath the hearth?"

She nodded.

"Then get them."

"The fire will have to cool first," she said placidly.

"The devil it will. If there's not enough room to shovel those coals aside, then empty out that pot and fill it with as many as it will hold. Dump them outside and come back for more. It won't take those stones long to cool once the coals are gone. Move, damn you!"

With a fatalistic shrug, Pétrie obeyed him, turning her halfbaked loaf of bread out onto a wooden rack on the table and moving steadily but with no undue haste. Diana smiled sadly at the girl's great show of dignity and wished she could think the slow pace would avail them some advantage. But there was no one to help them now unless the captain of the *Sea Maiden* worried enough to send someone to find out what was keeping them. And he, she decided, was just as likely to get the wind up for worrying about Simon's orders, and take the *Sea Maiden* back to Le Havre. Of course, Simon had quite possibly reached Paris by now, and might know of the "escape" but no matter how much she wished he were here at her side, there had not yet been time for him to make the return trip.

De Lâche moved to the door, opening it to step outside and shout, "Mama, Sophie!" A moment later, two women emerged hesitantly from the thicket and moved toward the cottage, the elder frowning slightly as though she did not believe her eyes, the younger allowing her pretty mouth to drop open and then hurrying forward to demand that de Lâche tell her whether he had indeed been arrested as they had been in Paris and, if so, how he had managed to escape.

Diana's eyes met Rory's. "You didn't tell them of your suspicions?"

His lips tightened. "I had no proof. All I was able to discover before I was arrested myself was that they had been taken. De Lâche, too, supposedly. That was a hum, of course. A neat little trap they set for us. We escaped through what seemed to be the rarest of chances, but with no way to help him. Then we found a farmer willing to hide us in his hay wagon and carry us to Le Havre. We said nothing to him, of course, about this place. When the comtesse said we'd make better time on horseback and that she had friends outside Louviers, we just slipped out of the wagon, not wanting anyone to be able to tell any soldiers who might follow that the man driving the wagon had known we were in his hay.

"De Lâche said he was not released until it was known you were outside Paris, and that he lost you in Louviers," Diana said quickly. "If he was following you, he must have known about the hay wagon."

"It took us a while to get the horses," Rory said slowly. "If our farmer was part of the plot, that's when he discovered our absence and informed de Lâche."

The voices outside had stopped, and Diana looked away from Rory to see that the women had noticed Darby, hitherto hidden from their sight by an outcropping of the thicket. He was attempting now to stagger to his feet, holding his head and looking sick. The women moved to help him, and de Lâche told them to hurry, his tone curt. Diana saw his sister look at him quizzically.

Mademoiselle Sophie Beléchappé, despite her sojourn in prison, was an appealing young woman with baby-soft brown curls clustered about a velvety, pink-cheeked face. She was small and rounded, wearing a dark cloak over a crumpled green woolen gown that had seen better days and that was totally unsuited to riding, and when she tilted her head now to look at her brother, she reminded Diana more of a child than of a woman. But moments later, when the others entered the room, Sophie's gaze came immediately to rest upon Lord Roderick, and her gentle brown eyes blazed with sudden shock.

"M'lord!" she cried, rushing to kneel at his side. "Oh, heavens, m'lord, what has befallen you?"

He reached out with his good arm to touch her face. " 'Tis naught," he said quietly. "Fortunately your brother has not my skill with a pistol."

"Bertrand!" She turned to glare angrily at her brother. "You did this to him? You!"

"Silence," de Lâche said harshly. "He will live. You must understand, Sophie, that his wound is as nothing compared to regaining Beléchappé. The emeralds will secure it to our family once again."

"You are a fool, Bertrand," said the woman who had entered behind Sophie. There was sadness in her eyes and distaste, as well. She was nearly as tall as her son and thin, too, but she carried herself with great dignity. Although her clothing was as mussed as her daughter's, madame la Comtesse de Vieillard stood as regally as though she wore smooth satin and ruffled lace instead of creased and muddied sarcenet beneath a muddied woolen cloak. Her dark hair, free of any sign of gray, was neatly confined in a frilled snood at the back of her head. Diana decided she was perhaps in her late forties, but it was hard to guess age when one was fascinated by the sharp, elegant features of madame's noble countenance and the intelligence in her fine gray eyes. "To think," Madame de Vieillard said in a full, melodious voice that seemed to fill the little cottage, "that your respected father had the right of it, that I spawned one who would actually seek to ally himself with that pig in Paris."

"Be silent," de Lâche said, glaring at her much as a child would who has had his fun spoiled. "You know nothing at all about the matter."

"You would give away your sister's dowry for nothing," she said. "Indeed, I believe now, though I did not wish to comprehend your behavior at Versailles, that you would have sacrificed your sister's honor to your cause."

He would not look at her. Instead, his temper flashed again and he ordered them all to sit, pushing Darby, who still clutched at his head, toward the hearth, where Pétrie had turned her attention from the new arrivals once more to her half-hearted business with the coals. "Find some rope," de Lâche ordered the sailor in English. "You will tie these people up with good sailor's knots, and if they persist in speaking you will gag them."

"Wha' did ye do wi' me dagger, ye bastard?" muttered Darby thickly. "I'd like t' kill ye fer this knot on me 'ead, I would."

"No doubt, but I tossed your little knife into the shrubbery, so you'd do better to do as I told you."

De Lâche had dropped the empty gun on the table, and Diana realized that he had no more bullets on his person. But he still wore his sword, and she was nearly certain there was nothing she could do to disarm him. She could have kicked herself for not thinking to retrieve the poker while he was engaged outside. She glanced quickly around the room. Rory and Darby were incapacitated, but perhaps if all four women were to attack de Lâche at once, they might be able to overcome his superior strength. At that moment, however, de Lâche signaled Darby, who had found a roll of crude twine, to tie her first, and Diana had nothing to do but glare at them both in frustrated silence.

There was only enough of the twine to tie their arms. When de Lâche indicated that Darby should next tie the comtesse, he explained smoothly that he was taking precautions to protect them from any rash action they might choose to take against him.

"I do not want anyone to get hurt," he said. "Do not bother with his lordship, man," he said, still in English, when Darby moved as one only half awake to tie Lord Roderick. "There is too little string, and he will cause me no difficulty. Not with his right arm incapacitated as it is." When all the women but Pétrie were tied and pushed down to sit upon the floor against the wall opposite the hearth, de Lâche took the remaining twine from the sailor, broke it in half, forced him to turn around, and bound his hands behind him like the others. Then he pushed him to the floor near Lord Roderick. "I am desolated to rush you, mademoiselle," he said then to Pétrie, "but if you have not placed those emeralds in my keeping within a space of five minutes, you will sorely regret the fact."

Pétrie looked at him, decided he meant what he said, and scraped the rest of the coals to one side. Then, fetching the poker from the floor by the wall, where it had landed when Rory knocked it from de Lâche's hands, she inserted the pointed end between two of the stones on the blackened floor of the hearth. Pushing downward, she pried one stone loose. It was much thicker than one might have expected it to be, and more time was required to work it free. She then pried up one more, revealing a deep space more than a foot square.

Pétrie gestured toward the opening. "The jewels are within, monsieur. Shall I remove them, or do you wish to do so yourself?"

"Get them," he ordered. His voice grated as though he no longer had much control over it, and his excitement was nearly tangible in that small room. The others watched silently as Pétrie, using her apron to protect her hands, knelt down, reached into the black hole, and drew out a square, gray marble box. Setting it upon the floor in front of her, she touched it experimentally with a bare fingertip, then lifted the lid. But when she would have removed the contents, de Lâche stepped forward. "Get over with the others," he said harshly.

Obediently, Pétrie moved away. Diana saw the girl's eyes drift toward the poker, which she had propped up against the stones of the fireplace. As de Lâche knelt swiftly beside the marble box, Pétrie reached for the poker, only to shriek with pain when de Lâche, striking like a viper, clamped a hand of steel around her wrist.

"Oh, no," he said softly. "Not with the end in view, my dear." With a vicious twist he sent her reeling toward the others, then plunged his hand into the marble box and removed a dark cloth bag. Diana half expected it to crumble at his touch, but it did not. Opening the bag, he withdrew an ornate necklace. The stones were dull-looking, needing to be cleaned, but when he rubbed one or two against the sleeve of his coat, the glowing green of the emeralds could easily be seen. There were other stones in the bag, but de Lâche was satisfied. He replaced the necklace. The comtesse sighed but did not speak.

De Lâche got to his feet and, with the last bit of twine, tied Pétrie's hands behind her. Then he picked up his cloak, slipped the bag of jewels into a spacious pocket in the lining, and swirled the cloak up and over his shoulders. His fingers moved automatically to the tiestrings, and when he realized they were broken, his gaze came to rest upon Diana. There could be no doubt of his annoyance, but she could not repress a saucy grin. He shifted his look to Pétrie.

"You have made difficulties for me once too often, my dear," he said. His tone was milky smooth again. "I have no time to attend to you now, but quite soon, when I am in favor in Paris, I shall have all the opportunity I require to deal with you as you deserve."

The girl bit her lip, but the comtesse was unimpressed. "When you are in favor in Paris," she repeated sarcastically. "Regard, my son, the likelihood that you will find that favor at the feet of Madame la Guillotine. You soil the honor of Beléchappé. I spit upon you."

The vidame laughed. "Take care, madame. In half an hour, perhaps a little more, the soldiers will come. You will be glad then, when you are charged with crimes against the state and with escaping from prison, to remind them of your relationship to me. You speak to the next Comte de Vieillard, you know, and I doubt I shall now have to await my so respected father's demise before that honor becomes mine." He picked up his pistol from the table and slipped it into another pocket in the cloak, then with a last glance around the room, he made a cocky gesture of farewell and pulled open the door, only to stop stock still upon the threshold, all his muscles tensing in shock beneath the velvet cloak.

"Well, well, what have we here?" inquired the Earl of Andover gently, adding when de Lâche took a step backward, "Nay, nay, my friend, do not retreat. I see that the cottage is already a trifle crowded, and dark, as well. I prefer to discuss certain matters with you in the light of day."

"We have nothing to discuss, my lord," said de Lâche, "not when I have nearly reached my goal. Not you, not anyone, can stop me now." He shrugged off his cloak and reached for his sword.

"As you wish," said Simon as gently as before. Then, in a louder voice, he called, "Rory!"

"Here," shouted his twin. "Speed the devil to his

own, Simon. He had the dashed effrontery to put a bullet through my best coat, and incidentally, through my shoulder, as well."

Diana, who had gasped at the sound of Simon's voice, barely stopped herself from calling his name and shrank instead a little closer to her brother-in-law, grateful that he had not mentioned her presence. Simon's anger with de Lâche over the wounding of his twin would be as nothing to his anger if he knew Diana was inside the cottage as well. And she knew that while a little anger might serve to give a man an edge, too much could blind him to his work. When that work was swordplay . . .

She could not see Simon now, but she watched de Lâche step from the cottage, his sword held loosely yet purposefully in his hand. Then she glanced at Rory. His lips were drawn together in a tight line. The sound of steel on steel rang out, and Diana closed her eyes, biting her lower lip. Her heart seemed to leap into her throat. She knew Simon had a formidable reputation as a swordsman, but that knowledge did little to assuage her fears.

"Simon will win," said Lord Roderick softly beside her, interrupting her tense thoughts. Sophie, on the other side of him, seemed perfectly relaxed, content to be where she was, looking not at all as though her brother's fate concerned her. The comtesse, too, maintained her calm dignity. Only Pétrie betrayed excitement. Her eyes were alight, and despite her tied hands, she managed to get to her feet and moved to the doorway to watch. Diana, unable to stand the suspense, tried awkwardly to clamber to her feet too. "No, Diana," Rory said, "he mustn't see you."

"I know, and he won't," she said grimly, "but I must see him. I cannot bear not seeing."

He said nothing further, and she made her way carefully to Pétrie, keeping behind the girl but positioning herself so that she could see the action outside. Tensely she watched as the two men danced backward and forward in the muddy clearing, their swords crossing and recrossing with nerve-jangling swiftness, the blades ringing together, then disengaging with a metallic, grinding sound that chilled her teeth. At first Simon seemed to be moving always backward, his sword meeting de Lâche's wherever it chanced to dart, parrying each stroke as it came but returning no thrusts of its own. Then, suddenly, just when she had begun to wonder if Rory could be wrong, if de Lâche might be the better swordsman, there was a noticeable change in the rhythmic pace of the clanging swords. The sounds came faster. And Simon was no longer defensive. He had changed his stance slightly and was thrusting with a quickness and precision she had not seen before. And now de Lâche was retreating, his steps not so agile as they had been before, his swordplay heavier handed.

He slipped suddenly, and she saw Simon shorten his thrust, letting the other man regain his balance. But when de Lâche, with a murderous look on his face, lunged immediately forward, Simon raised his wrist to the height of his face and, with a swiftness and agility that made the other man's moves seem clumsy by comparison, deftly turned the oncoming thrust aside and plunged his blade into de Lâche's breast. The thin man's eyes widened in shock, and he crumpled to the ground.

Diana realized she had been holding her breath and let it out in a long whistling sigh. She wiped clammy hands against her skirt.

Beside her Pétrie murmured, "Magnificent. He is a man, that one."

At the same moment, Diana saw Simon turn toward the cottage. Involuntarily, she stepped backward toward the hearth, but there was no escape. Seconds later, his large figure filled the doorway.

He glanced about quickly, blinking. It was darker in the cottage than outside, so it took a moment for his eyes to adjust. When they did, he was looking at his twin, but his gaze shifted immediately to the comtesse, then to Sophie, and then, at last, it came to rest upon Diana. Their glances seemed to collide, then to lock together, and she licked her lips, feeling her courage desert her as she watched his face go white with shock and fury.

15

To Diana's surprise, Simon didn't say a word to her. Instead, with what appeared to be a wrenching effort, he turned to Lord Roderick. "How badly are you hurt?" he asked tersely.

"My shoulder aches like the devil," his twin replied. "Like I said before, there's a damned bullet lodged in it. More to the point, however, de Lâche said there were soldiers on the way, that they would be here within the hour. I thought he meant to call them up himself, but that may not be the case."

"Then the bullet will have to stay where it is a while longer, I'm afraid," Simon said, untying Pétrie's hands, then bending to release the comtesse, Sophie, and Darby. "I don't doubt there are soldiers in the vicinity. I ran into a French patrol late this morning—about a dozen men—along the Paris road between Ébeuf and Louviers. That's how I come to be here instead of at the Tuileries. Discovered they were searching for an Englishman and two Frenchwomen who had escaped from prison in Paris." He glanced at Sophie, who had rushed to his twin's side. "Do you see if you can get him bandaged up to travel, mademoiselle."

"The French arranged our escape," Lord Roderick said. "I should have guessed how it was when they didn't even relieve me of the money I was carrying when they arrested me. Seemed providential, though, when we were able to make our escape." He broke off with a groan when Sophie, having removed the cloth which Diana had used, pushed a wad of muslin torn from her petticoat inside his shirt to cover the wound, which still bled sluggishly. Gritting his teeth, he went on to explain all that had taken place before Simon's arrival.

As soon as Darby was released, he moved without a word to help Sophie, taking Rory's neckcloth and tying it together with his own to fashion a crude sling, thereby earning a smile from the victim for his efforts.

"Thanks," Lord Roderick said. "What now, Simon?"

Simon had moved at last to Diana and was kneeling behind her. So aware was she of his anger that his touch sent chills racing up and down her spine. When he spoke, his tone was grim. "First, we must contrive to dispose of the body in the clearing," he said, "so it does not cause further trouble for Mademoiselle Milice and the others here at the château. I beg your pardon, madame," he added with a tight, rueful smile at the comtesse. "I wish for your sake that it had not been necessary to kill him."

"It is of no consequence, monsieur," said the comtesse regally. She had been talking rapidly with Pétrie a little away from the others and turned now to face Simon. She did not look at all discomposed by the death of her son, Diana thought, as she rubbed feeling back into her wrists. The comtesse went on, "He was a pig, monsieur. I deceived myself for too long, but I say it now, who should know. A changeling, without doubt. Certainly not a true son of Beléchappé. You must not think that I shall repine over the loss of such a one as that. I have been speaking to Pétrie Milice, who is loyal to our family, and she wisely suggests the removal of the corpse to our old cook's cottage. The soldiers will not disturb the old woman if she says she knows nothing. They think her of less than no account, and will believe her too frightened to lie to them. Then, once the soldiers have taken their leave, our people will see that Bertrand is buried on the land for which he intended to sacrifice his honor."

And so it was accomplished. Simon retrieved the emeralds from the golden cloak and then, with Darby's assistance, managed to fling the body over de Lâche's saddle to take him to the old woman behind the stables. The comtesse accompanied them in order to explain matters to her, while Pétrie, Sophie, and Diana helped Rory to mount his horse. Then, leaving Pétrie, with suitable recompense from Lord Roderick for her trouble, to put her cottage to rights and attempt to salvage her bread, the others rode to meet Simon, Darby, and the comtesse. When Darby explained somewhat consciously that the *Sea Maiden* lay at anchor just off the village of Deauville, Simon made no comment beyond saying that since he had sent his groom and Pettyjohn ahead to Le Havre, it was to be hoped that they would have the good sense to return to Portsmouth on the first available packet and await his pleasure there.

The comtesse, having little concern for Simon's servants, suggested tactfully at that point that it might be the wiser course to avoid the main road from the village to the château, since they seemed to be in momentary expectation of receiving a visit from a French patrol. Her advice was taken, and the six riders took a cross-country route to the harbor. The two crew members who had been left behind were waiting as ordered with the skiff. They looked astonished and none too happy to see their master with the others, and their glances each fell for one brief, uncomfortable second upon Diana, but neither man said anything.

It was immediately obvious, before the skiff was untied, that everyone could not fit into the boat at once, that two trips would be necessary. Thus, Diana, Sophie, the comtesse, and Lord Roderick went in the first load and were safely aboard watching the skiff being rowed hard for the yacht when a group of a dozen or so uniformed soldiers rode down to the harbor and along the shoreline only to pull up, frustrated of their prey, near the sea wall.

Diana, standing tensely at the rail, let out a long, relieved breath. Once again, the Warrington men had eluded disaster after intruding upon the affairs of a head of state. Sir William would have been proud, she decided, suddenly feeling very tired. A few moments later, the skiff reached the yacht, the men climbed up to the deck, and the skiff itself was hauled aboard. Less than five minutes later, the jib was up, the main sheet was filled with wind, and the *Sea Maiden* presented the village of Deauville with a clear view of her stern.

The skies were still overcast, but the wind was up and

almost warm, coming from the south. Diana saw Simon take the glass from the captain and put it quickly to his eye to scan the shoreline behind them. Clearly, he still worried about French patrol boats, but surely, she thought, the mounted soldiers had had no time to get word to such a boat, and there had been no large boats in the Deauville harbor.

She turned back to the rail to watch the roll of the sea being sliced into foamy breakers beneath the bow. It was a mistake. Now that she had begun to relax, her digestive system had no hesitation in reminding her of its delicate condition. She took a deep breath and swallowed carefully. Then, knowing it would be as well to put her mind to something else entirely, she decided to find out how Lord Roderick was faring. As she turned away from the rail, however, she came face to face with the broad chest of her husband. The noise caused by the wind in the sails and the rush of water below had permitted him to approach unheard.

"Simon!" She swallowed again, not daring to meet his gaze, knowing he must still be furious with her. Even so, she would not beg his pardon. Had she not gone to Beléchappé, she told herself, de Lâche must have got clean away with the emeralds, Pétrie Milice would undoubtedly have been hurt, and the chances were very good that Rory, Sophie, and the comtesse would all have been taken prisoner again. Perhaps Simon might have been taken with them. She squared her shoulders, wondering why he did not speak. Finally, she said, "I was just going to your brother, sir. Perhaps something can be done for him, to make him more comfortable."

"Darby is presently removing the bullet," Simon said evenly. "He has performed the service for others, and assures me that there is nothing particularly delicate about removing this one. It has not touched bone, nor has it caused a deal of damage. If my brother does not succumb to infection, he will be little the worse for this incident."

He spoke stiffly, formally, and Diana's pulse seemed to miss a beat. It was as if he had no particular interest in her, as if he were only imparting information. She nibbled her lower lip. "Still, I should go, Simon. Perhaps I can help."

"You are going to your cabin, madam, where you will lie down and recover your strength. You will be of no assistance to Darby. The last thing he needs is to have you being sick all over the floor while he attempts to operate."

"Sick! I am perfectly well, Simon," she said indignantly. But even as she said the words, her stomach tried to make a liar out of her. She drew another deep breath and let it out slowly, then said calmly, "I shall not defy your orders, sir. At least, I shall not interrupt Darby. But there is no reason for me to retire to my bed. I shall go to madame la comtesse and Sophie."

"You will, for once, do precisely as you are bid," he said coldly. "Sophie is with my brother and Darby in the galley, and there is no room for anyone else. And madame is recruiting her strength in the forward cabin." His hands came to rest upon her shoulders, and Diana waited for the bruising grip that he generally employed when he was put out with her. But his touch was gentle, and when he spoke again, his voice was no longer harsh. "You have a nasty bruise forming on your cheek and smudges under your eyes, Diana, and you are very pale. Moreover, a moment ago, there was a tinge of green in your face, which makes me doubt your good health. If you do not rest, you will collapse, and it is no longer possible for you to think only of your own wishes. You must consider the child. We must both consider the child. Therefore," he added, his voice hardening, "if you do not immediately go below and get into bed, I shall carry you and tuck you in myself."

She looked at him and saw that he would do precisely as he threatened. "Very well, Simon," she said with dignity, "I'll go." She gathered her cloak together at the front so that she would not trip as she went down into the companionway, and so conscious was she of maintaining her fragile dignity that she did not realize until she reached the door at the end that Simon had not followed her. Still, she was sure he would check soon enough to assure himself of her obedience, so once inside the small paneled cabin, she quickly doffed her cloak, slipped out of her rather damp skirt, and climbed into the narrow bed. As soon as she lay down, she knew Simon had been right. She was exhausted.

She had closed her eyes before it occurred to her that he had said nothing about her disobedience. Her eyes opened again, and she stared at the ceiling. Until recently, when she had defied him, he had roared at her afterward, threatening dire consequences should she ever do such a thing again. This time, barring his order to her to rest, he had said nothing. That he was angry with her could scarcely be denied. Just remembering the way he had looked at her when he had first walked into Pétrie Milice's cottage was enough to send cold shivers up her spine even now, hours later. She tried to think, to figure out what he intended to do, but her eyelids grew too heavy, and concentration became impossible. The bed rocked gently like a cradle, and even when she tried to force her eyes to stay open so that she could think, they refused to obey her. The ceiling persisted in fading to black, and her thoughts kept disappearing into the distant reaches of her mind until she slept.

At Portsmouth, Simon said nothing more than that she was to get into the chaise. Still sleepy, she obeyed him, thinking Sophie and the comtesse would join her. Not until the chaise leapt forward did she realize that she would remain alone. She had no wish to demean herself by shouting at the postilions to stop and explain their orders, especially since, looking out the window, she saw a rider whom she recognized with astonishment as Pettyjohn riding beside the chaise. He was Simon's man to the core, and she knew there was nothing to be gained by cross-questioning him except a loss of dignity, so she held her tongue, and when the chaise drew up at the White Hart in Salisbury, she knew where they were headed. Expecting no more than a change of horses, she was surprised when Pettyjohn opened the chaise door and invited her to step down.

"Am I to dine here, then?" she inquired, looking up at the magnificent Ionic portico of the newly restored three-story building. The great lamps on either side of the lower porch had already been lit against the growing dusk. Diana had heard of the famous inn, but she had never yet been privileged to dine there. Its reputation was excellent, however. She would give her courier no argument.

"You are to spend the night here, my lady," said Pettyjohn gently. "The master commanded that we stop before dark so that you not become overtired."

"You are taking me to the abbey, are you not?" Diana asked.

He nodded. "Yes, my lady."

"And his lordship? Whither is he bound, Pettyjohn?"

"To Langley Marsh, my lady, to see the comtesse and her daughter safe with the old count. Then, he will join you at the abbey." He watched her doubtfully, but Diana only shrugged.

"I trust the White Hart will feed me well," was all she said.

A number of people sat around a huge table loaded with steaming platters of food in the coffee room, but Diana was led to a private parlor, where Pettyjohn waited upon her. After a pleasant meal she retired to a comfortable bedchamber, where a cheerful chambermaid helped her prepare for bed, shaking her head in horror at Diana's lack of proper baggage. Without a blush, Diana explained that her coach had been attacked by highwaymen who had absconded with all her trunks, and the maid promptly offered to lend one of her own night gowns.

The following morning they were on the road early, and although her escort set a slower pace than she would have liked, they arrived at Alderwood Abbey by midafternoon. The weather had taken a chilly turn, and Pettyjohn, turning an eye skyward as he helped Diana descend from the chaise, suggested that like as not there was snow in the air again.

Her arrival in the new hall was greeted, as she had expected, in a mixed fashion.

"Diana!" shrieked Susanna, leaping to her feet without heed for the book she had been reading. It crashed to the floor. "Oh, Diana, we were so worried when the servants came from Osterley Park without you. Where have you been? Where is Simon?"

"Susanna, may I remind you once again that you are a lady?" her aunt said quellingly as she lifted her long-handled glasses to peer at her niece. "Pray, take your seat, and pick up that book. Such disgraceful behavior, I assure you, will not do in London."

"No, aunt," replied Susanna, but Diana was pleased to see that the anxious look was gone from the younger girl's face, as was the apologetic note from her voice. Clearly, Christmas had improved Susanna.

The marquess, seated as usual at his desk near the front wall, had said nothing. Diana made him a curtsy. "Sir, I hope I see you well. Simon and Lord Roderick follow me, but first they had to go to Langley Marsh to see the Comtesse de Vieillard and her daughter safely with the comte."

"I cannot think what you have been up to, Diana," said Lady Ophelia severely, "but I do believe you should have outgrown these outrageous starts of yours. Your servants were greatly confused at being sent on without you. I received a most unsatisfactory note from your brother's wife—no explanation at all—and another, a most distressing letter from Frances Villiers, fairly gloating over the doings at Osterley. Besides describing—I would not so far demean myself as to say *exaggerating*—the progress her dear son is making in his effort to captivate that tiresome Sarah Fane, she devoted an entire second sheet to your activities, Diana—gallivanting about the countryside with no proper escort one minute and disappearing entirely the next. I am persuaded you will wish to explain yourself."

Diana had no wish at all to explain, but she knew that if Lady Jersey had written to Lady Ophelia, she had no doubt written to others as well, and Diana's odd disappearance from Osterley would require some sort of explanation. She did her best to describe Lord Roderick's arrest in such a way as to make him appear the very embodiment of nobility, and then went on to describe Simon's efforts. Her own she glossed over, merely saying that she had come upon information that was vital to Simon's rescue attempt and had been forced to follow him to Portsmouth. When Lady Ophelia's expression grew more disapproving and the marquess showed no expression at all, Diana began to flounder and finally pleaded exhaustion and took to her bed, hoping that Simon would be able to do a better job of satisfying his relatives' curiosity.

Alone in her room, she tried to relax only to be overwhelmed by thoughts of her husband. Aside from the brief respite in the new hall, she felt as though she had done nothing but think of him for twenty-four hours. Even longer, if one counted her worry over his reaction to her visit to Beléchappé. At first, she had merely wondered what he had in store for her. He was angry, and he no doubt believed she would always flout his wishes unless he took strenuous steps to prevent her from doing so. That he had the power to prevent her from disobeying him if he chose to assert that power, was a little frightening. She did not wish to find herself under guard at Andover Court. Nor did she wish to be left at Alderwood Abbey under the marquess's authority. But Simon, by law, could command either alternative.

Even now the members of the *beau monde* were beginning to think of removing to London for the Season. Would she be left to kick her heels in the country? Moving to sit on the French daybed near the window of her bedchamber, she looked out onto the overcast world beyond and considered the likelihood that she would be forced to miss the gaiety of the annual whirl of activity that constituted the London social season. Lightning flashed on the distant darkening horizon. Would Simon dare to leave her behind and go to London himself, pleading the baby's safety as his excuse? She wouldn't let him. She would find a way to escape such captivity, for she couldn't bear the thought of Simon in London without her. It had been bad enough to be left on the *Sea Maiden* while he went to Paris. She would not allow him to leave her behind again.

She hunched her knees up in front of her chest, hugging them as she grimaced at the last thought and wondered how she could stop him. Simon had changed again. No longer did he merely bellow at her. Now, he seemed to act with a sense of purpose. And now, as she thought back, her own activities no longer seemed such innocent bids for independence. Not when she considered them as though someone else had done them.

Supposing, she thought now, staring out the window again, that she had not managed to tell Simon about Rory's deep involvement with Sophie? Simon would have ridden straight on to Paris in ignorance, thinking the Englishman the soldiers searched for in Louviers must be some other Englishman. Her own flight of temper had nearly kept that information from him. And later, when she had gone to the château, she had been in more danger than she knew. She would do the same thing again in the same circumstances, but she could not blame Simon for being angry with her. If first Rory and then Simon himself had not interfered, it was not inconceivable that de Lâche might even have killed her, and Pétrie, too.

By the time she fell asleep that night, Diana had come to the conclusion that, more than anything else, she wanted to end the squabbling, to live in peace with Simon. She remembered what it had been like during their courtship and the first, blissful, weeks of their marriage, when they had gotten along like a pair of happy children, delighting in each new thing they discovered about each other. She began to see, too, how the discovering process had grown to be a test of wills between them to discover whose was the stronger. Lydia's words came back to her then, as though Lydia stood beside her. She and Simon had been testing each other. The fact was as clear as could be, now, when perhaps it was too late. Perhaps matters had gone too far between them for Simon ever to forgive her. As she drifted into restless sleep, the vision of his face as he had looked, standing there in the doorway of Pétrie Milice's little cottage, returned, and Diana, half-asleep, stifled a sob in her pillow.

The storm that had been threatening since the day before finally broke during the night, and the winds lashed the abbey as rain poured down in torrents. But by morning the storm had passed with the violent but quickly spent power of a spring storm, leaving puddles in its wake but none of the snow that Darby had thought to see. Diana rang for Marlie and dressed, deciding to say nothing to the others about her delicate condition. She discovered, however, that Simon had not left the decision to her.

"I am sorry you left it to Pettyjohn to tell us your good news, Diana," said Lady Ophelia, gesturing to a hovering footman to pour them both a cup of tea. "I cannot think why you did not tell us yourself."

"I had thought to wait until Simon and I could tell you together," Diana said, forcing a smile. She waited uncomfortably for whatever might come next, and was surprised when Lady Ophelia said nothing other than that she hoped Diana didn't mean to quack herself, before commenting that their rather odd winter seemed truly to be turning to spring as it had been attempting to do since mid-December.

The day passed quietly after that, and Simon and Lord Roderick arrived during the afternoon. They closeted themselves with the marquess, however, and Diana did not see her husband until the entire family gathered for dinner, when the conversation centered upon the happy conclusion of Lord Roderick's affairs. Even Lady Ophelia seemed reconciled to the fact that he intended to marry a Frenchwoman, and Susanna drew a laugh from the whole company when she said that Simon ought to have known it was a case with Rory as soon as he learned his twin had gone to France without his valet. Simon argued that the lapse had no doubt stemmed from lack of funds rather than from any other cause, but Diana noticed that he had been at great pains to make his twin sound like a hero and to describe the emeralds in glowing detail. When he made it clear that the comte meant the emeralds to serve as Sophie's dowry, Lady Ophelia's eyes actually gleamed.

When the covers were removed, Diana followed her ladyship and Susanna back to the new hall, assuming that the gentlemen would follow. Half an hour later, a smiling Lord Roderick entered with the marquess, but there was no sign of Simon. Unable to contain herself, Diana asked Rory, quite casually, if he knew where his brother had taken himself.

"The library," he answered promptly. "Took a bottle of the best port. Said he wanted to think."

Without a thought for what any of the others might think, Diana hurried to the library. The room was nearly dark, but she found her husband sprawled in a chair before the crackling fire, his feet stuck out before him, crossed at the ankles, the bottle of port resting companionably on the little table beside him. He raised his glass.

"Good evening, Diana mine."

"Oh, Simon, are you drunk?"

"Not at all, sweetheart." He sat up straighter in his chair and beckoned to her. "Come and talk to me. I have solved Rory's problems but not my own, and I have made my head ache with thinking."

"With port, more like," she said softly, moving toward him. He watched her, his eyes glittering where they reflected the firelight. "You are very angry with me, are you not?"

"Aye," he answered, still watching her. "You have a talent for stirring my temper, sweetheart."

She stood by the little table, and the firelight made dancing patterns on her russet silk gown. Swallowing, she folded her hands together at her waist. "I-I wish to know what you intend to do, sir. You have made a number of threats in the past, you know, and I fear that this time, however good my intentions were, I have pushed you beyond what your patience will bear."

"I have made only one decision," he said, "and that is that in future we will spend more time at home."

Her hands gripped each other. "You *are* going to send me home! Oh, Simon—"

"Not send you, sweetheart, take you. We have spent too much time with our so-called friends. We'll do the Season in London, but we won't go until it's time for Rory's wedding in mid-March, and we won't follow the prince to Brighton this year. I want to get to know my wife without an audience."

She stared at him. "I feared I had made you angry enough to do something dreadful, and that you would say it was best for the child," she said slowly, still watching him as though she could not believe, even now, that he would not do some such thing.

Setting his glass down on the table, he held out his hand to her. "The firelight is making a halo around your head, sweetheart, and the absurdity is distracting. Come to me."

Taking his hand, glad of its warmth, she let him draw her nearer, then folded suddenly, in a swirl of skirts, to sit upon her heels at his feet. "Oh, Simon, I have been wrong to fight you. Lydia was right. I didn't understand what I was doing, and I wouldn't listen to her when she tried to tell me."

"So everything that has happened between us is your fault, is it?" Simon said gently. He gave her fingers, still nestled in his large hand, a hard squeeze.

Diana bit her lip, but she could not go so far as he seemed to want her to go. Not even her fear of what he might do could make her accept all the blame. "No, Simon," she said quietly, looking away into the flames. "I have done much for which I am sorry, but you have done things too."

"Diana," he said suddenly, "do you love me?"

"Oh, Simon." She turned back to him, tears welling into her eyes. "Oh, yes, Simon, so much. Enough for both of us if need be."

"But it is not the same as it was, is it? The way it was when we met."

"Not the same, no," she said softly, "but I have been thinking, too, and I don't think such feelings were meant to last."

"What do you mean?" His voice was tight, as though he controlled it with effort.

"What we felt at first was too strong, too fierce to sustain itself," she said. She turned toward the fire again. "Like fire." Her voice was low, but she had thought much, and she had things to say. "You know how it is when one first lights a fire, Simon, when the tinder catches in a huge, brilliant blaze?"

"Aye," he said. "There is a flash, and one has a wonderful fire. I remember the first time I lit one myself, as a child. I was proud. A magnificent blaze. But it soon went out, because I had not laid the kindling properly. The larger bits smothered the flame. Is that what has happened to us?"

"I think it nearly did," she said. "A good fire needs air. Remember when they were laying the Yule for Christmas? You were the one who said that."

He sighed. "You're right, sweetheart. I did. And you are going to say that I have not given you sufficient air to keep the fire breathing. You have said much the same thing before, have you not? Yet you say you still love me, so the fire cannot have gone out altogether."

"I thought it had," she said, looking down into her lap. "I told Lydia it had, that we no longer loved each other. She said we were only going through what every newly married couple goes through. But I didn't believe her, Simon. I felt stifled. And, too, I felt as if I was striking out in all directions at once, like one does when one is caught under a blanket and suddenly cannot breathe. But"—she felt warmth that had nothing to do with the flames crackling on the hearth rushing to her cheeks—"you have only to touch me, sir, to prove that the fire has not gone out. And when I realized where our quarreling might have led when it kept me from imparting vital information to you before you left for France, my feelings were such that—" She broke off to peer searchingly into his eyes, fearing more than anything that she would find only a wintery chill there. But she was wrong. The corners of Simon's mouth were turned up, and his eyes were glowing with warmth. He gave a little tug to her hand, and Diana flung herself into his lap. "Oh, Simon, I might have lost you!"

"And I, you, you stubborn, willful little wretch," he murmured against her curls. He pulled her tighter into his lap, one arm about her waist, the other hand moving to her chin. "Look at me, Diana. Do you dare to doubt my love? Have you any notion of the feelings that went through me when I saw you in that cottage and realized you were not, as I had thought, safe aboard the *Sea Maiden*? When I knew that had de Lâche bested me, you—aye, and our child, as well—would have been at that villain's mercy?"

She snuggled against him. "I saw the look on your

face, sir," she said. "I was certain you would beat me at the first opportunity. But you did not. You never do," she added simply.

"Perhaps this past year would have been easier for all concerned had I made good a threat or two, sweetheart, but I found, for all my fury, that I could never truly hurt you. No matter how much I wanted you to prove your love by submitting to my authority, I could not force you physically."

"I will submit now, Simon," she said gently. "I do love you. If you truly wish it, I will become the most submissive of wives."

He chuckled low in his throat. "Such an arrangement might indeed prove interesting, my love, particularly since it could never last long enough to become dull." She looked up quickly, indignantly, and he hugged her tight. "Ah, Diana, I do not wish it. It was wrong of me ever to demand it, to think it would prove anything. I only thought I wanted such a thing until that night you asked me why I'd married you and not another who would have bent easily to my will. Then," he added with a teasing smile, "I thought ahead to the future and realized I could never allow the mother of my daughters to set an example of meekness."

"Daughters, sir?" She raised her eybrows as haughtily as Lady Jersey at her most arrogant. "I'll have you know that no daughter would cause me the physical distress that your son has been causing me."

"Nay, I'll not argue the point with you, sweetheart, but it did occur to me that we shall no doubt have a daughter or two among our dozen children, and if any man ever tried to rule my daughter as completely as I tried to rule her mother, I'd take a horsewhip to him."

"But, Simon, you are a diplomat," she protested, amused. "Surely, you would reason with him first."

"Aye, and if he did not do exactly as I told him to do, *then* I would thrash him," he said firmly.

"Not if he truly loved her, Simon." She locked her gaze with his. "Surely, not then."

"No," he answered, lowering his head till his lips were but a breath away. "Not then."

About the Author

A fourth-generation Californian, Amanda Scott was born and raised in Salinas and graduated with a degree in history from Mills College in Oakland. She did graduate work at the University of North Carolina at Chapel Hill, specializing in British history, before obtaining her MA from San Jose State University. She lives with her husband and young son in Sacramento. Her hobbies include camping, backpacking, and gourmet cooking.

ROMANTIC ENCOUNTERS